DANCING BACKWARD 2: FINAL DESCENT INTO MALE SUBMISSION

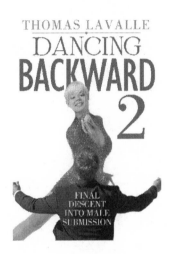

Thomas Lavalle

Juno Unlimited

ISBN: 9781798157602

Cover design: Jun Ares / Cover image: © Dreamstime

This is an adult erotic novel that explores and emphasizes some psychological aspects of female domination and male submission in a committed, consensual relationship. However, the story does contain descriptions of some fairly graphic scenes of "femdom" activities that could be pigeonholed under the heading of "B&D," i.e., "bondage and discipline." Readers under eighteen, and any who might find such material offensive, should avoid these pages.

Also by the author:
Dancing Backward: An Adventure in Male Submission
Dancing Backward 3: A Beloved Slave Reclaimed
Rapture and Capture: Three Tales of Irresistible Modern Goddesses

The author welcomes questions and comments on his blog:
thomaslavalle.blogspot.com
Or email: *thomaslavalle@gmail.com*

CONTENTS

EPIGRAPH

"That you may nurse and be satisfied with her comforting breasts,
That you may suck and be delighted with her bountiful bosom."
—*Isaiah 66:11 (NASB)*

CHAPTER ONE ~ HIS NEW LIFE

For Christopher, in the wee hours of that first morning of his new life as Kelly's slave, everything was strange. Like a drunk emerging from a monumental bender, he began, carefully and cautiously, to piece together all the lurid scraps of memory from the previous night, hoping to fit them into some kind of coherence.

Her foot was on his face. He had kissed that foot, both of her perfect feet, kissed them and shed tears on them. He had been slapped, many times, scolded and laughed at. His balls had been crushed in her hand. He had been stood in a corner for endless, excruciating minutes, forced to keep a penny trapped against the wall with the tip of his nose. But afterward she had opened her blouse and fed him one magnificent tit...

He relived the perfect happiness of that moment, but the memory was swept away by the Other Thing, the thing that explained the shameful nexus of pain all down his back and buttocks and legs.

He'd been beaten, like an animal is beaten. He heard and felt again in memory the merciless explosions of leather against his burning flesh. He had suffered the terrible wrath of Goddess Juno herself. He had suffered—and survived.

But not intact. Because the beating had taken something from him, something precious and irreplaceable, something he would never get back.

"You are not a man anymore." He spoke the words aloud, slowly and softly, knowing them to contain profound and terrible truth. "She took that away from you."

How fitting, then, that he'd spent the night here on the floor, at the foot of her bed, a place where a dog would sleep, and not in her bed like a man.

Never again in her bed.

Chris worked his right hand down inside the sleeping bag to feel the cold metal of the spiral cage she'd locked on him. The cage that kept him from touching himself, that even now prevented his penis from reaching its early morning fullness.

A man would feel outrage at this ultimate indignity; yet Chris was filled with twisted pride.

"This is your new life, slave."

Those were the final words she'd said to him last night—her voice husky, incredibly sexy and all-powerful—just before she'd closed the door and left him alone in the dark.

*

The dream had been a prolonged, panicky flight down shadowy streets from nameless pursuers. It ended in a cul-de-sac, with his back to a high wall as they closed in from all sides. He escaped by opening his eyes on predawn gray, in a familiar room rendered strange by his view from the floor.

But the dream panic lingered. His morning duties! Was it already too late? How could he have let himself fall back asleep and fail her again—after last night's terrible beating and his wretched tears of love and contrition?

He wormed out of the sleeping bag, scrambled to his feet, then let his panic dissolve as he took in her sleeping form and the ruby-red numerals of her bedside clock:

6:22

He hadn't overslept, thank God, but awakened nearly ten minutes *ahead* of his usual schedule. There was plenty of time to set out Kelly's clothes, arrange the towels and toiletries in her bathroom, then prepare her breakfast before kneeling to awaken her by kissing her foot, softly and reverently.

What Christopher truly yearned to do with those ten extra minutes was slip under the duvet and snuggle against the long warmth of his Goddess and breathe in the intoxicating scent of her ripe body. As he'd done on so many mornings in his old life as her househusband.

But those sweet glorious days were gone—forever! Chris heard again the imperious tone in which she'd announced the new sleeping arrangement:

"A lowly slave doesn't get to sleep with the Goddess who owns him! The idea is absurd!"

Lowly slave. No longer a derogatory figure of speech but a plain statement of fact. "Lowly slave" was what she'd turned him into, what he'd become.

Which left him, really, with only one ambition—to be the best slave possible for her.

As he stood there, captivated by the luxuriant slopes of her sleeping shape and embracing his implacable fate, there came a flood of love and longing for his Goddess that filled his slavish heart to bursting. And, alas, enlarged his penis to a crippling fullness as it assailed the steel ribs of the chastity cage. Talk about teasing and denial! This was "T&D" taken to the limit of what a man could endure.

Could his Goddess really be that cruel?

Yes! It was as if he heard her voice inside his head. *Get busy and do your chores.*

A step away from the master bath, he remembered that that, too, like her bed, was now off-limits. He about-faced and slipped silently out of her bedroom and down the hall to the small guest bathroom off the service porch. Inside, without turning on the light, he lifted the toilet seat and reached for his penis—and touched cold steel instead.

Whoops!

Christopher lowered the seat and then his rear end, but on first contact sprang up to escape the sharp pain. The deep bruising of his buttocks made it unendurable to put any weight on them. After several timid attempts, he made do by bracing his palms on the edges of the seat while squatting an inch or so above it and aiming his encaged penis sharply downward.

One way or another, he realized, he'd be forced to pee like a woman for the rest of his life. Another ignominy.

But that wasn't the way to think about it. Chris remembered something he'd read on a female supremacist website: *A good slave considers it an honor and a privilege to be allowed to sit down to pee like the superior sex.*

So this was an honor and a privilege. As it was to have his cock locked up by a Goddess like Kelly Ann Sheffield. And to be allowed to sleep on the floor by her bed. To be kept naked at all times and be permitted to kneel before her and kiss her feet whenever she went out or returned home. To scrub and clean and cook for her. And, yes, to be slapped and kicked and beaten by her, for purposes of discipline or training…

Or merely her amusement.

These thoughts sent Christopher into a submissive swoon—with immediate and painful consequences that were far from the kind of ecstasy he usually experienced in such a state. Needles of pain caused him to cringe and cry out as his engorging cock fought vainly to escape its steel cage. As for emptying his painfully full bladder, that obviously wasn't going to happen in his present condition.

He had to stop thinking about Goddess Kelly—right now!

He started to count in his high school Spanish. He was well past *doscientos* before the pain ebbed and his morning piss began finally to trickle out.

Moments later, blessedly relieved, Chris realized he couldn't brush his teeth. All his toiletries were still in the master bathroom. They needed to be transferred here, as per Kelly's instructions, and kept out of sight in the under-sink cabinet.

When he slipped back into her bedroom, he noticed her discarded clothing on the floor. Kelly never hung anything up—of course not. That was his job, which took precedence over anything else he might be doing. Her skirt he draped over a chair for later pressing; the silk blouse, bra, panties and wadded pantyhose she'd gagged him with last night all went into the hand-wash hamper. As usual, just touching these sacred objects—especially Kelly's bra, a floral lace underwire model in her usual 44GG—infused Christopher with feelings of reverence and, oddly, of inferiority.

*

The final thing Chris routinely did before awakening his Goddess was to fetch her newspaper from the welcome mat outside their fifth-floor condo and lay it, top fold up, beside her coffee mug. And good thing he did!

Because he found himself staring at the *Wall Street Journal Weekend* edition.

Somehow, after last night's cruel beating and corner time and then being locked into the chastity cage, Chris had lost track of what day it was. Had he awakened his Goddess before seven o'clock on a Saturday, instead of letting her sleep in, she might have flayed him alive.

Heaving a sigh of relief, Chris put his breakfast preparations on hold and, with sponge and spray cleanser, began attacking kitchen surfaces. Moments later, he was startled to hear her call from the bedroom:

"Slave, come here!"

He hurried into the bedroom, saw the bedclothes flung back.

"In here!" He hurried into the master bath. The recessed ceiling spots were half-dimmed, bathing Kelly in soft pastel light across the room. She was seated on her toilet throne, wearing only a long pink sleep shirt that was enticingly unbuttoned. Her gorgeous dancer's legs were wide open to his avid gaze.

"Crawl here, slave, and clean me."

His heart beating with submissive excitement, Chris dropped and surged forward on his knees. He hesitated as his shoulders made contact with her shins, but Kelly, grabbing him by the ears, tugged him forward between her spread thighs, then planted his face into her glistening bush.

"Show your Goddess what a good job you can do. Don't miss a drop."

Blind now, but with every other sense alive, Chris set to work with his tongue—and so eagerly that Kelly had to laugh aloud. She'd suddenly thought of Nubbin, the white Westie pup who'd been her girlhood playmate. Nubbin would lick anyone in sight, but especially favored his moppet mistress. Really, was the high-strung little terrier any more frantic with his tiny tongue than her darling slaveboy? God knows, she'd spent years training him to be a devoted and skillful cunt-licker, but he seemed even more galvanized by this brand-new vaginal assignment.

In truth, the initial tongue taste of Kelly's strong morning urine had triggered a gag reflex in Christopher, but submissive eagerness had carried him through. After a few seconds, the acrid droplets became for him a magical elixir, and he was transported into such a bliss state that even the painful waves from his confined penis were as nothing. Finally, it required a sharp slap on the back of his head to interrupt his efforts.

"Are you *deaf*, Christopher! I said 'That's enough!'"

"Sorry, Goddess. I—I—"

"I know, I know, you got carried away." She used his ears again as handles to tip his head upward, then stared down into the piss-moist face. "Apparently you like the taste of my golden nectar."

"Yes, Goddess. I do."

"Like it or love it?"

"I *love* the taste of your golden nectar, Goddess." His shining eyes offered their own eloquent testimony.

"How fortunate for you! Because I'm thinking of making this one of your regular duties. And perhaps we can even take it a bit further, and I'll teach you to drink directly from my sacred fountain without spilling a drop. Would you like that, slave?"

Chris glanced down again, unable to sustain her goddess gaze. His assent was mumbled.

She tilted his face back up, this time with a fingertip. "You're being shy this morning, slave. Are you trying to hide from me?"

"No, Goddess." But of course he was. He felt like a little boy kneeling before her, his face in her hands, her glorious breasts inches away, bulging out from the open silk shirt.

"Good, because you never can hide from me, you know, and you mustn't try. You are to confess *everything* to your Goddess, every day. Perhaps I'll have you start a slave journal in which you write down your secret thoughts and innermost longings and so on. You know, like a high school girl confiding her heart and soul to her bedside diary. Do girls still do that, I wonder, or do they just post everything on Facebook? Never mind. Just tell me, how do you feel about things this morning? Are you happy? Are you cured of all your little mutinies and, shall we say, serial fuckups?"

"Yes, Goddess. I am."

"And you accept your destiny as my slave? You realize that it's the one thing that can give your life real meaning and purpose?"

"Yes, Goddess, I do." Not knowing why, Chris felt his tears welling up again and knew he could do nothing to stop them.

"It's all right to cry, little slave. Perhaps they're tears of happiness and relief, knowing that you've finally found your rightful place in life at my feet. Could that be it?"

"Yes, Goddess." It was true. Chris felt fulfilled and idiotically happy.

"Even though you've seen how cruel I can be when I feel it is necessary?"

"Yes, Goddess."

"Good. You're making real progress, slave, though you still have a long way to go. Now, let's have a look at your new present."

Kelly leaned down and took his encaged penis in hand, then flicked the tiny padlock that secured the spiral cage to the base ring."

"This makes a little clicking sound, doesn't it? When you walk? Even when you crawl?"

"Yes, Goddess, it does."

"Perhaps I should attach a little bell to it—to the lock, I mean—to help me track your movements. What do you think of my idea?"

"Whatever you wish, Goddess."

"Well, I *know* that. But don't *you* think it would be funny? Don't you want me to have fun at your expense?"

"Yes, Goddess. I think you should do it. Definitely."

"Perhaps then I will."

But Kelly spoke absently, because her French-tipped fingernails were now probing the ridges of tender cock flesh trying to expand between the steel spirals.

"And what about little Johnny Wobble? Is he trying to flex his muscles in there?"

"Yes, Goddess."

"But he can't, can he?"

"No, Goddess, he can't."

"But he'll just keep trying, won't he?"

Kelly giggled, relishing her role as his tormentress. But she turned serious moments later, bidding him get to his feet and turn around. She wanted to inspect the damage she'd inflicted on his hindquarters last night with the heavy weightlifter's belt. It was mostly out of curiosity, she admitted to herself, but she did emit a tiny gasp of solicitude as she saw all the angry welting and bruising discoloring his buns and the backs of his thighs. She really *had* laid into him! Thank God his skin did not appear broken at any point.

"Really, Christopher, it's not as bad as I feared." Kelly traced her fingertips lightly down one of the long welts. "Is it still painful?"

"Yes, Goddess."

"A little or a lot?"

"A lot."

"Can you sit down?'

"No."

"Good. You'll be able to get more of your chores accomplished that way. Besides, the furniture is off limits to you anyway, you know?"

She gave his deeply bruised right butt cheek a tender pat, but followed it with a stinging swat. Chris yelped and jumped forward.

"Sorry, sweetie, I just couldn't resist that! I seem to have discovered a slight sadistic streak. Perhaps you've noticed."

She stood, brushing Christopher aside as she moved to the granite countertop and began fluffing her white-gold pixie hair in the long, theatrically lighted mirror.

"Flush the toilet, then pay attention to my instructions. I'm not sleeping in, as you can see. I'm going to the Muscle Factory after breakfast. Don't run out to the French bakery, I don't care for a croissant this morning. Just make me an omelet—two eggs and some diced bell pepper and tomato and grated cheddar. Do you have all the ingredients?"

"Yes, Goddess."

"Good. Have it ready with my coffee in twenty minutes. I'm going to shower and shampoo now, but the instant I turn off the water I expect you to be standing right here with a warmed bath towel. Use the microwave and—"

"I know how, Goddess."

Kelly whirled and slapped his face. "You *dare* interrupt me? You forget your place this soon—after last night?"

"I'm so sorry, Goddess. I—"

"Not as sorry as you will be when I get home. And I'm going to punish you right now, too. I was going to have you be my little boudoir boy and apply my after-shower body lotion. Isn't that one of your favorite things in all the world?"

"Yes, Goddess."

"Well, you just lost out this morning. But maybe I'm being kind, since you'd only get all worked up inside your little corkscrew. In any case, I'll dry and lotion myself. Now you run along and lay out my workout outfit. The black-and-gray yoga pants with the bamboo print, I think, and a black sports bra. No panties—I'm gonna try going commando for workouts. Socks and Nike trainers. I'll do my makeup after I eat. Got all that?"

"Yes, Goddess."

She tipped her head toward the bathroom door. "Okay. You're dismissed."

As Chris moved cautiously behind her, Kelly feinted quickly as if to swat him again. Then giggled as she watched his unmanly flinch mirrored before her.

"What a wicked lady I've turned into!" she thought, wondering what further indignities she could subject him to this morning. Was it all in aid of making a more devoted slave or just because it amused her? Perhaps both, she thought, giving herself the benefit of the doubt.

*

Seated in the breakfast nook Kelly Ann Sheffield made quick work of the omelet as she scanned the *Journal* headlines.

"Very nice, Christopher. But I really should've had you use three eggs so there'd be a few bites left over for you. You'll have to make do with licking my plate. Here, slave."

Kelly held out the empty plate out. Chris, who'd been standing nearby like a good waiter, moved forward quickly and, bending from the waist, began to lick the faint yellow traces of egg. After he'd thoroughly cleaned the residue, he continued to lick, making the white porcelain surface shine. He kept at it until she took the plate away.

"That was your breakfast, slave, Probably your lunch as well. That's also for interrupting me when I was giving you instructions. If you eat anything while I'm gone, I'll make you confess and punish you severely. Don't doubt me."

"I won't disobey you, Goddess. Ever again."

"Well, we'll see, won't we? I'm not sure when I'll be back. I may go shopping after my workout. Shall I tell you where?"

"Yes, Goddess, please."

"I'm going to a sex shop with my new friend, Carmen. And I may bring home some more special little items that I'll want to try out on you. Get the general idea?"

Chris nodded, but was afraid to speak.

"Good. That will give you something exciting to think about while you're doing your chores. And don't forget, you are to remove all your clothes and any other possessions from my bedroom—I think we'll call it the 'Mistress Bedroom' from now on. Just put all your things in garbage bags, like I had you do when I moved you out of your crummy college apartment. I'll sort through them later to see if there's anything worth keeping. Also, roll up my sleeping bag carefully and put it back in its stuff bag. You won't be using it again. You'll either sleep on the rug with a few blankets, or I may get you a yoga mat or maybe even a futon. I'll see how I feel about that."

Five minutes later, having applied her makeup, Kelly was ready to leave for the gym. Her naked slave was waiting at the front door, kneeling far forward, face to the carpet. He kissed her Nike trainers, right and left, as she presented them.

Kelly nearly complimented Chris on his dutiful execution, but thought better of it. After all, he was simply showing appropriate deference. She did reach down and tousle his hair before turning to the door. "Work hard all day for me, slave. Make me proud to own you."

Then she was gone.

Rising too quickly, Chris felt lightheaded and had to steady himself with a quick hand to the doorframe. His heart was full of love, and his penis was writhing like a crazed serpent. But more than anything he was eager to get to work. When his Goddess returned, he wanted her to see evidence of his fanatic devotion everywhere she looked.

*

CHAPTER TWO ~ RECONSIDERATIONS

In her high-heeled western boots, the stocky, middle-aged woman teetered a full head higher than her much younger male companion and outweighed him by maybe fifty pounds. As she browsed the store aisles, she kept the pale boy close beside her with periodic jerks on a chain leash snap-linked to the dog collar around his neck.

Even here in Xanadu, which catered to a bewildering range of sexual kink, this explicit display of female supremacy and abject male submission had turned some heads. It was definitely distracting Kelly as she watched discreetly from the next aisle over.

"Cute couple, huh?"

The murmured sarcasm was from Carmen Gallegos. The Cuban-American bodybuilder had taken Kelly to this big suburban sex emporium to help her pick out a "few essentials" for Chris' ongoing training and discipline. "I especially like that she's got him in a muscle shirt," Carmen went on, "to show off those spindly arms. I bet she makes him wear her brand, too."

"You're not serious?" Kelly whispered back.

"Fuck, yeah! Take another look. That's no urban cowgirl, not with those scuffed-up boots and that tobacco pouch hanging out of her breast pocket. She's the real deal. Remember, Latigo Canyon is only a couple miles from here, and that's like wall-to-wall horse ranches."

A second look confirmed Carmen's observations. Kelly also noted the muscular set to the woman's jaw, the breadth of shoulders under the faded denim ranch shirt, and the big bunched fist clamping the chain leash.

"See what I mean?" whispered Carmen.

"Okay, so she's the real deal." Kelly feigned nonchalance, but her mind had just begun unspooling its own S&M video in which the scrawny, skulking youth was rough-stripped of his saggy tank top and torn jeans, then hog-tied and pinned bare-ass beneath a big leather boot as the woman reached toward a nearby fire pit for a glowing, red-hot iron.

Kelly pulled the plug on the inflammatory images before they could earn their full triple-X rating.

But Carmen had more to say. "If she hasn't branded that poor bastard yet, I'll bet he's got a buttload of scars from her spurs and riding whip. When we get to the back aisle, you'll see a whole wall of saddles and bridles for ponyplay."

A scuff of boots and a jingle of metal drew Kelly's attention back to the odd couple. The boy was shuffling sideways toward his keeper, Kabuki style, head down, but evidently not fast enough. She snubbed the chain tighter, sliding her fist against her captive's dog-collar, then jerked him up on his toes.

She held him up there, goggle-eyed, sneakers barely touching the floor. Then she leaned in to whisper in his ear, punctuating her message with an evil chuckle. The boy's pale face visibly darkened. He began to nod desperately.

When she released her throttling grip, the boy dropped and sagged against her, clutching in vain at her broad hips and heavy thighs before sliding down in a heap between the steel-tipped toes of her ranch boots. Taking a couple quick wraps of chain around her fist, the woman jerked him back to his feet, then onward toward an array of strap-on dildo harnesses.

Carmen breathed softly: "Holy shit!"

*

Kelly was glad to have the women's bathroom at Xanadu all to herself. She locked the door and settled in the only stall, ignoring the naughty French postcard posters shellacked across the walls. More flagrant images were swarming in her mind, incited by the hard-edged little scene she and Carmen had just witnessed. She was seeing Cowgirl and Ponyboy again, this time with herself and Christopher in the leading roles, but with a major wardrobe upgrade. Her version included some Tony Lama ostrich boots she'd seen in a catalogue along with jodhpur twills and a rakish, grouse-feathered Stetson, plus a rhinestone-studded leash for Chris. And the big, swirly "KS" she had monogrammed on all her bath towels was now emblazoned on her pet's naked ass.

"I'd never do that to him, of course!" Kelly protested aloud, informing herself and the empty room. Nor would she ever take him out on a leash in public.

That there was a streak of cruelty in her dominance, she'd always known. But she'd defined it as "playful"—little-girl mischief all grown up, something that excited her boyfriends as much as it did her. "Wicked Witch of the North" was what one spiteful high school rival back in Minnesota had called her, and not without cause. But even with Chris, Kelly had kept that despotic side of herself in careful check.

Until four days ago.

It had been unleashed then by another scene of extreme female dominance. The scene had played out on a security monitor at a deserted airport baggage claim where she'd landed in the wee hours after a twice-delayed flight home from her last sales trip. She'd glanced up at the small black-and-white screen in time to see a busty, stylishly suited middle-aged woman deliver an ass-kicking to a much younger man who was squatting at her feet, tending her luggage. The well-aimed toe of her stiletto pump had sent him sprawling facedown. Without squandering a backward glance, the woman had high-heeled off the screen, leaving her underling to gather up her several bags and hurry after.

Kelly's reaction to those few seconds of accidental voyeurism had been almost as violent as the little scene itself. To her shock and surprise, she'd wet herself on the spot, though confused as to why the sight of casual female cruelty had triggered such heavy vaginal secretions—along with what turned out to be a whole series of erotic aftershocks. That very night the Wicked Witch of the North had been released from her long hibernation, and Kelly had vowed to turn her too often neglectful househusband into her obedient 24/7 house slave.

With her new dominant friend, Carmen Gallegos, as guide and cheerleader-in-chief, Kelly had embarked on the project with the same methodical zeal that had marked her meteoric rise as a sales executive in her first two years out of college. In fact, the progress she'd achieved with Chris in just three full days had astounded both Carmen and herself.

Just to hit the high points, Chris had lost the right to wear clothes when at home, along with other basic personal privileges, such as sitting on furniture or sleeping in her bed. She now required him to address her as Goddess Kelly and to be on his knees, ready to kiss her feet, whenever she left the condo or returned.

And last night she'd not only locked his cock in a steel cage, but given Chris his first real taste of corporal punishment.

The problem was, as Carmen had warned, Kelly wanted more. The power rush from these last three days, at first merely intoxicating, had already become addictive. At the office, in the midst of scrutinizing regional sales numbers, she found herself devising additional indignities to inflict on her slave. Hence this morning's shopping visit to Xanadu with Carmen.

But now, after this unexpected glimpse into the depths of her own brutish tendencies, Kelly was having serious misgivings.

How far was she really prepared to take all this? Yes, men were inferior to women—she'd always known it, even as a little girl growing up in Minneapolis—but did she want them treated as livestock? "Adult Fun 'n' Games" was Xanadu's slogan, but a lot of the stuff in these well-stocked aisles would go nicely in a medieval torture chamber.

And if she was aroused by the idea of searing her initials into the flank of a captive male, what barbarism was next? Ritual castration? Snuff films? Was she be any different, really, from those high-born Roman ladies who whiled away their afternoons in the Colosseum being fanned by slaves while watching Christians devoured by lions?

And then there was the big horsewoman out there in the store aisle. The ass-kicking domme at the airport had been glamorous, an older, raven-haired version of Kelly herself. But this big moose-jawed bitch had all the feminine allure of a jail matron on steroids. Is that what Kelly wanted to turn into? And did she want her sweet Christopher to become a sad sack like that pathetic guy she was jerking around?

The inner verdict was emphatic. "No" on both counts.

A quick release of urine rinsed away her sexual secretions, and she tried to rinse her mind as well. She blotted herself and stood, taking a deep breath as she snugged the tight yoga pants back up over her flaring hips.

Time for a new resolve.

You just galloped right up to the edge of a precipice, girl. Now back away slowly and turn around. And steer a new and safer course, for yourself and Christopher, one step at a time.

*

"So what just happened back there?" Carmen asked, twisting around to guide her white SUV out of its slot in the big strip-mall parking lot Xanadu shared with a mattress store and a Thai noodle shop.

"What do you mean?"

"Look, Kelly girl, this isn't going to work if you hold out on me. I'm on your side, remember?"

"I know, and I'm incredibly grateful for everything you've done. Like taking time out this morning to—"

"Never mind that. Just tell me what's up with you. You come back from the john and all of a sudden you want to leave."

"I know it's weird, Carmen, but I just had to get out of there. I couldn't look at any more of that—stuff, merchandise, whatever."

"Was it something to do with Ms. Bull Durham?"

"You mean Ms. Bull *Dyke*, don't you?"

Carmen shook her head. "I've seen her in there before with a couple different subbie guys, so I'm guessing she's straight. You know, kinky but straight."

"It's not her orientation. It's—it's the way she yanked that poor doofus around. But, yeah, it was her. I don't want to turn into her."

"Like *that's* gonna happen. For starters, you'd need a face transplant—like from a pitbull."

Kelly had to laugh, then resumed her earnest tone. "Let me try and explain. It's not because the way she yanked him around grossed me out or offended me—though I guess it did, on one level. It's because *it also turned me on.* And when you talked about the poor guy wearing her brand—I mean, the way you said it, the idea suddenly didn't sound farfetched at all, more like a fait accompli."

"A fate *what?*"

"It means something that's already happened. Like if you yanked his pants down, you'd definitely see this big burn scar on his butt. But here's the thing, Carmen. Whether she's actually done that to him or not, my conscience tells me it's sick, right? And yet just visualizing her doing it to him was making me wet—big time. *That's* why I had to get out of there. Now do you understand?"

"I don't know. Let me think about it." Carmen drove off the lot and swung left toward the nearest freeway onramp. "By the way, that big plastic bag I tossed in back has a few items I picked up for you on my way out. You can pay me later if you want 'em."

"You didn't have to do that, Carmen. But thank you."

"De nada."

Kelly slumped back, folding her arms beneath the heavily hammocked thrust of her breasts, then glanced over at her new friend. The vibrant Latina sat high and proud in the raised bucket seat, small square hands clenching the wheel, brow furrowed in concentration. She'd told Kelly that she'd rushed out and bought the brand-new SUV, a Buick Enclave, right after the popular "American Ninja" cable TV show signed her to a second season.

Carmen Gallegos definitely had star power. She radiated charisma and sex appeal, with a fashion sense every bit as eye-stopping as her world-class physique. A fringed buckskin minidress, worn over workout shorts and sports bra, bared generous sections of golden skin and muscular curves. The sexy Pocahontas look was accessorized with a jangle of silver bracelets, a beaded headband and a rainbow-hued Guatemalan scarf tied around her glossy black ponytail. Oversized Daylgo-orange sunglasses added a final touch of flash.

For Kelly, accustomed to being the automatic center of attention wherever she went, being upstaged by a female companion—even momentarily—was not only a novel experience but a welcome relief.

It wasn't until they were on the freeway, heading back over the coastal hills, that Carmen spoke again:

"So let's see if I got this straight. You got turned on. Big time, like you said. And that turned you off?"

"I know, it makes no fucking sense."

"Then help me understand. So far I got you sitting on the shitter and suddenly you have some kind of holy vision, some kind of, what's that word, epi-, epi-"

"Epiphany?"

"Right. You had one of those?"

"You could say that, I guess." Kelly chuckled. "More like looking into a time-warp mirror and seeing myself ten years from now. Hell, ten days from now. And not liking what I saw."

"But you've always dommed guys, you told me yourself. So none of this kinky shit is new to you. I just gave you some more techniques. Where's the problem?"

"I never went so deep into it as I have these last few days with Chris, with your help, that's what's new. And it's such a slippery slope—having him totally in my power. I've taken him down into submission so far, so fast, it scares me, Carmen. It's like coming around a bend and finding yourself roaring down a long steep grade with no brakes."

"To me, Kelly, that just sounds like fun. Like a roller coaster. Are you afraid of those, too?"

"Are you kidding, I *love* them! I thought *everybody* did, till our ninth-grade class—this is back in Minneapolis—went to Valleyfair. That's a big amusement park about twenty minutes out of the Cities. And I made this boy I liked go with me on the High Roller. He literally begged me not to, but I made fun of him till he went. Then, on the first big drop, he threw up all over himself and kept crying and screaming the whole rest of the way—and not because he liked it. He was actually shaking when we got off. I broke up with him then and there. Talk about being a heartless bitch."

"Shit, I'd have made him go again. But maybe there's your answer, Kelly. That no-brakes feeling you're having with Chris, like you can do anything you want with him, just look at it like a big thrill ride. Too much fucking fun to miss."

"But nobody gets hurt on a coaster, Carmen. Scared shitless maybe, but not hurt. But with Chris, I can really hurt him. I did already, like I told you this morning."

"Like I told you, you should have checked with me before you used that fucking lifting belt on him."

"I know I should."

"By the way, I picked up a lightweight leather strap for you." Carmen jerked a thumb toward the bag in the back seat. "The Fraternity Slapper, it's called. Guaranteed not to leave bone bruises."

"I know, I know. I'm a monster."

"I didn't say that. Look, is Chris actually complaining this morning?"

"I think he's too terrified to complain. I'm telling you, I've totally broken his spirit."

"Don't be too sure. Subbies love to fake that stuff, playing possum. It's like Whac-A-Mole. You think you've stomped them flat, crushed the last bit of macho pride right out of them, and up it pops two minutes later, grinning and reaching for the TV remote."

"I know him, Carmen, he's not faking. You told me I needed to make him fear me, and I did, and he does. Scared shitless probably."

"So maybe he *is* in a state of shock after what you did to him. And, obviously, so are you. All I'm saying is, don't overreact. You'll both get over it, and go from there."

"I don't know about that."

Carmen glanced over sharply. "So what are you saying? You want to call the whole thing off?"

"I'm seriously thinking about it, Carmen. You say I'll never turn into that scary-looking Xanadu lady. Okay, obviously not on the outside. But on the inside, I think it's already happening."

"Listen to me, Kelly girl, I do way heavier stuff on Hector than you've ever thought of doing to Chris, including the way you clobbered him last night. And do I look, you know, depraved?" Carmen looked over with her doll-cute features so comically contorted that Kelly cracked up.

"You look like you just dropped a barbell on your tits."

"Not me, babe! Next time you come to the Muscle Factory, you can watch me bench one eighty-five without even grunting. *And* I'm a black belt in Tae Kwan Do. I told you that, right?"

"Right. *And* you also told me you're a bad-ass stuntgirl who jumps off buildings. *And* you were a cheerleader, too, just like me."

"*You* were on the cheer squad?"

"All three years of high school."

"Yeah, I bet you were one of those candy-ass blondes who just shook their big tits and their pompons while I did all the scary aerials."

"Sounds about right." Kelly laughed.

"The thing is, I'm still a cheerleader, *your* cheerleader, and don't you forget it."

"But what if all that rah-rah spirit is just wasted on me?"

"I'll decide that. What I think, Kelly, is you're making this way more complicated than it needs to be. What if I just ask you some simple questions, and we'll see where that gets us, okay?"

"Fire away."

"Let's start with this one. Do you want to dump Chris?"

"Of course not. What made you ask that?"

"Just checking. From the pictures you sent me, he's an awfully cute guy, and I might like to own him."

"I bet you would. But I saw him first and I'm keeping him, one way or the other."

"But maybe, with this big change of heart you're having, you're gonna let him sit around now and watch TV all day like he used to while you bust your butt at work."

"No way! I make sure he's got a nice long list of chores to do."

"Or else?"

"Absolutely."

"So you still expect him to clean your house?"

"*And* cook my meals. *And* handwash my undies. All that stuff."

"And do a good job of it?"

"He damn well better!"

"Good! I can see you haven't lost your mojo. Now let me ask this. When you're away on your sales trips, do you want him splooging into your dirty panties like you told me he did yesterday?"

Kelly shook her head, but suddenly began chuckling as Carmen's method became obvious.

"What's so funny, blondie? This is serious shit."

"You're talking just like a lawyer, you know? Leading your witness through a series of clever questions exactly where you want to take him—I mean *me.*"

"So I watch a lot of *Court TV*, so what? Let's keep going. So, are you going to keep him locked up?"

Kelly hesitated before saying "Yes." Then added, "At least for now."

"Good! Now what about, you know, making sure he knows his place? Do you want to have to discuss every fucking thing with him, like if you tell him to do something, or do you want instant agreement from him, instant obedience?"

"Obedience, every time."

"Whether he agrees or not?"

"Exactly."

"So you like having your word the law?"

"Of course. What girl wouldn't?"

"I'm asking the questions, remember? Now let's talk about

punishing him, discipline, whatever. Which you never used to do, right?"

"Right."

"You'd just tell him how he fucked up and how upset you were and he'd swear to do better and then go right back to fucking up again, with the result that nothing ever changed. Have I got that about right?"

"Exactly. Which is why I came looking for you. I wanted Chris to be more like your Hector. Doing your bidding, even anticipating your needs."

"Maybe the smartest thing you ever did, girl. Because all that shit I told you to do to Chris over our two-hour sangria lunch—making those new house rules and slapping him around, and even kicking his junk, and strapping his ass, though I didn't mean a fucking razor strap. Everything I told you, it worked like a fucking charm, right?"

"You know it did, Miss Smarty Pants."

"What can I say? That's how guys are. They're simple creatures, just little boys. They need our strict guidance, and our strict punishment when they don't do what they're told. So now let me ask you this. How do you like making Chris ask permission to speak?"

"Mostly I like it, but not always."

"What do you mean?"

"I like having that power over him, sure. Being the only voice in the room, so to speak. I don't like being interrupted, and he used to do that way too much. But, believe it or not, a girl can get tired of hearing just 'Yes, Goddess, No, Goddess.' Chris can be witty and funny, and sometimes I miss that."

"So why not give him permission whenever you want to hear from him? Or set regular times when he's allowed to talk. As long as you make it clear there's no arguing or questioning your decisions or opinions, and especially your authority."

"Yeah, okay, that could work, I guess."

"Now let's look at it from Chris' point of view. Do you think, deep down, he wants to be your slave? Or do you even care what he wants?"

"I do care. And, yes, I think he wants it, and that it fulfills him and makes him happy."

"So why deny him that? And why deny him the kind of severe punishment he needs to become the best possible slave to you? I mean, when you beat the shit out of him with that big slab of leather last night, you told me that afterward he was full of love and gratitude, slobbering all over your feet. That's how subbies are. Train 'em like dogs and you can't go wrong."

"But what about me, Carmen? What about what beating the shit out of him does to me?"

"Don't worry. I'll keep an eye on you. And when we go back to Xanadu, we'll stay the hell away from the aisle where they sell the cattle prods and branding irons."

*

Kelly stood beside the door of her Audi in the Muscle Factory parking lot where Carmen had just dropped her, watching the bodybuilder guide her white SUV back into traffic, heading for an afternoon photo shoot.

Suspended from Kelly's hand was a big pink plastic shopping bag, drooping with the weight of all the items Carmen had picked up for her. Which she shouldn't have done.

What Kelly should do now was throw the bag in the trunk without even looking inside.

Instead, trying to suppress a flutter of visceral excitement, she opened her car and slid behind the wheel, tossing the bag on the empty seat beside her.

Okay, just take a quick look, then into the trunk.

She reached into the bag and fished out the first item. It was the "Fraternity Slapper" Carmen had mentioned. The flexible leather strap was virtually weightless compared to the heavy belt she'd used on Christopher.

"Forgive me, baby," she whispered aloud and set it aside.

Next was a riding crop, braided leather over some kind of flexible rod with a wrist loop and a heart-shaped leather flap at the business end.

The heaviest item was a long-handled wooden paddle, shaped and sized like the big paddles for the French "Jokari" game Kelly had played as a child. A gold-foil label said "Brand Spanking New." Thinking about the awful impact it would make on Chris' bare bottom made her feel queasy.

And excited.

The last item—not counting two pairs of Velcro-adjustable locking cuffs—was a cane, a thin rod maybe thirty inches long of real rattan with visible bamboo joints. Kelly wrapped her fingers around the whipcord grip and gave a tentative flick to her wrist. The whippy little stick whistled through the confined space, sending shivers down Kelly's spine.

Dear God! Why was Carmen tempting her with all this stuff? Kelly examined the sales slip. The Cuban bodybuilder had spent nearly a hundred and sixty dollars! One by one Kelly stuffed the items back in the bag, cinched the drawstring and placed the bag back on the passenger seat. She took several moments, then, to recover her resolve, which had been so firm and fixed when she'd walked out of the bizarro netherworld of Xanadu into the daylight of normalcy.

She wasn't going to use *any* of those nasty little implements on Christopher! She'd played along with Carmen's clever Q and A, and, yes, the Latina had made some valid points. But that didn't erase the unholy vision that Kelly had seen so vividly in her mind's eye back at Xanadu. Of herself as some kind of demented Cruella de Vil and Christopher reduced to permanent wimp status at her feet.

What you should do right now, Kelly instructed herself, is drive around to the alley and deep-six the whole bag of diabolical tricks into the nearest dumpster. She could settle up with Carmen later.

But when Kelly turned the key, igniting the muscular growl of the Audi's big V-8, she found herself steering away from the alley and out toward the street, then turning toward home. With the big pink bag still prominent on the seat beside her.

It was eleven forty-four, and she wanted to see her Christopher.

She missed him terribly.

*

CHAPTER THREE ~ DOMESTIC INTERLUDE

Chris thought back, trying to recall how many times in the past he'd gotten hard while doing housework. It had happened, of course, but not often, and never before like this. In the nearly four hours since Kelly had left for the gym and he'd set to work in naked chastity, his engorged penis had writhed continuously and painfully against its spiral cage, trying and failing to erect itself fully.

What a bizarre form of self-flagellation she'd devised!

At one point he actually looked down and cursed himself. "Stupid bastard, can't you forget her for five fucking minutes?"

But, of course, his cock wasn't listening to him. It was attuned to the siren song of its real owner, a goddess who was miles away, but whose mystical influence followed him from room to room and chore to chore.

So, this, too, was his new life. A constant throb in his steel-sheathed member and a permanently inflamed butt from corporal punishment, which, as Kelly had explained last night, would be a regular part of his life going forward.

Yet the more he pondered his abject and unmanly fate—and how could he not?—the hornier it made him, which just kick-started the pain cycle all over again.

Chris parked his Swiffer mop and thought back to his old househusband life. Those lazy slob days when he'd done the barest minimum of housework with the TV always on in the background and his cock swinging free and flaccid in cargo shorts or sweatpants.

A househusband could get away with shit like that, he thought, as he towed the vacuum cleaner to Kelly's bedroom. A slave couldn't.

"Make me proud to own you."

Those words—said just before she'd exited this morning—had been looping through Christopher's brain ever since, helping to keep him on task and at maximum effort.

He plugged the powerful vacuum into a bedroom socket, switched it on and began painting the Chinese Art Deco rug that bordered the big Spanish four-poster bed with slow, careful strokes the way Kelly had taught him.

Make her proud to own me.

Once he'd dreamed of making Kelly proud of him as a man and husband—even, in his wilder fantasies, as an equal breadwinner.

But none of that was ever going to happen. Even if he'd applied himself back in college and gotten his graphic design degree and landed a respectable job in his field, he was never going to make a name for himself. He simply lacked the talent. And the ambition. And the drive.

What he was, Chris was forced to admit, was an aimless, amiable guy who'd lucked into Kelly's fantastic orbit and been sucked up just like the *Millennium Falcon* into the Death Star. Except, unlike Han Solo and the *Falcon*, Chris had no desire to escape.

In exchange for living with his voluptuous goddess, he'd given up his freedom and his manhood.

And he'd do it again in a heartbeat.

Polishing her big bathroom mirror about an hour earlier, Chris had glimpsed a furtive face peering out at him through the expanding hole in the Windex mist. Peering out, but not quite willing to meet his gaze.

What shameful secret was that face hiding? Had she taken away his soul, too?

Maybe, Chris thought, but I don't care.

He finished the last corner of the carpet and flicked off the vacuum's motorcycle roar. In the room's sudden silence, he spoke a solemn vow:

"I'll surrender everything to you, Goddess Kelly, if that's what it takes to make you proud of me."

The answer was so simple, so stunning, that Chris was flooded with a sense of joy and certitude. Yes, he thought, this is what I am and all I ever want to be.

Hers.

He looked around the large bedroom that, up till last night, he'd been privileged to share. And suddenly remembered her commandment to remove all his clothes and all his possessions from what was now exclusively the Mistress Bedroom.

Why hadn't he done that already?

In a whirlwind of submissive zeal, he hurried to the service porch and returned with a roll of big Hefty bags and began unspooling and tearing them off at the perforations. Moving swiftly down the long walk-in closet, past all the arrayed splendor of Kelly's wardrobe, he reached his own tiny allotted section and began stripping everything he owned from the hangers, dumping them at his feet. He gathered up several hats and caps nested on an overhead shelf and a half-dozen pairs of shoes from a floor rack, then squatted to empty all three drawers from a small dresser at the end of the closet, scooping out socks and shorts, t-shirts and sweaters, bathing suits and belts.

Next, from under what had been his side of the bed, he retrieved several pairs of running shoes and sandals before clearing out the entire contents of the bedside table, leaving only a short stack of approved magazines in the small cabinet—recent issues of *Good Housekeeping* and *Bon Appetit* with household tips and recipes Kelly wanted him to prepare for her. His college subscription to *Sports Illustrated* she'd canceled long ago.

In ten minutes Chris had filled six garbage bags and removed every trace of himself from the Mistress Bedroom. He stood there, feeling a momentous sense of accomplishment, knowing himself fully committed now, like a man taking monastic vows. His sacred service, of course, was to an earthly goddess. But, like a novice monk, he was permitted nothing from his old life.

Literally nothing. Even this shiny metal dingus she'd fastened on his cock didn't belong to him.

Suddenly, then, his roving gaze found something he'd missed wedged behind the now empty bedside table. Kelly's old MacBook Pro, a hand-me-down from her last computer upgrade.

What was it she'd said last night, that flippant remark about his being permanently logged off? Could she have really meant it? Could she have already done it?

Chris had to find out. He retrieved the laptop and sat on the edge of the bed. Or started to. Because, at the first fiery contact of his butt with the mattress, he sprang to his feet.

The blazing pain subsided quickly, but his distress remained. He'd just broken another of her new rules—sitting on her furniture. Something he'd have to confess and be punished for.

Which, of course, she had every right to do. But, with the certainty of his punishment, Chris decided he might as well complete his crime. Kneeling on the Chinese carpet, he put the MacBook on the floor in front of him and booted up.

His desktop panorama of Yosemite Valley was now defaced with a never-before-seen password popup.

Kelly had shut him out completely.

Somehow being stripped of Internet access hit Chris harder than being stripped of his clothes and possessions. Why couldn't Kelly have installed one of those parental control programs that block adult sites, letting him at least check out the news and sports?

Of course he knew the answer. She'd told him. She intended to keep him completely isolated from the outside world, her abject prisoner. But even maximum security prisoners were allowed Internet access these days, Chris was pretty sure. Not slaves, apparently.

Chris shut off the Mac, now useless to him, and placed it atop the bedside table for Kelly to do with as she pleased. Then he remembered his iPhone. He hurried to the kitchen and happily snatched it from its charger on the counter.

One awakening touch confirmed the worst. His web browser, email, news feeds, all had been removed. Even his weather app had vanished.

Kelly had left the phone and text-message icons. Exclusively for contact with his Goddess and no one else, as Chris quickly verified.

As for her home-delivered *Wall Street Journal*, for her eyes only, that always went directly into her briefcase after breakfast.

Chris supposed there was no way Kelly could disable the big flat screen. But she'd made it clear that his punishment for any unauthorized watching would be off the charts.

Again came the clarifying thought: A slave doesn't need to know what's going on in the outside world. His entire universe is circumscribed by his owner. All his thoughts are to be focused on her—her commands, her wishes, her needs, what he can do next to serve her.

In other words, go back to your chores.

Chris cinched all the drawstrings and began dragging the bags down the hall to the service porch. It took three trips, two bags at a time, shoving them all into a corner so they didn't block the washer and dryer both churning and spinning away on their separate cycles.

Kelly had said she'd go through the bags later and decide what, if anything, to keep. Meanwhile, he had one outfit only, the one he'd been born with.

Chris grabbed his cleaning caddy and returned to the bedroom, using a rag and dusting spray to wipe down the just-emptied dresser drawers, then the bedside table. Next he began sliding Kelly's hanging clothes into the vacated space, making room for easier access and new purchases. He hoped she'd also be pleased with the additional storage space in the emptied dresser and shoe racks and on the overhead shelf.

He picked up his cleaning supplies and left, but was back ten minutes later with fresh bed linens, having just ironed the pillowcases. As he carefully made up her bed, Chris thought, not for the first time, that, really, "Queen-sized" was the proper way to describe her huge mattress. "King-sized" should be used for the next size down. And with her slave demoted to the floor, Kelly could really feel like a queen, having all that cushy acreage to her royal self.

Chris gave the thick duvet a final tug to align it perfectly, then fluffed her pillows and pillow shams, arranging the smaller throw pillows in front just the way she liked.

The digital bedside clock informed him it was nearly noon. Which meant his Goddess could return at any moment without warning, and he must be there waiting, naked and knee-bent, when she opened the door.

In a submissive panic now, Chris hurried back to the service porch to set up the iron and ironing board. The wicker basket still held a backlog of unpressed clothing; but, even more important, by stationing himself here, he'd be able to reach the front door in a matter of seconds.

As soon as the iron started steaming, Chris pulled out a lime-colored linen blouse and set to work. He started with the yoke as he'd been shown, carefully tugging and smoothing the material to avoid pressing in wrinkles.

And as he worked, for his own physical comfort he tried not to think of his Goddess. But, of course, he could think of nothing else, especially while listening intently for the sound of her approaching footsteps.

CHAPTER FOUR ~ POINT OF NO RETURN

Rushing up all five flights to her condo, Kelly threw open the door—and nearly tripped over her prostrate slave. In her eagerness to get back to Chris and make a new start with him, she'd momentarily forgotten he'd be waiting right there on his knees to kiss her feet.

As he was doing now, lips pressed passionately into the sweaty nylon mesh of her sports shoe.

"My sweet boy," she murmured, setting her gym bag down and closing the door. "My sweet, sweet boy!"

As she looked down at his groveling devotion, Kelly experienced that familiar surge of erotic power accompanied by fluttery feelings in her stomach.

But this time she fought those feelings. If she didn't, she reminded herself, if she kept indulging this seductive power trip she'd been on the last four days, sooner or later she'd become just like that hard-eyed, steel-toed bitch at Xanadu.

A glam version, to be sure, but inwardly the same.

Kelly forced her focus on the ugly welts and purple bruises that marred Christopher's naked buttocks and the backs of his thighs.

All of it her handiwork.

Did she feel no guilt, no shame, for what she'd done to her "sweet, sweet boy"? And how could she even think of using additional weapons on him—paddle, cane and crop? (Just to make sure she didn't, she'd left the big pink Xanadu bag locked in the Audi's trunk.)

Marshaling her resolve, Kelly withdrew her Nike trainer from beneath her sub-husband's face. When his lips pursued avidly, she prodded his head away with her toe and spoke firmly:

"That's enough, Christopher. We're going to have a little talk now, you and I." He looked up, face radiant with adoration. "Follow me to the loveseat."

Kelly started across the room but swung back on hearing a flurry of knee bumps and palm slaps. Chris was crawling quickly after her exactly as she'd trained him to do.

"No, Christopher, on your feet. Like a man."

He got up, but awkwardly, as if he'd somehow forgotten how it was done. The drooping spiral cage, Kelly noted, was approaching horizontal, being pulled upward from his groin by his excited penis.

"Come on, then, Christopher. But you must try to calm down. We're going to talk, not play."

Kelly moved to the burgundy velour loveseat and sat, crossing her legs before patting the cushion beside her.

Chris came to her, but did not sit down. He just stood there, his distress obvious.

How could he sit beside her? It wasn't a matter of the pain involved in putting weight on his inflamed ass; gladly would he suffer that for her! No, it was because the very idea had become unthinkable to him—placing himself on the same level as his Goddess and Owner, as though he were in any sense her equal. The only proper place for him now was at her feet. Could this be a test of his submission, to see if he had truly accepted his innate inferiority?

And so, casting his eyes downward, he began to lower himself.

"No, Christopher! I want you up here beside me. And, no, I haven't forgotten the rule about the furniture. I'm making an exception for this little talk, and I expect you to obey me in this, as in everything else. Is that clear?"

"Yes, Goddess," he said, reluctantly straightening himself.

"Also, I'm giving you temporary permission to address me in the old way—not as Goddess, but simply as Kelly, or even Kell. Won't you like that?"

"Yes, Goddess—I mean Kell."

"Okay. Now sit down."

But, before he could obey, she grabbed his cock cage. "No, wait! I want to take this off first."

Slipping two fingers down into the deep cleavage beneath her sports bra, Kelly fished out a thin gold chain, which he hadn't seen before. But, as she lifted it over her head, he instantly recognized the tiny brass key that slid down the chain into her fingers.

Uncrossing her legs, Kelly leaned forward, key in hand. It took a few seconds of frowning concentration before she successfully slotted the key and opened the miniature padlock with a snick-click, freeing Christopher's cage from its base ring.

Setting the lock aside, she fastened her fingers around the steel sheath. "Now," she said, flashing a wicked smile, "to release the kraken!"

Her first sharp tug achieved nothing—except a yelp of protest from Chris. The spiral cage, visibly caught in his swollen flesh, did not budge.

"It seems we're going to need a bit more force, sweetie." Kelly tightened her grip.

"No, Goddess, please!"

"Hush, Christopher. Don't be a baby! It will only hurt for a second. One—" The hard yank came on "two."

This time Chris screamed. It felt like his cock was being ripped out by the roots. But the contraption was off, thank God, releasing his cock to slap straight up against his belly.

Kelly set the cage on the lamp table beside the tiny padlock, then smiled at his rigid salute. "Well, to quote an old line, I guess you're glad to see me. But we're not quite through."

Leaning forward, she worked first one testicle, then the other, back through the stainless steel base ring. This allowed her to slide the ring up and off his upright cock and set it, too, aside. Seizing his erection now, she pulled him close.

"Here's another rule we're definitely going to relax. You know your cock isn't particularly impressive size-wise, Chris, but I like having it totally exposed and vulnerable to me at all times. So whenever I'm home, I'm probably going to set you free. That doesn't mean that you get to touch yourself. This still belongs to me," a quick, hard squeeze buckled his knees, "and I'm the only one allowed to touch it. Of course, whenever I leave, you'll be locked up again, because, as we both know, you can't be trusted. Understand?"

Chris nodded, but in truth he'd barely registered her words, so excited was he to feel himself once again in her Goddess grip. He stood there, ramrod hard and trembling before her, his cock-tip now leaking precum.

"You may sit down now, Christopher, beside me," she said, releasing him. "But don't you dare drip on my upholstery."

"Please, Goddess!" Chris glanced yearningly at the floor. "Please, can't I go to my usual place?"

"Oh, Christopher, how could I have forgotten! It still hurts you to sit, doesn't it?"

"It's not that, Goddess. Please! It wouldn't feel right—sitting beside you, on the same level."

His tone was so imploring, his face so distressed, that Kelly finally relented.

"All right, sweet slave. You may kneel here in front of your Goddess, if that's what your little heart desires."

"Thank you, Goddess!" Chris dropped to his knees, then, to show his gratitude, bent to kiss her shoes again, right and left.

Well, their talk was certainly off to a shaky start! Kelly thought, as little shivers of excitement continued to spread throughout her body. Even worse for her prior resolve, she had to admit that it did feel much more natural to have him down on his knees, helplessly erect and looking worshipfully up at her.

Even so, she was determined to proceed with her plan. She ruffled his hair as she began: "Christopher, you're making this extremely difficult for me. I came here fully intending to relax some of the rules I've imposed."

"Because of last night, Goddess?"

"Yes, because of what I did to you last night—and would have gone on doing if you hadn't collapsed. Have you looked at your ass in the mirror today?"

"Yes, Goddess."

"Well? Do you want more of that? Do you really want to find out how much crueler I can be? Do you?"

There was a long pause as he looked down, unable to sustain her searching gaze. His answer came finally in a whisper:

"I *did* look in the mirror, Goddess, and… and… I'm *proud* to wear those marks you put there. I'm so lucky to be owned by you, Goddess. Even to feel your cruelty."

"You don't want this to stop? Is that what you're saying?"

"Yes." He glanced up, his expression once again pleading. "And please don't take away any of my new rules. You said there were a lot more, Goddess, and—and—to be the best slave I can be, I want to obey them all."

"Damn you, Christopher!" Kelly reached down and slapped him hard, a stinging blow that whipped his face sideways and left a livid handprint.

"Th-thank you, Goddess," Chris stammered when he was able to focus.

"'Thank you, Goddess,'" Kelly mocked in sing-song disgust. "Of course! The perfect slave response!"

She sprang from the loveseat, stepping around him to pace the floor. "What the fuck am I going to do with you, Christopher?"

When he didn't respond, she stormed back and seized a fistful of his hair, yanking his head back until she was staring down into his eyes.

"You stupid little bitch! Can't you see I'm offering you your freedom! Tell me you want it! Tell me now—before I destroy you!"

"Please, Goddess! I don't want to be free! I want to be your slave. Forever!"

"Damn you! Damn you!" And, with a fist still coiled in his hair, she slapped him even harder. "You really want this?"

"Yes, Goddess. More than anything." Chris was weeping now. Kelly knew all was lost.

"You know there will be no going back from this?" The question, she realized, was as much for herself as for her slave.

"Yes, I do."

"Oh, God," she cried aloud, "I tried to stop this! God knows, I tried!"

She let go of his hair and sat down again, sagging heavily against the backrest, then heaved a deep sigh that fully stressed the spandex halter top. Her heart was galloping, her emotions a seething maelstrom. Somehow she had to get a grip. There would have to be safe and sane limits, she knew that. But right now she couldn't think of any. She wanted absolute power over Christopher, and she would have it. And just thinking about that was getting her hotter and wetter by the second.

Kelly's regard had been heavenward. Now she lowered her gaze back to her kneeling slave. Tears glistened in his worshipful eyes and tracked both cheeks.

"Are you going to punish me now, Goddess?" he asked in tremulous voice.

"What are you talking about?"

"This morning, Goddess. Remember? I interrupted you when you were giving instructions? And you said you were going to punish me as soon as—"

"Shut up, Christopher! I know what I said, but you're not running things. And don't worry, you'll be punished, and punished severely. But right now I need to use you for something else."

She took his face in her hands roughly. As he flinched in obvious expectation of another slap, she bit his underlip till she tasted blood, then forced her tongue deep into his mouth. He yielded to her dominant kiss, moaning softly and insistently. Otherwise he remained utterly passive in his passion, hands at his sides, as he'd been trained.

Finally she broke the kiss and, still holding his head in her hands, looked deeply into his submissive soul from point-blank range:

"I think we should have a little ceremony now. To seal the deal, so to speak. What do you think?"

His "Yes, please," was soft and fervent. He began nodding like a bobblehead toy.

"It's not a collaring. I'm afraid I don't have a collar for you yet, slave. You'll have to wait for that."

He kept nodding, gravely now, while trying to swallow a lump in his throat.

Taking hold of his still vertical erection, she rubbed her thumb over the ooze-slick tip, then used the shaft as a handy tiller to steer him around, knee-walking him in a half circle till his back was about a foot from the loveseat.

"I want you to arch all the way over backward, but keep your legs folded behind you." Kelly guided him down carefully till the back of his head touched the cushion. Chris felt like a human pretzel with the strain on his lower back, plus shooting pains in his legs as his thigh muscles bunched and tightened.

"It really hurts, Goddess!"

"You begged me for this, slave, so now you'll damn well suffer for my pleasure. I want your arms behind your back, wrists together. We'll have to pretend for now that you've got cuffs on. Okay, that's perfect. Don't move!"

Kelly did a little shimmy as she worked her bamboo-striped tights down over the voluptuous swell of her hips and ass, then down her muscled thighs and calves. Finally, bending down, she tugged and kicked her Nikes free of the clingy material to stand over her slave, naked from waist down. She was much too far gone to deal with taking off her shoes and socks or even unhinging her super-sized sports bra.

"Oh, God, Christopher, I'm so fucking wet!"

By way of demonstration, Kelly swiped two fingers through her cunt lips and wiped the lubricous residue across his upper lip. Next, with her back to the loveseat, she straddled her slave's backward-arching body and, using both hands to spread her ass cheeks, lowered herself onto his upturned face.

She wriggled around a bit, making sure her labia fully covered his nose and mouth, though obviously aware he'd need to breathe from time to time. Right on cue she felt his tongue tip probing ever so gently for her swollen clit. In her frenzied state, there was no way she could sit and wait for his oral efforts to take orgasmic effect. She began rocking her hips violently, grinding her crotch against her slave's face and watching his unfettered cock saw the air in its futile, spastic dance.

Ponyboy and Cowgirl, indeed!

And, she was definitely in the saddle, posting to and fro while squeezing her massive tits through the sports bra. Every now and then she would lift her hips a bit, reminded by Chris' desperate bucking and thrashing that he needed to grab a breath. But then, she was already gasping for air herself.

This is what he's for, she thought, *my sweet, sweet boy!*

Kelly loved that delicious feeling—of being in total control over Christopher even as she prepared herself to surrender to the primal forces gathering and building deep within her. Enhancing her pleasure was the fact that he'd just consigned himself, body and soul, to her permanent keeping.

Just thinking about this sent her careening through the last barrier into a long, shuddering freefall.

Afterward, as her arc of ecstasy subsided into deep purring contentment, Kelly found her thoughts turning to various cruel and delicious ways she could satisfy her slave's need to be severely punished. To meet his more immediate need, though, she lifted her hips, allowing him to gulp great lungfuls of oxygen. In a further act of charity, she reached down and quickly squeezed him off, sending him into predictable spasms, both physical and emotional. Usually Kelly was amused by all the gushy and ardent things boys blurted out on those rare occasions she allowed them to come, but Christopher was truly in a state. And soon his passionate avowals grew so tiresome that she was forced to muffle his mouth, once again, beneath her descending buttocks.

*

CHAPTER FIVE ~ CARMEN'S VISIT ~ 1

Phone conversation later that day:

KELLY: Hi, Carmen! Look, I know you're on a shoot, but can you give me a minute?

CARMEN: We're on break now, so I can give you five, no problem. Ten, now, that might be kind of iffy. What it is, it's this caveman-cavewoman commercial for Achilles. Ever heard of it?

KELLY: Should I have?

CARMEN: Fuck no! It's this new, supposedly macho-type cologne for like totally clueless guys. Smells like bug spray to me. I pitched Hector for the cave-guy gig, but turns out his comp card shows his shaved head and all his gang tats. So they hired this blond steroid monster from Down Under, and they stuffed his junk into this leopard-skin G-string. Me they got in this redhead wig looking like Wilma, you know, from *The Flintstones*, only with a whole lot less fur. I swear, my *chi-chis* are practically falling out. Lucky they're not Kelly-sized or, believe me, this thing would never get on the air. And now what I'm gonna do is shut up so you can fill me in on the deal with Chris. I assume that's why you're calling.

KELLY: Right.

CARMEN: So how did it go when you got back?

KELLY: Long version or cut to the chase?

CARMEN: Better cut to the chase, seeing as how they could call me back for reshoots any minute. You back on track with him?

KELLY: Yeah, and full speed ahead—on everything you and I talked about.

CARMEN: I knew it! You just had to work through it, babe, that's all.

KELLY: I guess I did. This morning at Xanadu somehow I lost the courage of my convictions.

CARMEN: Either that or you wimped out.

KELLY: *Touché!* But I really did try to talk him out of it, Carmen, out of the whole thing.

CARMEN: Which makes absolutely no fucking sense, girl. I mean, from everything you tell me, he's a sub, and we know you're a born domme. And, in my book, that spells happy-ever-after.

KELLY: I know, I know. But I was curious to see how he'd react. Or, maybe, if he'd try to convince me that this is what he really wants, too. And he did exactly that.

CARMEN: How?

KELLY: Well, for starters, he wouldn't even sit beside me to talk about it. He told me he belongs on the floor, at my feet.

CARMEN: All right, give the boy credit for having learned his place.

KELLY: I do. In fact, Carmen, you know what? I may be falling in love with him all over again.

CARMEN: No shit? So, do you like want him to fuck you now?

KELLY: No, it's not like he's my stud muffin or anything like that. I'm falling in love with having him underfoot, you know, as my slave. My total slave. It's fantastic!

CARMEN: You had me worried there for a second.

KELLY: I'm just saying, it's so clear now—that what Chris really wants is to be my property, to do whatever I want with. These last four days, I think they've made it clear to both of us, just what our roles are.

CARMEN: You know, Kelly girl, that's really hot, what you're saying?

KELLY: It is, isn't it? And without you, it would never have happened.

CARMEN: Just call me Little Miss eHarmony. So, did you try out any of those new items I picked up for you?

KELLY: No, but I'm getting sopping wet just thinking about it. And here's the weird thing. Chris really *wants* to be punished. Even after what I did to him last night.

CARMEN: Maybe *especially* because of what you did to him. You'd be surprised how many subbies turn into pain sluts.

KELLY: I don't think Chris is that far gone yet. I think he's just really turned on by my power over him. He actually went out of his way to remind me of some silly shit he did wrong this morning to deserve more punishment. Like he was afraid I was going to forget.

CARMEN: So give the boy what he wants—and needs. Is there a problem?

KELLY: The thing is, like I told you, I bruised his booty big-time. I'm afraid I'll do permanent damage if I swing too hard or use the wrong implement, or weapon, or whatever they are.

CARMEN: I believe the technical term is "impact toys."

KELLY: Whatever. But maybe I should give it a couple days, you know, and let him heal first?

CARMEN: Wanna know what I think?

KELLY: Duh! That's why I'm calling.

CARMEN: I think you're making the same mistake most novice dommes make. You're afraid you're going to hurt the poor guy. So, instead, you go way too easy on him. And then it becomes just a game to them and pretty soon the guy is playing you.

KELLY: How can you say that? I told you, I beat the shit out of Christopher! I mean, I had him screaming into his pantyhose gag until he threw himself at my feet, begging for mercy.

CARMEN: Okay, so you used the wrong tool on him. But now, all your maternal instincts are kicking in and you want to take pity on him. Am I right?

KELLY: Well, yeah, pretty much.

CARMEN: Remember me telling you, once you get a guy down, you're gonna be tempted to ease up, but really that's the time to step on him even harder and keep him down?

KELLY: Sure, I remember.

CARMEN: Know where I got that little morsel of femdom wisdom?

KELLY: From the Internet?

CARMEN: No. From *mi abuela.*

KELLY: Who's that, your auntie?

CARMEN: My grandmother. My little roly-poly, gray-haired Cuban grandma. Mercedes was her given name, but everybody called her Mercy, which is kind of funny, since she was a real dictator, just like Castro or Bautista, when it came to her husband. I mean, we all knew growing up that Grandpa Gusto, may he rest in peace, was henpecked and pussy-whipped. And I'm talking big-time. But what none of us knew, and I didn't find out till I was like seventeen and Mercy took me under her wing, was Grandpa was actually her slave. She didn't use that word, of course, but, looking back, it's obvious that's what he was. Gus worked in a furniture factory—this was back in Ybor City, the Cuban district of Tampa—and every Friday afternoon—that was payday—Grandma would drive right up to the factory gate and Gus would hustle out and hand over his paycheck already signed. I guess this was before direct deposit, you know? She told me once he never saw a penny of anything he earned. Zip-zero-*nada.* What she used to do was give Grandpa exact bus fare to and from work every day but no lunch money because she always made him brown-bag it. And, believe me, there were no boys' nights out for Grandpa Gus, not ever! That poor bastard came straight home from work, dropped his toolbox, tied on his frilly apron and started right in on his chores. Or else!

KELLY: No wonder you turned out such a firecracker! Mercedes sounds fantastic!

CARMEN: And, remember, Kelly, this was in a culture of like total machismo. The young feminists should put up a big statue to my *abuelita*, Grandma Mercy, right in the town square of Ybor City, with her fat arms folded and holding her trusty carpet beater.

KELLY: Is that what she used on your grandpa?

CARMEN: Every Sunday, right after they came home from Mass. She told me she made him drop his pants and bend over so she could wallop his ass with that carpet beater. She showed it to me once. I'm telling you, that thing had to be lethal! A lot heavier than you'd think, made out of twisted, braided fibers of sugar cane.

KELLY: Did you ever see her use it on him?

CARMEN: You know, I really wish I had! And if I'd asked her, maybe she'd of let me watch, or even let me try my hand. Of course, the old guy was, what, already in his sixties by then, so maybe not. But she definitely wanted to tell me all about how she kept him down and ruled the roost. She saw the way boys flocked around me, and she especially liked how I treated them—you know, like shit under my shoes? "Carmelita," she told me once, "men love bitches. So be one!" And, you'd better believe, I've taken her advice!

KELLY: So she was your mentor?

CARMEN: Yeah, just like I'm yours. Except when it came to corporal, like how hard and how often and all that stuff, I basically had to teach myself, trial and error, you know? It took a couple years and a shitload of wailing on guys to get my confidence up.

KELLY: Well, hint, hint. I was wondering if—

CARMEN: Hey, they're waving at me. Gotta go, girl!

KELLY: Carmen, wait! Is there any way you could maybe show me—

CARMEN: Show you what? Oh, of course! You'd like me to come over there and show you how it's done—on Christopher?

KELLY: I'd love it if you could. Is that too weird?

CARMEN: Fuck, no! That's what girlfriends are for. Are we talking tonight by any chance?

KELLY: Tonight would be fantastic. Of course, anytime would be—

CARMEN: Hang on. It's what, about four now? And we're supposed to wrap here by five. We're about thirty miles out in the boondocks, but if I don't go home first, I could maybe get to your place by six-thirty or seven. Would that be too late?

KELLY: We'll be right here waiting for you, and one of us will be naked and handcuffed. Will you be hungry?"

CARMEN: Starving!

KELLY: I'll get Chris to make his famous Chinese chicken salad for both of us. He's gotten really good at it.

CARMEN: Hey, they're getting fucking frantic over there. I really gotta go.

KELLY: You're the best, Gallegos.

CARMEN: I know.

*

Chris had spent the last half-hour in the Mistress Bathroom cleaning grout lines on the white tile floor. It was a hands-and-knees job, section by section, requiring the consecutive application of baking soda, vinegar spray, stiff brush, cleaning rags, sponge bucket and large towel. On some sections, Kelly had stressed, he'd need to repeat the six-step process several times to achieve satisfactory results. Chris had just finished the area around the Goddess' Throne for the third time and was now knee-walking backward to start on the next section.

Painfully backward. The ache in his knees and shins was so acute that he'd all but forgotten the steady throb from his wounded buttocks.

This is the new normal, Chris reminded himself. *Learn to love it.*

"Slave!"

All thought was swept away by the imperious summons from directly behind him.

Chris whipped his head around. His owner was leaning back against the open door, arms folded, one knee outthrust with foot braced behind. She'd changed into skintight, hip-hugger jeans and was spectacularly bra-less beneath a peekaboo tank top with maximal cleavage. Her expression was one of amused contempt—prompted, no doubt, by the unsavory sight of her slave's battered buttocks and dangling ball sac.

"Is that all you've done?"

"I'm starting to get the hang of it, Goddess. I promise I'll get faster."

"You'd better. But right now I need you to fetch something for me." She clapped her hands. "On your feet."

Chris scrambled up, chagrined to see his penis pointing directly at his Goddess.

"You get worked up scrubbing my bathroom floor, do you, slave?"

Chris lowered his gaze and his voice. "I guess I do, Goddess."

Her throaty chuckle further stiffened him. "Well, perhaps I'll arrange to have you spend more time in here. You can turn it into a gleaming shrine." She strode forward and handed him the keys to the Audi. "Run down to the basement and fetch the pink plastic bag from the trunk. Don't look inside, just bring it straight back."

"Goddess, I—I don't have any clothes."

"I'm aware of that, slave. I saw the garbage bags on the service porch and the extra room in my wardrobe. I'm quite pleased, by the way. But didn't you leave yourself *anything* to wear?"

"No, Goddess. You said to remove every—"

A stinging slap silenced him. "Don't keep telling me what I said! Just answer my questions."

"Thank you, Goddess! No, I didn't leave myself anything to wear."

"What about the Armani suit I got you for those rare occasions when I permit you to attend cocktail parties or business dinners? Don't tell me you stuffed *that* in a garbage bag, too?"

"Yes, Goddess. I—I wasn't thinking." Christopher shut his eyes and clenched his face, anticipating another slap. He was not disappointed. The open-handed blow came from the other side, jarring him off balance and delaying his mandatory "Thank you, Goddess."

"Mindless obedience will usually keep you out of trouble, slave, but not this time. What you did was beyond idiotic." Kelly shook her regal head in exasperation. "You'll need to go through those garbage bags and retrieve the suit, *and* the neckties I bought you at the same time, *and* the dress shirts, *and* the blue blazer, *and* the gray flannel slacks, *and* the leather belt *and* the black dress shoes—and don't forget the dress socks. After everything is cleaned or pressed, I'll have them put in storage for you."

"Yes, Goddess." Chris turned to go, but his upper arm was seized. "You can do all that later. Right now we've got to put something on you so you can run down to my car. Stay on your feet and follow me. You have permission to walk."

Chris scurried along in her wake, first into the Mistress Bedroom, then into her big walk-in closet. He stood near, watching Kelly click her way down the long hanging rack in quest of something suitable. Except he wasn't watching her nimble hands or her patrician profile, but the luscious wobble of her hefty left breast, liberally exposed through the tank top's gaping armhole. The enticing vision brought him fully erect.

"Well, what do you think, slave?" she demanded.

Chris instantly adjusted focus. She was holding up a shorty kimono of plum satin.

She couldn't be serious! Or could she?

"No, I guess not," she answered her own question, quelling Christopher's panic. "As much as I'd love to do it to you, sweetie, we mustn't scare the neighbors."

She replaced the kimono and stepped sideways, swiping and clicking through the next batch of hanging clothes, then the next, and the next. Finally, nearing the rack's far end, she extracted a big fluffy bathrobe. Chris recognized it as a posh souvenir brought back from a recent business trip to Dubai. The terrycloth had a white-on-white checkerboard pattern with the iconic logo of the Burj Al Arab Hotel. Kelly flung the robe toward him carelessly, but Chris used extreme care to catch it. Woe unto him had he let it touch the floor!

"Belt that on and go barefoot. People will assume you're headed for the pool." A double palm clap signaled his dismissal.

*

Chris was back in five minutes. He'd followed instructions not to look in the bag, but he'd smelled leather right off. He'd also felt of the contents, enough to form a pretty good idea of what sort of stuff was inside and how and on whom it would be used. Enough to feel a stab of real fear along with the usual submissive excitement.

He found Kelly in the kitchen, sitting on her heels in front of the open refrigerator. "You need to do a better job arranging these shelves," she snapped without looking up. "What are my yogurts doing way down on the bottom?"

"I promise I'll be more careful, Goddess." When she straightened up, shutting the refrigerator door, Chris reached out with the plastic Xanadu bag and the car keys. "Here, Goddess Kelly."

But he was left holding the bag. She just glared back, arms folded beneath the intimidating thrust of bosom.

"What's wrong, Goddess? What did I do wrong?"

"For starters, slave, why are you still wearing my robe? You know you're never to wear clothes before your Supreme Goddess!"

"Oh, God, I forgot! I'm so sorry!" In his panic to divest himself of the garment, Chris shrugged it off and let it slide backward off his shoulders. This was another mistake, but the realization came a split-second too late. As he whirled to retrieve it, Kelly's swinging right palm caught him behind the ear and sent him tumbling against the lower kitchen cupboards.

Dazed and fearful, Chris could only look up and sputter his "Th-thank you, Goddess!"

"Get my robe off the floor this instant and drape it over that chair. Carefully! *Now* you may hand me the bag and my keys."

Properly naked and back on his feet with plastic bag in hand, again Chris approached his Goddess. But a narrowing of her gray eyes told him he was still on dangerous ground. He tried to retreat, but again it was too late. She was on him like a cat, pummeling his face with both hands.

"You forget your place!" she shouted over his anguished cries and mumbled thank-yous. "How dare you present anything to your Goddess in such a rude and disrespectful way! Do it correctly, exactly as you were trained!"

How could he have forgotten that, too? Chris fell to his knees, prostrating himself while extending the bag upward with both hands. Kelly snatched it from him and tossed it on the countertop along with the car keys.

"That is the *only* way you are ever to hand anything to me, or to any female guest I may have. Naked, on your knees, head down."

"Yes, my Goddess."

"And it's not just when you're presenting something to me, or serving me, that you are to bow down. *Any* time I ask you to approach me, or I approach you, you are to get on your knees and abase yourself. Is that sufficiently clear?"

"Yes, Goddess, it is."

"Let that be a constant reminder of your inferior place in my household. Where is that place, slave?"

"Always at your feet, Goddess."

"Exactly!"

"But—but—"

"But *what*, slave?"

"Wh-what was that you just said, you know, about—about female guests and—?"

"Oh, you noticed that, did you? What was it you wanted to know?"

"It's just that I never heard anything like that before, Goddess. About my serving other women."

"Are you questioning my right to have you do so?"

"No, Goddess, I would never—"

"Because if I wish to display my naked, obedient slave to one or more of my girlfriends, or even casual female acquaintances, rest assured that I will do so without consulting you. Is that clear? Or do I detect a slight look of disapproval on your face?"

"No, Goddess, b-b-believe me!" But his stammering protest could not stop the blow he'd seen coming. Kelly was standing directly over him now, her left hand arcing down and impacting flush on his right cheek. A plaintive wail burst from his lips, followed by another abject thank-you.

"I will not have my authority questioned by you, in any way, ever! You begged to be my slave, and you will live by my rules! Is that understood?"

"Yes, my Goddess."

"And get that injured look off your face. Don't you dare play the pitiful victim with me, slave. I'm making all your pathetic, sniveling dreams come true! Isn't that so?"

"Yes, Goddess, it is."

"So, slave, tell me this. Do you think my last slap was too hard or too cruel?"

"No, Goddess, absolutely not."

"Are you the one who decides how hard or how often I'm allowed to slap you?"

"No, Goddess."

"Is there any limit to how many times I'm permitted to slap my property?"

"No, Goddess, there isn't."

"Right on all counts."

Kelly stepped back from her chastened slave, heaving a deep sigh as she leaned her hips against the counter. Despite what she'd just said, she decided that a limit on face-slapping had indeed been reached—at least for the moment. Her palms were smarting from all the impacts, and both sides of Christopher's face were now puffed and inflamed.

Kelly noted with satisfaction, however, that his penis retained a semi-rigid salute, another sign of her limitless power over him.

But there was another reason to move things along. She was feeling extremely pre-orgasmic. Something would have to be done about that—and right away. She addressed the cowering figure:

"Will you ever again forget to kneel when you come before me, slave?"

"No, Goddess. Never."

"Good." She clapped her hands. "Kneel up."

Chris did as told, and Kelly came toward him—and kept coming till she stood only inches away and he was staring at her dimpled navel through an artful slash in her tank top. Her fingers snaked around the back of his head, and his face was guided forcefully downward into the crotch seam of her jeans.

"Is this what you worship, slave?"

His "Yes, Goddess" came out slightly muffled and congested, almost a choking sound. Glancing down, she noted a telltale shuddering of his shoulders.

"Are you starting to cry again, little slave?"

"No, Goddess, it's just that—that—"

"Don't lie to me!" She tipped his face up. "My God, you *are* crying! I hope they're tears of joy."

"I'm sure they are, Goddess."

In truth, Chris didn't really know why he was feeling weepy again. These last few days his emotions had gone wildly out of control. Out of *his* control, at any rate. Like every other aspect of his life, it seemed, they had come under his Goddess' dominion.

But all these considerations were forgotten as he worked his nose into the cleft of her jeans, praying she'd allow him past this final barrier.

"It's time to please your Goddess, slave," came the longed-for directive. "Unzip me and pull my pants down."

With eager fingers, Chris unbuttoned her pants and slid the zipper tab reverently downward before tugging and peeling the rough denim fabric over her swelling hips. She wore no panties.

"That's enough, slave!" The waistband had only reached mid-thigh, but her golden triangle was fully revealed. "Now get your face in my bush where it belongs."

Christopher needed no encouragement, only permission, Kelly knew, when it came to performing oral worship. She also knew that her playfully bossy behavior—insulting, intimidating and slapping him silly—only heightened his servile craving for her.

So, she'd given him a bit of hell. Now, with a forward thrust of her pelvis, she offered him the gates of heaven.

At this point, Chris could neither speak nor think, see nor hear. Nor did he feel the additional pain of the Spanish tiles on his already abraded kneecaps. He was scarcely aware of Goddess Kelly's fingers knotted in his hair, then sliding down to caress his painfully swollen face.

He was keenly aware of her pervasive and pungent female scent, and he gloried in the slippery wetness that coated his face as his nose and tongue probed her labial folds. Soon enough he was inside her holy of holies, licking and sucking and swallowing her juices to his soul's content.

Realizing that his Goddess was already in a state of extreme readiness, Chris quickly settled into a rhythmic tonguing of her swollen clit—and too soon felt the first muscular contractions that signaled imminent climax. Unfortunately, this meant he was going to be short-changed in his cherished cunnilingual duties. It seemed his

Goddess had discovered a whole new way to have her slave bring her right to the edge—by using him first as her whipping boy. Or slapping boy.

Which was something to bear in mind, he thought, something that might help him endure the shocking pain of future punishment sessions. By suffering her cruelty, he would be helping his Goddess achieve higher levels of sexual gratification. And wasn't that what male slaves were for?

Chris was keenly attuned to Kelly's powerful body—to the clench of her abdominal muscles, the grunts of visceral effort, the sudden clutch of talon fingers on his painfully sore jaw, and finally a more violent bucking of her hips that began to whipsaw his head.

And he was straining, too, not unlike a zealous husband in the delivery room, counting breathing cadences to his sweat-soaked, gasping wife. Except, of course, Chris was only midwifing her orgasm, not a baby.

Any second now, he thought.

It started with a wail as heart-wrenching as though she were being beaten, just as he had been last night. But there was no pantyhose gag to muffle these piteous cries. Would the neighbors think him a wife-beating brute?

Gradually, then, her despairing ecstasies softened into a rapturous rise and fall that Chris always found utterly captivating. This was what he lived for—the incredible privilege of being present during these exalted moments of female ascendancy. His Goddess was now in another realm, he knew. A multi-orgasmic realm that only females could enter, and which males could never experience—except vicariously, as he was doing now in the clench and clasp of his female ruler.

Little by little her exquisite sighs died away, and her body went slack. Chris made a grab to steady her, but she had staggered back against the high kitchen countertop, giggling as though tipsy. Chris kneewalked forward, hoping to plant his face back between her legs, but Kelly pushed him away roughly. She pointed down at her hip-hugger jeans, which were still stranded at mid-thigh.

"Get these off me now, slave."

Christopher made quick work of it, shucking both pantlegs down those gorgeous dancer's legs to puddle at her ankles, where, with a balancing hand on his forehead, Kelly was able to step out of them.

"What time is it now, slave?"

"Almost five-thirty, Goddess."

"Oh, shit! You've barely started on the bathroom floor, and now I need you to switch to ironing. Can you get through everything still in the wicker basket in, say, half an hour?"

"I'll—I'll try, Goddess."

"Well, I'd rather you didn't rush and end up scorching one of my silk blouses. Take your time, if you have to, just do as much as you can between now and six. That's when you'll need to start dinner preparations. You'll be making Chinese chicken salad for two. Have you got all the ingredients?"

"Yes, Goddess, I'm pretty sure."

"You better be *damn* sure—*before* you start your ironing. If there's something you don't have, call Pink Dot and have it delivered A-S-A-P. Have you got all that, or do I need to have you repeat it back?"

"No, Goddess. I can remember."

"And don't forget to put my jeans in the hamper and hang my Burj bathrobe back in the wardrobe." On impulsive then, and contrary to her resolve, she reached down and slapped his face again—hard. "Why are you still on your knees? Get up, slave! There's a lot for you to do and very little time."

"Yes, Goddess." Christopher scrambled up, grabbing her jeans off the floor.

"One thing more, Christopher."

"Yes, Goddess?" He turned back, longing for even a word or gesture of affection from this fantastic creature whom he worshipped and adored.

It was not to be.

"Your little pee-pee seems to be sticking straight up. Is that supposed to impress me?"

"No, Goddess."

"Good, because it's not impressive, you know. It is kind of cute, I suppose, in a horny adolescent way. It's almost dripping, isn't it?" With one bare foot she swiped at his rigid shaft, starting a comical, tick-tock wobble. "You'd really like to come, wouldn't you?"

"Yes, Goddess, I would."

"If we had more time, I'd make you beg, but it's not going to happen anyway, is it, slave?"

Chris shook his head. While being endlessly teased and denied drove him out of his mind, he accepted that Goddess Kelly had the divine right to do that to him. What *did* hurt him, and keenly, was being denied the idyllic aftermath of her passion. Those intensely intimate moments of cuddling and devotion; or, every bit as sweet, those times when she would lapse into après-sex slumber while he remained motionless at her breast or between her legs, barely breathing, till she awakened.

"Poor baby," Kelly was still cooing at him. "Not only is it not going to happen tonight, but, the truth is, I can't really say when it *will* happen. Maybe not for a very long time. Which means I should probably lock you up right now. But I'm thinking of leaving you out a little while longer. Would you like that, slave?"

"Yes, Goddess."

"Then hadn't you better thank me?"

"Thank you, Goddess."

"But when you're out of my sight, don't you dare touch yourself. Or you'll be a very sorry, sorry slave indeed."

"I won't, Goddess, I swear."

She flashed him a wicked smile before clapping her hands twice to dismiss him.

*

As she watched her slave out of sight, Kelly was savoring her usual post-orgasmic charge from sending him back to his menial chores with his balls in full burst mode. Yet she also felt a small pang of regret. Not for this minor cruelty, but for an earlier kindness—a silly egalitarian gesture she'd made after coming all those times while face-sitting him on the loveseat. If only she hadn't given Chris that quickie hand job, think how incredibly desperate he'd be right now!

Which gave her momentary pause. How long, she wondered, might she extend his enforced chastity and sexual frustration? For weeks, certainly, but what about months or even years? Could she be that cruel with her Christopher? Probably not, but it was delicious fun to think about, especially knowing she had the supreme power to do it.

It was definitely something to ask Carmen about the next time she saw her. Which, Kelly reminded herself, should be in just about an hour from now.

And wasn't *that* going to be a big surprise for somebody?

*

CHAPTER SIX ~ CARMEN'S VISIT ~ 2

Chris hung up the ivory linen wrap-blouse and reached into the wicker basket for the next item to be ironed. This turned out to be her Versace pants, floral-printed and ankle-cropped in stretch cotton. He turned the riotously patterned legs inside out, then dialed the iron to its lowest setting. Kelly had gotten them on the Via Veneto, which was apparently a fancy shopping street in Rome.

She'd gotten them on sale. For just under twelve-hundred dollars. Or was it euros? Chris proceeded with extreme caution, trying not to be paralyzed with fear.

Of all his chores, ironing had been the one he'd disliked the most. And, perversely, the one he seemed to spend the most time on, since Kelly insisted that not only her clothes be pressed, but her pillowcases and dish towels, too.

But his attitude had changed drastically these last few days, along with everything else in his life. It wasn't that he'd learned to love ironing or gotten a whole lot better at it. His technique was still clumsy and his concentration uneven. And just now, with all the chores Kelly had piled on him, plus the beatings and slappings she'd administered, Chris was having a tough time just staying on his feet with eyes focused.

No, the difference was his attitude. He'd stopped kidding himself that such menial work was beneath him. How could anything be beneath a lowly slave? How could *any* task undertaken in the service of a Supreme Goddess be anything but an honor and a privilege?

Chris had learned something else under his new regimen. Not

only was Goddess Kelly to be worshipped, but everything she owned was to be considered sacred. Which meant each item of clothing merited the utmost care. Which is why he'd been slapped so hard for letting her bathrobe fall to the kitchen floor. And why she expected her Versace pants to be completely wrinkle-free each and every time she pulled them on.

This had become the new purpose of his life. What could be more important than caring for the clothes and personal items of a Goddess? What, for instance, could be more important than maintaining her vast collection of shoes in logical arrangement and near-new condition, cleaned, polished and repaired as needed?

Or hand-washing and air-drying her sacred undergarments, then folding them perfectly and placing them lovingly into lingerie drawers that were always neatly arranged?

Or washing and pressing her designer blouses and skirts and dresses to the very best of his ability, and fetching her dry-cleaning from down the street as soon as it was ready, so she never had to think about it?

What could be more important than laying her ensembles out on the bed each morning, and, if asked, making thoughtful, alternate suggestions?

Or ensuring that her bathroom counter and mirror were kept as spotless as in one of the luxury resort hotels Kelly represented, with all her toiletries and cosmetics arrayed for easy use and her combs and brushes always freshly cleaned and free of stray strands of hair?

Chris was learning to take great personal pride in completing all these chores and daily routines for his Goddess. By doing so, as she'd pointed out, he was not only giving some meaning to his own existence, but actually making a small contribution to her professional and social success in the world. With her mind freed from such trivial concerns, she could concentrate more fully on the great challenges facing her each day in her executive career.

Which is why, despite his fatigue, Christopher was getting painfully hard again, just thinking of the absolute power his Goddess exercised over him, and the many ways she'd demonstrated that power these last few days. Demoting him from househusband to slave, stripping him not only of clothing, but of basic human rights and privileges. His pitiful objections had been met with insults and derision, face slaps and crotch kicks. Then, the biggest comeuppance of all, last night's brutal thrashing with the thick leather belt.

Yet the crueler her treatment, the greater his submissive arousal—or so it seemed. It actually excited him, for instance, to be confined in this little alcove off the kitchen—what Kelly called her service porch—naked and sweating over the ironing board. While his Goddess lounged in the adjoining room, watching her favorite shows on the DVR.

She was only about twenty feet away—so near, in fact, that she'd ordered him to keep the door closed so she wouldn't be annoyed by the steam iron's intermittent hiss. While he remained on constant alert for the sound of a summons, in case she should require additional service.

Chris made a final inspection of the Versace pants, draped them across a hanger and hung them on a short utility rack with the other finished ironing.

Next out of the basket was a rolled-up towel, still damp. Inside, also damp, was an aqua blouse of cotton chiffon. Making sure the iron was still on its lowest setting, he stretched the delicate fabric across the ironing board, then covered it with a damp cloth to prevent it from drying out while being pressed. He repeated the process, section by section, with painstaking care.

As he worked, every so often he would glance up, between the dangle of hand-washed panties, pantyhose and bras drying on the overhead clothesline, to a small cork board on which Kelly had pinned a printout in extra-large type. It was entitled "SLAVE MANTRA," and Christopher was learning it, section by section. He located the part he was currently working on and began to repeat, quietly and reverently, the following phrases, letting each sink into memory:

"Goddess Kelly is my Queen and Goddess... She is powerful... I bow to Her and kiss Her feet...Her power is absolute over me... She is great and powerful... She protects me... She owns me... It's her right to own everything... I obey Her totally... She is in absolute control... She speaks and I listen... She leads and I follow... Her decisions are final... I'm afraid to cross Her... I'm afraid of Her anger... I'm afraid of displeasing Her... I bow down and worship Her..."

This was, of course, mind control, but for his own good, as Kelly had explained to him patiently. "You mustn't think for yourself, slave. It only gets you into trouble, as you should know by now. I'll do all your thinking for you. All you have to do is obey."

He glanced upward again, this time at a small digital clock just below the corkboard. 6:26. The Chinese chicken salad was ready to serve, as per Goddess Kelly's instructions, whenever she gave the word. She'd said to prepare it for two and set two place settings, including stemware. This was a puzzle, since Chris was no longer permitted to eat with his Goddess, or even to sit at table, for that matter.

Did she intend him to dine beside her one last time, the way she'd asked him to join her on the loveseat earlier? As a fond farewell to the way things had been—before finalizing his slave status forever?

These wistful speculations were shattered by the door chime, which gave him a nervous jolt. Answering the door was *his* job, but not now surely—not stark naked like this with his cock sticking straight out!

He parked the iron, listening intently. And heard, to his great relief, the unmistakable creak of the recliner mechanism, then his Goddess' bare feet padding to the door. There was the double click of the bolt being retracted and the knob being turned, then the soft sweep of weather-stripping across carpeting.

The door was open. Who could it be?

He heard a female voice, Hispanic and high-velocity, too fast for Chris' mind to process as Kelly fired back her own word burst. Women, as Chris kept being reminded, could so easily outthink and outtalk men. Next came Goddess Kelly's husky chuckle—a sound that never failed to thrill Christopher—followed by an explosion of soprano cackles.

A name popped into Chris' head. *Carmen.* The "new friend" Kelly had gone to the sex shop with this morning, when she'd picked up all the scary stuff in that plastic bag.

It had to be her. A "female supremacist." That's how Kelly had referred to her new friend last night. He knew now who the other place setting was for.

But why was she here? Just for dinner? Several other possibilities sprang to mind, triggering excitement and apprehension. One way or another, he was going to find out. And maybe very soon. Because the two women were coming closer now as they headed for the living room, giggling like schoolgirls as they talked over each other.

"What was so difficult about *your* day?" Kelly was saying as their steps approached his closed door. "All you had to do was stand there and look sexy."

"Yeah, for four hours straight, deep-frying in the sun. While Mr. Muscles from Melbourne kept fluffing his three-word lines. Look, I'm fucking famished. Where's this famous Chinese chicken salad you were talking about?"

"It's ready. I'll have my slave serve it. And pour us some chilled Chardonnay."

"Sounds heavenly! Where do you keep him, by the way?"

"He's right inside that door, ironing my clothes. Let me show you."

The door to Christopher's alcove began sliding back into its recess. An instant after, Chris found himself on full, naked display before the two women.

In his shock, he completely forgot his brand-new slave protocol—until a flicker of fury in Kelly's gray eyes brought it all back. He dropped to his knees, touching his forehead to the floor in front of Carmen's platform sandals.

"Kiss her feet, slave," came Kelly's haughty command.

Chris raised his eyes just enough to focus on the tanned, clear-lacquered toes peeping out of Carmen's sandals. He touched his lips to one sexy foot, then the other. Her toes were unusually long and elegant.

"You may lick them, slave," Carmen said matter-of-factly.

"Don't forget to thank her for the privilege," Kelly added. "You may address her as Goddess Carmen."

"Thank you, Goddess Carmen."

Licking the day's accumulated sweat and dust from these lovely toes sent Christopher into a submissive swoon. He realized, with some surprise, that it didn't feel in the least unnatural to be on his knees before these two superior women. It felt like he was exactly where he belonged, far beneath them.

"Remain on your knees, slave," his Goddess commanded, "but kneel up, so you can look up and admire Goddess Carmen's great beauty. But you're not to speak unless given permission."

Christopher did as told, feasting his eyes on the vibrant young Latina above him.

"Have him stand up," Carmen said, "so I can inspect him full-length."

"You heard Goddess Carmen. On your feet, slave, but now keep your eyes down."

Again Chris obeyed, but the visual impact of what he'd just seen remained vivid in memory. Even in platform sandals, Carmen stood several inches lower than his own barefoot Goddess, who'd changed into black leggings and a gray knit top with plunging v-neck. Of course, when it came to cleavage—well, that was strictly no contest. But Carmen's fringed buckskin minidress, with its tight-belted waist, showcased a lusciously contoured figure, especially her bronzed, sleekly muscled legs. These were absolutely sensational.

Her best features, though, were blazing dark eyes and a blinding white smile. Chris could easily believe Carmen was an actress. It looked, in fact, like she was still wearing theatrical makeup.

"So what's he doing out of his cage?" came her sultry voice.

"I like having him completely vulnerable to me when I'm home," Kelly explained. "Also, I wanted you to be able to check him out."

"No problem."

A slim hand appeared in Chris' downcast circle of vision. A golden hand, adorned with silver bracelets and a vintage ring of Navajo turquoise, the fingers now encircling his rudely pointing penis.

"Carmen, look! I think he's trying to get extra hard for you. What a little show-off! But he's not as impressive as Hector, is he? Not even close."

"No, but I like his shape. Hector's kind of crooked, you know? Like a wet cigar. Why do you let him have hair down here?" Carmen released his penis with a painful sideways slap, then wound her fingers tightly in his pubic hair and yanked so hard that Christopher cried out. "Why don't you make him shave it all off like we talked about?"

"I'm definitely thinking about it. Of course, it'll make him look like a little boy, but then he's never really been much of a man. Have you, sweetie?"

"No, Goddess." Chris kept his eyes down. He was fully rigid now from being handled so dismissively by this sexy, superior Latina.

"Make sure he shaves everything—cock and balls and ass cheeks, and don't let him forget his underarms. And punish him if he misses a single hair. That's what I do with Hector."

Kelly chuckled. "Did you hear all that, slave?"

"Yes, Goddess."

"Right now, though, I want you to hurry up and serve our salads. After you pour us each a glass of Chardonnay."

"Yes, Goddess, I'll—"

"Quiet! And I expect to see excellent service from you tonight. You won't be eating, of course. Right after we eat, and you do a quick cleanup, you're going to get that severe punishment you've been asking for all day. Have you got all that?"

"Yes, Goddess Kelly."

"Then get going." Her hands clapped twice in dismissal.

"Wait! Before he leaves, why don't you have him curtsy to acknowledge your orders?"

"Don't tell me you make Hector curtsy."

"Fuck, yeah! Next time you're over, I'll make him do it for you. He's gotten really good at it. Put him in one of those black satin maid uniforms with lace trim and a white pinafore, and, I swear, that cholo could fit right into *Downton Abbey*."

"I know I keep asking you for favors," Kelly said when she'd stopped laughing, "but could you show Christopher how it's done?"

"No *problemo*. Here, slave, watch closely. I'm going to curtsy several times, then it's your turn."

Given permission to raise his face, Chris again found himself distracted by the impact of the sexy Latina and forgot to study the quick and graceful up-and-down movement, which she did with one foot behind the other and a single dip of her head. When it came Chris' turn, he got his feet wrong and almost lost his balance. This drew a derisive snort from Kelly and a hard slap from his instructress.

"Watch again, slave, and this time pay attention! I'm going to do it in slow motion, and I expect you to copy everything I do." Turning to Kelly, she asked, "What do you want him to say when he curtsies? I have Hector say 'Yes, Ma'am' or just 'Yes'm.'"

"Christopher says 'Yes, Goddess' to everything, but with a curtsy, I suppose 'Yes'm' does sound a bit more obsequious."

For the next several minutes, Chris was put through his servile paces while his Goddess looked on in fascination. He couldn't help recalling his first painfully awkward lessons in dancing backward. But Kelly had seldom slapped him for those early missteps, certainly not as often as Goddess Carmen was doing now. By the time he finally managed to execute the simple movement to her grudging satisfaction, his cheeks were aflame and he'd been reduced to tears of pain and frustration.

"That's not bad, slave. But it's still clunky, like you're just going through the motions. Make it quick and super-respectful, like saluting a general."

"I'm a lot higher than *that*, as far as he's concerned!" Kelly objected.

"Of course, you are. And he's, what, a woman's slave, the lowest rung on the ladder. And basically a sissy boy, if you want to turn him that way."

Finally he was dismissed, with a final swat on his naked ass from the laughing Latina and a horselaugh from Kelly.

"So tell me," Kelly said when her slave was out of earshot, "what do you think of him?"

"Definitely a keeper."

"He's a lamb, actually, and I'm having so much more fun with him, thanks to you, Carmen. But why do I get so hot watching you slap him around like that?"

Carmen flashed a delightfully wicked smile. "Just wait. You ain't seen nothin' yet."

*

The dominant beauties sat chatting and gesturing with their chopsticks between crunchy mouthfuls of the delicious Chinese chicken salad with fried wonton noodles. Chris stood a dozen feet away at the sideboard, as he'd been trained, watching without seeming to watch. He'd seated the ladies at the dining room table, lighted the white pillar candle in its glass bowl between them, served the salads, refilled their wineglasses and now remained on high alert.

He feigned outward calm, but inwardly Chris was pulsing with excitement at being their waiter for the evening. He got so carried away with his role that, for a delusional moment, he imagined himself impeccably attired—in white tuxedo jacket and black bowtie— forgetting that he wasn't attired at all, but standing there jaybird naked with a rampant hard-on.

While being completely ignored.

Being a servant to these Goddesses now felt utterly natural, even a naked servant, not worth a glance unless he was required for a refill, say, or an additional condiment. What did seem bizarre now was the idea of eating at table with them, or with Goddess Kelly. How had he ever imagined himself worthy of such equal status?

Crouching at their feet and being hand-fed table scraps, or putting his face in a dog bowl full of their plate scrapings, all these he could easily imagine in this new order of things. And, knowing the caprices of his Goddess, Chris was fully prepared for such a summons. Though, in his present state of excitement, he couldn't imagine himself swallowing anything. He was far too spellbound by the candlelit glory of their animated profiles and delectable forms against the sparkling backdrop of city lights out the windows.

And, of course, he was a nervous wreck from thinking about what these two fantastic females were planning to do to him after dinner.

At the moment, however—from what Chris could glean from their rapid-fire exchanges—they were swapping the latest celebrity gossip. About some Chinese kung-fu film star whose shockingly undersized "wangdoodle" had been caught on iPhone video and had now gone viral all over social media.

"Serves him right," Carmen was saying. "The egotistical asshole got shit-faced on meth and coke at his own wrap party and started Donald Ducking!"

"What the fuck is Donald Ducking?" Kelly wanted to know.

"You know, doing the no-pants dance? Naked from the waist down?"

This ignited more laughter and started a hilariously raunchy contest to see who could come up with the most politically incorrect, Asian penis-size joke. The terms "spring roll," "candlewick" and "egg noodle" all got dishonorable mentions.

Whoever said girls couldn't talk dirty, Chris thought, or didn't like to objectify the male of the species? And what a delightful privilege it was to eavesdrop on unfiltered girl talk.

"But did you get a look at his ass?" Kelly was saying now.

"I already said he was cute. Are you fishing for more compliments?"

"No, of course not. I mean all those welts and bruises."

With a start, Chris realized the raunchy conversation must have veered when he wasn't tracking. The Goddesses were obviously discussing *him* now—his ass, *his* welts and bruises.

"Honestly, Kelly, like I said, you're making way too much of a fuss about it. Hector gets a lot worse from me on a regular basis. And

I regard it as doing him a favor. He says he wants to be my slave. Okay, a real worthy ambition. But talk is cheap, and we know guys will say anything. What I also know, and Hector doesn't, is that he's gonna need a shitload of physical persuasion to achieve his goal of being a good slave to me. And that means being punished every single day of his inferior life. Know what Grandma Mercy always said?"

"Ah, another gem of femdom wisdom from your *abuela?*"

"You wanna hear it or not?"

"Forgive me, Carmen. Yes, please tell me what your wise grandmother always said."

"She told me that even a good man can be improved with daily beating."

"What about a bad man?"

"Twice a day—just for starters!" Laughter exploded again. "I'm still not sure which Hector is, but, believe me, I rarely miss a day with him."

"What about today?" Chris saw Kelly's eyes go to the antique ormolu clock beside him on the sideboard.

"Today is not over yet. And Hec knows it."

"Well, then, maybe we'd better get on with things. If you're sure I'm not going to do any permanent damage."

"Don't worry. He's your property, after all, so we'll be careful not to do permanent damage."

"Okay. Slave," Kelly raised her voice fractionally, "serve our coffee in the living room. Right away. Then clear the table and put everything away. Leave your complete cleanup till later. We'll expect you to report for punishment in no more than ten minutes."

"Yes, Goddess Kelly."

*

CHAPTER SEVEN ~ SECOND PUNISHMENT

After a hectic cleanup, with the table cleared, perishables put away, dishes stacked in the sink and his stomach in a mad whirl, Chris was ready. It had taken less than five minutes. But Goddess Kelly had said no sooner than ten. Or had it been no *later?* His brain, hopelessly addled, could not recall which. Fearful of coming out too soon or too late, he peeked into the living room.

Goddess Kelly and Goddess Carmen were on the loveseat, sitting almost primly, half turned toward each other with knees nearly touching, saucers on laps, coffee cups in hand. Carmen was talking and gesturing with her free hand, Kelly nodding vigorously.

Women always had so much to communicate!

Chris ducked back into the kitchen, deciding to split the difference between five and ten and give it at least two more minutes before appearing for his punishment. In the meantime, he did some more putting away, wiped down the kitchen counters, cleaned the stovetop (though he hadn't used it), then rinsed plates and silverware and put them in the dishwasher.

Eight minutes had elapsed by the stove clock, and his heart was pounding. Taking an extra-deep breath, he left the kitchen.

Walk or crawl? The protocol was not clear to him. But, overwhelmed by a conviction of his own inferiority and sensing it would be best to propitiate these Goddesses, he dropped and approached on hands and knees, head down.

Before dipping his eyes, however, he'd glimpsed—with a jolt of genuine fear—the neat array of punishment implements on the low glass-and-chrome coffee table in front of the loveseat. These, obviously, were the items he had felt inside the plastic drawstring bag.

Riding crop, leather strap, wooden paddle, thin bamboo cane. Like surgical instruments laid out in an operating room. Beside the cane were two pairs of what Chris recognized as flexible plastic cuffs, with Velcro closures and attached D-rings.

Dear God, were they *all* going to be used on him?

Without really knowing why, he picked the spindly bamboo rod as the one capable of inflicting the most pain. At least there was no actual whip. Though that, too, might be in his future.

Fear now gripped him by the throat. But Christopher kept crawling stealthily forward, knowing there was no escape for him. He had begged for this only a few hours ago—for Kelly to treat him cruelly, to spare him nothing in order to make him the best possible slave.

Kelly, with her back to him, was asking Carmen about taking a Pilates class.

Should he wait here, a few feet away, for a formal summons? Or should he just crawl up to his Goddess' nearer foot and kiss it?

But that might be construed as an impertinence. Or, worse yet, an interruption. Women were never to be interrupted when they were speaking, *any* women, *any*where. For a lowly male to interrupt two Goddesses would be unthinkable. So he waited, head down, letting the delightful music of female conversation wash over him.

"Slave, I see that you're ready." Goddess Kelly set cup and saucer down on the glass table. "Crawl to me."

Chris felt her palm gliding over his upturned bottom as he crept forward to kiss her bare feet. He loved his Goddess' touch, but even her caress was painful just now on his welted flesh. How could she expect him to take *more* punishment?

"What do you think, Carmen? We could do it just like this, with him kneeling between us."

"It would be better, I think, with him hanging right here." She patted the back of the loveseat. "You'll see why in a moment."

"Up, slave!" Kelly pulled painfully on his earlobe.

Christopher leaped to his feet and, forcibly steered by the ear, scrambled after Goddess Kelly around to the back of the loveseat, then let himself be draped over it like a Gumby doll, head down in the velour cushions. Why didn't she just tell him to get into the same position as last night?

Despite his fear over what was to come, Chris was fully erect, with the sensitive underside of his penis rubbing now against the top of the loveseat. In fact, he was in imminent danger of ejaculating. Should he say something? But that chance was about to vanish:

"Open your mouth, slave!"

He obeyed and got it stuffed—with a pair of panties. Fresh panties, by the taste and smell and texture. But what else could they be? He'd just hand-washed all her soiled ones and hung them to dry. The panty gag was secured with several wrappings of pantyhose that were then cinched tight at the back of his neck. Next, after a quick succession of harsh, rasping sounds—Velcro strips being peeled apart—his wrists and ankles were circled and strapped with the flexicuffs, both women working together, their movements swift and synchronized.

Twisting his head on the seat cushion, Chris was just able to catch an upside-down glimpse of Kelly's hands on his left wrist cuff, feeding what looked like his own utility clothesline through the cuff's D-ring, then tugging his wrist forward. Quickly, as the process was repeated on each cuff, Chris found himself effectively bound, spread-eagled and helpless. Both wrists had been yanked forward and outward, then tied off, probably to the loveseat's front legs, while both ankles had been yanked far apart and secured most likely to the rear legs.

It was a scary predicament, and Chris was properly frightened. More than anything, he was beside himself with excitement. This was a submale fantasy come true—to be trussed up naked and panty-gagged, completely at the mercy of two sexy, Supreme Goddesses. There was no way he could cut short this punishment session as he'd done last night, throwing himself at Goddess Kelly's feet. All he could do was thrash and convulse against his bonds.

And would they even notice? Or care?

"You're really good with those ropes," Kelly was saying. "I can't even move his hands."

Chris listened to himself talked about in the third person, as though he were of no consequence. *Because I'm not*, he thought, more and more accepting of his inferior status.

"I've had lots of practice," Carmen was saying, "from like the age of twelve."

"Seriously?"

"Damn right! My cousin Jaime was an Eagle Scout, and I made him teach me ropework. And, in case you're wondering, yeah, I *did* practice on him a bit." Carmen's evil chuckle reminded Chris of a cartoon villainess. "I was a devil child, didn't I tell you?"

"Could you teach me?"

"Show you the ropes?" Carmen giggled, then went on: "But why? Are you planning to open a commercial dungeon or something? What you should really do—if you want to make this part quicker and easier—is go back to Xanadu, or just check online, for a custom bench with straps you can buckle him into in about five seconds, so he can't move. You can get one that looks just like a regular home workout bench and keep it in that extra bedroom with all that other gym equipment you got. And while you're at it, get him a ball gag."

"Duly noted. Thanks, Carmen."

"Hey, girl, better check his dick! I saw something move down there."

Chris felt a hand slip between his ass cheeks and grip his throbbing erection. "He's getting ready to shoot—all over my upholstery! I better ice him down quick."

"Don't bother, Kelly. When we crop his balls, his cock will go kaflooie. In fact, let's start right now. Remember how you did it to Hector?"

"That hard?"

"He's just a slave, remember? He exists to serve you, and to be abused and degraded for your pleasure and amusement. And it's time he learns you mean business. Here, take the crop and then give his junk a good solid whack or two till his dick shrivels up. Unless, of course, you want to ask his permission first."

"As if!" Kelly snickered. "No, don't worry. I've got this."

Chris held his breath and clamped his jaws, tensing his abdominal muscles in advance. But none of this prepared him for the actuality of the blow. When the business end of the crop struck his exposed testicles, his body convulsed and his breath exploded into the panty gag. Then he just slumped in his bonds as waves of crippling pain radiated outward from his groin. Even Goddess Kelly's barefoot kicks to his balls had not hurt this fiercely.

"Well?"

"That did the trick, Carmen. It's the incredible shrinking penis again."

"Good. Why don't you go ahead with the crop now and maybe the leather slapper after that. We can save the paddle and the cane for another lesson?"

"Sounds like a plan. But weren't you going to show me how?"

"Yeah, I was, but you'll learn a shitload more doing it yourself. Go ahead and start marking him up, and I'll just keep an eye on things. And let yourself go. He's your toy, right, so have fun with him."

"Where do I start?"

"I'd concentrate on the backs of his thighs. His ass cheeks are already lit up pretty good."

The instant she adopted Carmen's nonchalant, "let yourself go" attitude, Kelly felt liberated from unnecessary concerns over doing it incorrectly or injuring her slave. She felt fully empowered to exercise her dominion over Christopher, and—as Carmen had reminded her—to have fun doing it.

In fact, "fun" was too pale a word, she realized, as she slapped the crop tentatively against her thigh and walked to and fro behind her captive. In the immediate aftermath of that first whip-snake strike against his ball sac, Kelly had begun to feel the familiar, aphrodisiacal "high" that came from sexual dominance.

The crop was ever so much lighter than the heavy weightlifter's belt, which meant it wouldn't inflict nearly the same degree of damage per strike. And yet, the whippy little implement felt so much better in her hand, which meant she could wield it far longer. So, if she wasn't careful, the cumulative damage might be just as severe.

"You asked for this, slave," Kelly said aloud, admiring his thoroughly beaten buttocks.

She trailed the tip of the crop ever so lightly over the inflamed, injured flesh, watching his butt cheeks quiver in fearful expectation. The teasing had come naturally to her last night with the heavy belt in hand, but it was so much more fun with the crop. She caught Carmen's approving smile. She would have liked to prolong this playful prelude, but out of concern for her mentor's time, Kelly opted to cut it short.

The first blow was directed at the back of her slave's left thigh, a mere flyswatter snap with a lot of wrist action. Chris' reflexive flinch was out of all proportion to the light impact. The slap of leather on flesh was also negligible, certainly inaudible to her neighbors. What would happen when she pumped up the volume?

"I'm going to turn on some music," she explained to Carmen, retrieving the satellite TV remote from the small table between the recliners. She found the rock oldies audio channel and increased the volume on Elton John's "Alligator Rock" till it was bouncing off the walls.

Instantly energized by the happily thudding piano chords of the early Elton, Kelly swung her head and hips in tempo as she began cropping Chris' thighs, occasionally venturing north to work over his already battered butt.

"¡Qué guay!" Carmen shouted, whatever that meant. "Work it, babe!"

Kelly didn't worry about technique, steadily ratcheting up the speed and force of the blows till her slave began to jump and writhe with each strike.

She also tried not to glance over at Carmen too often, but each time she did, she was heartened by flashing eyes and quick nods of approval. *She knows exactly how I feel*, Kelly thought, putting even more force into each swing.

The primal sensations that gripped her now went beyond mere intoxication. Last night, she'd felt mostly contempt for this cringing male who, recognizing his own inferiority, was letting himself be beaten like an animal. And, honestly, there was more than a trace of that scorn tonight. Yet, again and again, as she wielded the flexible lash, seeking out new fleshly terrain to be marked and claimed, Kelly began to feel a deep tenderness for Christopher and the complete surrender of his manhood that made her ascendancy possible.

He truly knows his place, she realized, *and glories in my power over him every bit as much as I do!*

This was the kind of gender supremacy that had shocked and excited her four days ago at the airport, seeing "Cougar Domme" give the boot to her kneeling "Muscleboy," and again this morning at Xanadu when the older, Western-garbed domme jerked her scrawny toyboy around at the end of a chain-leash. It was nothing less than modern-day, femdom slave ownership, an outrageous and unapologetic lifestyle—and one that Kelly now coveted for herself.

And Christopher wanted it, too—to be totally owned by her. At least he claimed he did. She was simply testing his sincerity, wasn't she, lash after lash?

"Better check his face," came a quick prompt from Carmen.

Kelly stopped herself. She was a bit dizzy, breathing very fast and very deeply, as though she'd been running. She reached over the back of the loveseat and grabbed a fistful of her slave's hair, twisting his head around. She was surprised to look down into wretched, tear-stained features. Because of the gag, and being so caught up in her own torrential emotions, she hadn't guessed he'd be sobbing. Gratified by his suffering, she bent down and kissed each of his streaming eyes. Poor, sweet helpless boy, caught in her deadly web!

But Kelly didn't want to stop just now. The video speakers had begun blasting out Bob Seeger's "Old-Fashioned Rock 'n' Roll," one of her favorite oldies, and her Goddess body itched to resume its punishment dance.

But, as she pushed her slave's face back down, there came a gentle touch at her arm. Was Carmen calling a halt so soon?

Not to worry. Her friend was handing her the leather strap with a conspiratorial smile. "Go ahead and warm up his ass a bit with this. But you're definitely in the home stretch."

She's right, Kelly thought, trading the crop for the light leather slapper. Her arms weren't tired in the least, but her chest was heaving, maybe as much from excitement as exertion, and a quick down-glance showed her big tits pasted against their low-cut, sweat-damp confinement as though she were in the finals of a wet t-shirt contest.

But she was very close now to what felt like being a truly seismic climax, and she did want to get the feel of the leather slapper. With Carmen's sanction, she began to target Christopher's already inflamed butt cheeks, being mindful not to break the skin. But if the lashes were slightly moderated now, the words she began shouting at her quivering slave, to punctuate each strike, were merciless:

"You belong to me, slave—forever and ever!" "I own you, every part of you, and I will break you down!" "I demand total obedience from you, at all times!" "You're my property, my chattel, and never forget it!" "Surrender to your Goddess, surrender everything to me!"

Finally exhausted, she stopped and bent far over, hands on hips, like a marathoner having just staggered across the finish line. Gradually her gasps subsided into an easy in-and-out cadence that perfectly matched the song now pulsing from the speakers, the

Pointer Sisters' "Slow Hand."

Carmen appeared beside her, taking the leather strap from limp fingers.

"I came," Kelly said matter-of-factly, between gulps of oxygen.

"I know. It was very sweet."

"Does that happen for you, when you're playing with Hector?"

"Not always, but yeah, sometimes. It's very special when it does. It scares him, hearing the sounds I make, because I'm not ladylike like you. But I like him to be scared. It makes him worship me even more."

"Did I—did I go too far, do you think?" Kelly glanced over at her slave.

His whole backside, from the top curve of his butt cheeks down to his hamstrings, was a fiery sunset of hot pinks, deep reds and darkening purples.

"Don't worry about. You don't let him sit down anyway, right?"

"Right, so that works out, doesn't it?"

"Just give him some TLC after his corner time. But I think you've both learned enough for one night. And, besides, I really want to get back to Hector and start teeing off on his glutes. By the way, I got a great Cuban salsa mix you might want to try next time. I could loan it to you, if you like."

"Sure, I love salsa, and I'm down with Cuban motion."

"You're not too bad. For a white lady."

"I'll take that." Kelly laughed. "And thanks for putting up with all my mood swings today." Kelly slipped her arm through Carmen's as they moved toward the door. "I couldn't have worked my way through it without you."

"Yeah, well, I've got one last present for my new BFF." Carmen had parked her blue-denim totebag on a chair near the front door. She dug into it now and lifted out a tall gift bag of silver foil, handing it to Kelly.

Kelly was surprised by the bag's solid heft. There was a sliding, shifting weight inside and the slithering jingle of chain. Her curiosity was aroused. "What is it?"

"A little surprise for bedtime," was all Carmen would say. Then, with a little wave and a big grin, Carmen Gallegos sashayed out the door, her platform sandals clacking off toward the elevator.

Kelly closed the door, then turned and leaned heavily back against it. Across the room, slung like a piece of meat over the small sofa and still pinioned by four taut ropes, lay her naked slave.

She'd trolled that off-campus ballroom dance class three years ago, hoping to find at least one guy worth the plucking from among the herds of shy, shambling stumblebums, and this is what she'd come away with. And what she'd turned him into.

Her helpless captive. And, at the moment, a quivering mess.

And she wasn't done with him.

*

CHAPTER EIGHT ~ BEDTIME

When Chris was finally released from his corner time and crawled to Kelly's feet, the physical relief he felt was enormous. Moments later, however, as he began to kiss and lick his Goddess' beautiful bare feet, his tears came back in a rush and he was overcome with other emotions—of contrition, gratitude and slavish love.

The world, he knew, would not consider these normal responses to being severely beaten and humiliated. But his world had been turned upside down, and such feelings were fast becoming the norm.

The pain Goddess Kelly had inflicted—on top of his earlier injuries—had been excruciating. He rejoiced that it was over—although his whole backside was still on fire—and looked ahead with real fear to his next punishment. Despite this, he was truly thankful that she'd favored him with her cruel lash and allowed him to grovel at her feet.

How much simpler his life was now that he'd accepted his inferior slave status. He had only to remember his place and do her bidding.

"Enough, slave." The lovely foot was withdrawn from his lips and reinserted under his chin, tipping his face up toward hers as she leaned forward.

"Why are you crying again? Are you ashamed of what you've become?"

"No, Goddess," Christopher said, enraptured by her shimmering gray gaze. "I just feel so lucky to be your slave, and—and—"

"And what?"

"And I want to thank you, Goddess, for punishing me and teaching me what I am and should be."

"You're very welcome," Kelly said, genuinely pleased by his answer. "Since that's how you feel, I'll make it a point to punish you as often as possible. Does that make you even happier?"

"Yes, my Goddess."

"Good, that's certainly what I want to hear. But right now I think you need hydration before you pass out and become unable to serve me properly." She slid her foot from his chin to his cheek, then nudged his head sideways like a soccer ball. "Look what I've brought you, slave."

Chris saw it now, on the floor beneath the lamp table—a big glass mixing bowl brim full of water. She must have placed it there during his corner time.

"It'll have to do until we can get you one of those big shiny steel bowls from PetSmart and stencil 'SLAVE' on it. Go ahead, drink your fill."

Chris *was* thirsty. He knee-walked forward and tipped his face carefully, extending his tongue into the water.

"No, not like that, slave! Hands behind your back, then put your whole face in the water and gulp! Like *this.*" She trod the back of his head, shoving his face under the surface.

Chris began gulping, but panicked as water began rushing into his nose as well as his open mouth. He needed desperately to clear his nostrils and gulp air, but steady downward pressure kept his face submerged. By the time she relented, and he lifted his face free, he was choking and gasping and snorting, all at the same time.

And Kelly was making almost as much noise as he, in a giggling fit at his predicament. Chris sat back on his heels, hands still behind his back, feigning a smile, as though he, too, saw the humor. He did not, though he supposed he must have looked ridiculous with his bright-red ass in the air and his head down in the big bowl, choking and sputtering.

"Did your little tummy get filled with water, slave?" Kelly inquired with mock concern.

"Yes, Goddess," Chris lied, not wishing to be dunked again. What he really wanted now was a towel to dry his face and hair, and a Kleenex and the use of his hands to blow his nose.

"And now I bet you're hungry, aren't you, sweetie? Unless you secretly scarfed some of that yummy Chinese chicken salad while you were making it for us."

"Goddess, I would never do that!"

"I hope not! I'd hate to think of what would happen to you if I ever learned of such a thing. But I seem to recall that Goddess Carmen and I both had second helpings, so there can't be any left for you, can there?"

"No, Goddess, there isn't."

"Then you'll just have to go to bed hungry again tonight. Will you be able to endure that, slave? To please your Goddess?"

"Yes, Goddess, of course."

"Well said! Of course, you will. You'll endure whatever I say, even if it seems unfair. Especially if it seems unfair, I should say. And it does amuse me to treat you cruelly, surely you've learned that by now?"

"Yes, Goddess, I have."

"In fact, I seem to recall your begging me to do exactly that earlier today—over and over with tears in your eyes. Begging me to treat you cruelly. Hmm?"

"Yes, Goddess, I did."

"Well, that's settled then. You'll go to bed hungry. But what about your Goddess? I seem to have worked up a bit of an appetite, and burned oodles of calories, beating your cute little slave butt. Do we have any fresh fruit left?"

"Yes, Goddess."

"Must I ask you *which* fruit we have?"

"Sorry, Goddess! There's a box of fresh strawberries... and a few blueberries left. I think they're still good. And a half cantaloupe."

"Any pineapple?"

"No, Goddess. I'm sorry, I—"

"Never mind. Just cut everything up into bite-sized chunks in a little dessert dish and bring it to me with a dessert fork and a glass of Pellegrino. Save any extra for my breakfast. And don't you dare pop one into your mouth!"

*

While Chris was in the kitchen, preparing her dessert, Kelly reached down on the other side of the recliner and brought up the tall silver gift bag from Carmen. Inside, as she'd guessed, she found a leash-length of chain exactly like the Xanadu lady had used to jerk her slave around, with a choke-collar that would tighten when pulled.

Lifting it out, Kelly felt a quiver of carnal excitement, picturing it on Christopher. It would obviate the need for a slave collar, at least for now.

But the bag was not quite empty. Kelly reached in and pulled out a piece of paper, folded in four, and a small D-ring snap-fastener, the kind called "carabiners." Unfolding the paper, Kelly found a handwritten note from Carmen above an amusing, explanatory sketch. Kelly began to read:

"I stopped off at my apartment on the way here (I couldn't help myself!) & grabbed these for you. Here's my idea…"

As she read on, Kelly felt her mouth stretched wide in her wickedest little girl smile. What a treasure Carmen was! This was exactly how she would have her slave sleep from now on.

Kelly stuffed leash and carabiner back in the silver bag just as Chris came out of the kitchen. He was crawling awkwardly but carefully, on knees and elbows, enabling him to bear the little dessert dish and glass of sparkling water in his hands before him.

Kelly snorted in derision. What a ridiculous mode of locomotion! To serve her properly, she decided, he should remain on his feet, carrying the items on a little tray.

"Stand up now, slave," she snapped, accepting the glass and dish from his outstretched hands, "and show me your curtsy."

It was still only passable. "You'll have to work on that. And I suppose you'll need a little apron or something to pluck at with your fingers when you dip down. And, honestly, I prefer you completely naked before me, as you know. We'll just have to see. I may save the curtseying business for when you're serving me and my female guests, like tonight, and otherwise just have you prostrate yourself. Are you getting all that?"

"Yes, Ma'am."

"No, *not* 'Ma'am,' I prefer Goddess. Get back down on your knees and say it properly!"

He dropped, touching his forehead to the floor. "Yes, Goddess."

"Now crawl back into the kitchen and finish your cleanup. After that, use the bathroom—the utility one, of course—and do whatever you need to do, but don't dawdle. Brush your teeth, use the toilet, but don't bother showering. It's okay if you stink, since you won't be sleeping in my bed or even close to it.

"But before any of that, turn around now and let me see what I've done to you. Well, well! Apparently your Goddess went easy on you, slave, because your skin doesn't seem to be broken anywhere. You don't require any Band-Aids or Neosporin. Now get going, and, as soon as you're ready, report to me in the Mistress Bathroom. Don't take longer than ten minutes."

*

Chris knelt the instant he crossed the threshold into the Mistress Bathroom, nearly crying out at the sharp pain of the tiles on his abraded knees. Which reminded him that he'd be right back here on his knees tomorrow, for another hour at least, finishing up the grout-cleaning job.

Kelly was standing with her back to him, in front of the right-hand sink—*her* sink when they'd shared the bathroom; both sinks, of course, were now exclusively hers. His cock stiffened at the voluptuous hourglass figure displayed in the black tights and gray knit top, and at the deep cleavage revealed in the theatrical mirror as she studied her cell phone, while her fingers were busy texting.

The regal face in the mirror glanced up, then turned and focused down at him, unsmiling: "Wait right there, slave. Head down."

Chris did as told, fighting the overwhelming urge to place his palms under his kneecaps to ease the pain. Minutes passed while he listened to the soft, rapid tapping of her fingers on the small screen.

She's texting Carmen. Giving her an update and probably getting back new bizarro ideas to try on me.

That sexy hot Latina scared the shit out of Chris. The way she'd reached out when she'd first seen him and grabbed his erection, then twisting her fingers in his crotch hair and telling Goddess Kelly to have him shave it all off—like *she* owned him. Chris was convinced that this whole recent avalanche of events—turning him from househusband into full-time slave and whipping boy—had been triggered by Kelly's coming under the sadistic influence of Carmen Gallegos.

But he'd asked for this, too, hadn't he? And deserved it. What's more, Chris had to admit, these last few hours, teased and tormented by two glorious Goddesses, had exceeded even his wildest submissive fantasies.

So, as he'd been instructed to do whenever he was "parked" without a specific assignment, Chris did his best to switch off his own thoughts and began silently repeating phrases from his slave mantra:

"This is Her house… I belong to Her, I'm not my own… I am Her slave and Her property… She is everything while I am nothing… She is mighty and powerful and I am weak… She commands and I obey… She is wise and makes good decisions… I don't second guess Her… I don't talk back… I serve Her and submit…"

A hand clap broke Christopher's slave reverie and snapped his head up. His Goddess was standing over him. She reached down and, as he was about to flinch, caressed his cheek, which was still painfully swollen from the many hard slaps he'd received that day from both Goddess Kelly and Goddess Carmen.

"We're going to do something new, slave. I think you were less than truthful when you said you'd drunk your fill. Frankly, I think you coughed most of it up. You'll get better with practice. But we really should get some fluids into you before you sleep, so I'm going to provide them to you. Can you guess what I'm talking about?"

"Yes, Goddess, I think so. I hope so."

"Oh, you do? Well, tell me then, what do you hope is going to happen next?"

"Am I… am I going to drink from you?"

"Yes, you lucky boy, that is exactly what you are going to do! You're going to learn to drink my golden nectar directly from its source. Does that frighten you?"

"No, Goddess, not really." Chris was maybe a wee bit apprehensive, but more than anything, he was anxious and eager to try this. In truth, it felt to him more like a special privilege than a punishment. What better way to show total devotion to his Goddess than to drink her tangy essence directly from its sacred font?

"Well, you did seem to like my taste this morning, didn't you, when I allowed you to lick me clean after I peed?"

"Yes, Goddess, I did."

Kelly looked thoughtfully down at her slave. This wasn't going at all like Carmen had said. The Cuban bodybuilder had just texted about the thrill she got from making Hector drink her warm piss every morning, despite the fact that the acrid liquid made him gag. According to Carmen, she kept a tight grip on his collar the whole time to keep him from pulling away.

It looked like that kind of coercion wasn't going to be needed with Christopher.

"Knees together, slave," she said, stepping forward to straddle him. Then discovered, with him kneeling up, his mouth was way too high. She pushed down on his head. "All the way down, slave!"

Chris cried out when his inflamed butt landed hard on his heels, but she held him there. It turned out to be the perfect height, placing his mouth level with her crotch.

"Good. Now peel off my tights."

When he'd bared her from the waist down, Kelly kicked the little heap of stretchy fabric across the tile floor. Then she grabbed a handful of Christopher's curly hair and yanked his head backward. When he was staring straight up, she inched forward and settled her pussy lips on his upturned mouth.

"You can embrace my calves, if you like, slave. Good, hold on tight. Now open wide. All the way. I don't want you to miss a single drop. Are you ready?"

Chris' murmured assent tickled her labia.

"Good boy. Here it comes."

She released only a spurt at first, and was gratified that Chris swallowed all of it. Feeling the greedy pressure of his mouth against her, she quickly let out a bit more. Then a great deal more.

His eyes were now shut, she saw as she glanced straight down past her luxuriant golden triangle.

Was he in a total bliss state already?

She reached down and felt the muscles of his throat and his Adam's apple working. But not fast enough—for some of her piss was trickling down his cheeks—and, with his head tipped far back, into his eyes and eyebrows and hair, even into his ears.

That's okay, she decided, *it's his first time.* She let it all go then, way more than he could handle, though he tried his best, gulping and swallowing valiantly. She and Carmen had killed a bottle of Chardonnay between them, so her bladder had been quite full, and she intended to empty every ounce of it into her slave.

Don't worry, Carmen had reassured her in another text, *drinking your piss will be good for him. It's sterile, plus it's got proteins & hormones & lots of other goodies. Some people call it urine therapy. You can Google it.*

Maybe it was healthful for him, and maybe he *did* crave every drop, but it still gave her an incredible power rush to do this to him—to stand over her slave and bend back his head and use him as her private urinal, letting her golden nectar flow straight down his throat.

How fitting! I make my male sit down to piss while I stand—and deliver!

Christopher's eyes remained shut as Kelly released everything she had. His upturned face was drenched now with the overflow, and his arms were still locked around her flexed calves like a child hanging on to Mommy for dear life.

Then—too soon!—it was over with the final series of spurts. But she kept his face pressed tight to her, encouraging him to lap up all the remaining droplets. She ran her fingers through his wet hair, saw his eyes opening, lustrous with devotion.

"I'm very, very proud of you, little slave," Kelly said tenderly. "Don't you think you did a good job—for your first time?"

"I'm sorry, Goddess, that I spilled so much. I—I—"

"Hush, darling boy. And don't worry. You'll get better and better at it. Soon you'll be drinking from me without wasting a single drop. But if I can offer some advice, I think perhaps your mistake is trying to keep up with me by swallowing, instead of just opening your throat and letting my stream flow right down into you. Next time let's try that, shall we?'"

"Yes, Goddess."

"But right now, because I'm so pleased with you, I'm going to give you another special reward. Perhaps you can guess what it is."

Christopher *could*, but he was almost afraid to say it. "Do I get to keep licking you, Goddess?"

"Right again, sweet boy, that is exactly what you get to do. Keep licking your Goddess, like a good little pussy slave, and make her come and come and come."

It was a command Chris was only too happy to obey. But he had only to take her across the finish line—a very short distance in time, as it turned out—before her anguished outcries filled the room, followed by an exquisite series of little-girl sighs that touched his heart and made him want to protect this heavenly creature from all the world.

Kelly had been rocking slowly to and fro where she stood, using both hands to wedge his face into her cunt. Now, with a final ecstatic sigh, she released him, trailing the fingers of one hand caressively down his cheek before stepping away.

Chris knelt in rapt adoration, his cock at full rigid salute. But what he craved more than anything was just to hear more tender words from his Supreme Goddess.

But she was already turning away, stripping off her gray knit top and flinging it across the floor tiles. As she pranced like a dancer past the mirror, he caught a quick reflection of her bouncing breasts in all their glory. She paused with one foot on the raised threshold of the shower.

"Scrub the floor where you spilled my nectar, slave, then wipe it perfectly dry so I don't slip. Then go take a shower yourself own. But make it all the way cold, I don't want you using any of my hot water. And let's make that the rule from now on. Also, the cold spray will help shrink you so I can lock you back into chastity for the night. Got all that?"

"Yes, my Goddess."

"Good. As soon as you've done all that, report to the Mistress Bedroom and wait for me on your knees."

*

Chris was waiting, as directed, in the Mistress Bedroom. From habit, he'd chosen his old spot on the Art Deco throw rug beside her big four-poster. This was his default station each night before being given permission to climb in beside her.

Permission that would never be his again, from what she'd said. Just thinking about that—what he'd once had and now had lost forever—made him dizzy with longing and regret.

Presently he heard the door open. Barefoot steps padded toward him across the carpet, then stopped. His heart was racing. What was she going to do to him now?

"I thought I told you to take a cold shower, slave."

The accusatory tone made him cringe. Hesitantly, not daring to glance up, he offered his defense:

"I—I did, Goddess."

"*All the way* cold?"

"Yes, Goddess."

"Then why are you sticking out like that?"

"I—I started thinking about you, Goddess Kelly."

"Look up at me, slave!"

She towered above him, magnificent and unattainable, snugged into that same white hotel robe she'd made him wear. On her it was a queenly garment, belted loosely and open enticingly above and below.

Chris wanted to prostrate himself again, to escape the coming wrath, whatever it might be. Until he saw the telltale twitch of her lips, curling now into an indulgent smile.

"You're totally hopeless, aren't you, puppet?" Her voice had softened into a throaty purr. "My hopeless little puppet."

"Yes, Goddess, I am."

"And you've been that way since our very first dance, haven't you? No wonder I had to make you my slave. What else could I do with you?"

"Nothing, Goddess. I—I don't want to be anything but your slave."

"I know, I know. Manifest destiny and all that. Look, unless you want me to kick you in the balls again, you'd better go fetch some ice, or maybe a champagne bucket of ice water, and bring it back here, so I can shrink you, then stuff you back in chastity." She clapped her hands twice in dismissal.

When he returned, Kelly was seated on the edge of the four-poster with the spiral cock cage and the little padlock beside her on the duvet.

"Set the bucket down, then squat over it and lower your balls into the water."

Chris squatted, but hesitated as his butt cheeks touched the bucket's rim, with his testicles dangling just above the icy surface.

"Why are you stopping, slave?"

"Goddess, it's really, really cold!"

She sprang up and, with one lunging step, delivered a sharp slap to his face.

"You dare disobey me?"

"No, Goddess," he cried out, "I'll do it right now!"

But his Goddess wasn't in a mood to wait. With a downward shove on his shoulders, she plunged his genitals into the ice water, nearly tipping over the bucket.

Chris yelped in shock and tried to leap up, but she held him down, arms locked on his shoulders. He clutched at her robe, begging to be let up. She waited till his pleas grew truly desperate before she relented.

"Okay, I think that should do it," she said, hoisting him to his feet. "Let's have a look at you."

She bent and poked a lacquered forefinger at the shriveled nub of his penis, then at the almost retracted testes. "Shit, maybe I overdid it. I think you're actually too small to lock up! Hey, wake up in there!"

Kelly used both hands, slapping his balls several times, then rolling his cold, shrunken member between her palms. Sooner than he would have believed possible, Chris felt the throb of returning blood, and with it a flood of submissive lust that caused his rapidly thawing penis to stir and raise its head.

"Glory be, he's alive!" Kelly said with a salty chuckle. "Sorry, little guy, it's back in the slammer for you." Chris watched her nimble fingers slide the base ring down over his uncoiling cock, pull his balls through, one after the other, then twist on the spiral cage and secure it with the tiny padlock.

"Now, as soon as you mop up the water you spilled, I'll show you where you'll be sleeping."

Moments later, frightened and excited both, Christopher followed his Goddess into her long walk-in wardrobe, admiring the graceful swing of the heavy robe with each stride. She flicked on the lights, bathing the long rack of hanging garments down the left side in bright fluorescence. Higher up, a storage shelf also ran the closet's full length, with custom shelving and shoe racks along the right. Facing them at the far end was the small chest of drawers Chris had emptied of his own clothing just yesterday.

Kelly stopped about halfway down and snapped her fingers, pointing to the oak floor. Chris hurried forward and knelt, then looked up at a tall silver gift bag now in his Goddess' hand. He watched her reach into the bag and draw out a long chain leash with a choker loop on one end, the kind used for training dogs. His heart nearly skipped a beat as he guessed what was to come.

"Tip your head toward me, slave."

As he did so, Kelly dropped the loop of chain over him and cinched it tight. He could breathe, but swallowing was impeded. The metal jingled as he turned his head to glance up at his Goddess. Her eyes were asparkle.

"Well, slave, how do you like your new collar?"

"I love it, Goddess Kelly." In truth, it was one of the most transcendent moments of his life, as thrilling as any childhood Christmas morning. Rather than feeling demeaned or degraded, Chris felt a soaring pride at his new status, conferred by this simple noose of metal. If there was pride of ownership, couldn't there be an equal pride in being owned, especially owned by a Supreme Goddess?

"It's not a real slave collar, of course. That will come later—if you prove yourself truly worthy. This is just for making sure you stay put. But maybe I'll loosen it, just a bit."

She stepped close, humming softly to herself as she adjusted the choker noose. His Goddess was truly pleased with herself, Chris thought, as his cock writhed vainly in its cage.

"Am I—am I going to spend the night here? In your closet, Goddess?"

"Obviously. Do you have any say in the matter?"

"No, Goddess, of course not."

"Then don't ask tiresome questions. You'll sleep wherever I put you. If I want to, I can put you naked out on my little balcony and leave you there all night. Is that clear?"

"Yes, Goddess."

He watched now as she fed the O-ring at the other end of the chain through a hanging metal loop that supported the long clothes pole, then doubled it back on itself, using a carabiner to clip the links together.

She'd tethered him to the bracket directly above, giving him just a bit of slack.

"Now lie down."

He tried, but his neck chain snapped taut with his head still several inches off the floor.

"Here, let me adjust that." He looked up and saw her unclip the carabiner, then back out several inches of chain before refastening. "Now try again."

This time Chris was able to rest his cheek tentatively on the hard floor, as long as he kept it directly beneath the carabiner.

"Better?"

"Yes, Goddess." He remembered to thank her. But the euphoria of only moments ago was fading fast, replaced by incipient panic. Did his Goddess really expect him to sleep like this?

"Lift your head, slave," came the command from above. He did so, and felt a welcome softness of pillow slide beneath his cheek. "There, that's better, isn't it? And here's something else." There was a soft whump as a folded blanket landed close beside him. "You can sleep on that or under it, or fold it in half lengthwise and crawl inside. Well, what do you say? Aren't you going to thank your Goddess for taking such good care of you?"

"Yes, I'm sorry, thank you, Goddess Kelly, for taking such—"

"That's enough. And here's your cell phone, fully charged. Tomorrow's Sunday, remember, so your Goddess will be sleeping in. But I want you to set your alarm just as though tomorrow was a weekday, so you can get an early start on your chores. In fact, let's make it six—and have that be your wakeup time every day from now on so you can get more done for me in the mornings. Are you listening, slave?"

"Yes, Goddess."

"Good. I'm leaving your hands free. If you have to go to the bathroom, you have permission to take off your noose and go take care of your needs. But then you are to come straight back here and get back into your collar and pull it tight. I may wake up and check on you. If you are not exactly where I put you, you will be a very, very sorry slave. Do I make myself clear?"

"Yes, Goddess Kelly."

"You have a lot to think about. Things have been moving swiftly for you these last few days, haven't they?"

"Yes, Goddess."

"And they will continue to do so. There will be many more changes for you, stricter rules for you to obey. This is going to be your life from now on—real domestic slavery, not fantasy playtime. You do realize that?"

"Yes, Goddess."

"And do you still love and worship your Goddess?"

"Yes, Goddess, I do."

"Then you may kiss my foot before I leave you for the night."

Her naked foot stepped on his pillow, several inches from his face. By craning his neck, Chris was just able to reach her toes with his lips.

"I love you, Goddess Kelly!" he breathed between ardent kisses. "I love you so much!"

"I know you do, slave." But her foot slid back a few inches. Chris lunged forward with his face, but the quick-snap of the chain brought him up just short. Kelly's throaty chuckle floated down from above.

Then the lovely foot turned, pivoting. She was walking away. Chris twisted his head around in time to catch a fleeting glimpse of her vanishing white robe. He heard her bare feet squinch on the hardwood, the door handle turning, then the slap of her palm on the light switch, plunging his world into darkness as the door clicked shut.

He felt instantly bereft and abandoned. If only she'd let him sleep on the floor beside her bed like last night!

Then the door was opened again, and a lance of outside light shot through. Was his prayer being granted? Had she a change of heart? As he turned toward the light, something soft, nearly weightless, struck him just above the ear.

"Did that hit you, slave?" her playful voice called.

"Yes, Goddess."

"Can you reach it?"

"Yes, I have it."

"It's all for you, sweet boy. From your Goddess. Treasure it, you've earned it."

His fingers identified the fabric, by weight and texture, as the door closed and total darkness returned. She'd tossed him the worn, sweaty tights he'd peeled off her before she'd pissed in his mouth. The ones she'd worn while flogging him and working herself into a near frenzy. The cotton-spandex mesh would be deeply impregnated with her pungent woman scent.

Working his hands along one wispy leg, he located the crotch, then pressed it reverently to his nostrils. Again and again he inhaled, till his entire sense of self was lost in the aura of female power and majesty.

Wholly at peace then, and utterly exhausted from his day, Christopher lay his fabric-shrouded face on the small pillow and surrendered to blissful sleep.

*

CHAPTER NINE ~ RETURN TO XANADU

Chris hadn't driven in five days, not since the night he'd been late picking Kelly up from the airport. And this morning, just like on that fateful drive home, Kelly sat behind him in the big Audi sedan instead of beside him, making explicit his new servant status. She'd even taken permanent custody of his drivers license.

His chauffeur's uniform, such as it was, consisted of a t-shirt and sweatpants, both gray and saggy, which she'd had him retrieve from the Hefty Bags crammed full of his discarded clothes, along with a pair of flip-flops.

Beneath the sweatpants, he wore only his chastity cage. And, as of this morning, he didn't have any pubic hair. He'd been ordered to shave his crotch and genitals in accordance with Goddess Carmen's recommendation. Only after considerable pleading on his part had his Goddess allowed him to spare the fuzz on his butt cheeks, but only because the area was still so painful to the touch.

Seeing himself completely hairless down there, in stark contrast to his Goddess' full, coppery-blonde bush, had plunged Christopher all the way back, in humiliating memory, to junior high—to that first day he'd undressed in a boys' locker room shared with high-school guys. He remembered the steamy communal showers and the sweaty aisles jammed with naked, swaggering jocks. Guys with hairy chests and crotches and big swinging dicks. Guys who shouted dirty jokes and snapped rolled wet towels at Christopher and his mostly hairless classmates, at their ass cheeks and little-boy peepees.

Christopher had thought those memories safely buried, but here they were right back again, and, thanks to Goddess Kelly, as painful as ever. She had already stripped away his manhood, but this latest emasculation, instigated by Goddess Carmen, went further yet, making him actually look and feel prepubescent. And, just like those long ago locker-room bullies, Kelly seemed to take every opportunity to swat his naked ass and flick his genitals until he yelped and cringed like a sissy boy.

This morning she hadn't even bothered to tell him where they were headed. Once they were underway, she'd given only minimal directions, glancing up from her cell phone. Such as: "Turn left at the next light." Then, "Stay on this street until I tell you to turn." And then, "Get on the freeway up ahead—the east onramp."

Of course, as he reminded himself, a slave didn't need to be told where he was driving. Why should a Goddess waste her precious time on pointless details? He'd find out when they got wherever she wanted to go.

Right now they were heading east, toward the valley, the freeway traffic sparse on a Sunday morning. Which gave Chris the chance to steal an occasional mirrored glimpse back at his Goddess. Whenever she caught him at it, she'd flash a knowing smile, obviously relishing his helpless fixation on her beauty.

She was dressed, today, in tight white stonewashed jeans above cork-soled platform sandals and had chosen to go daringly braless under a white ribbed-cotton tanktop with gaping side cleavage.

So stop looking back at her, you dumb fuck! All it did was keep his cock straining against the bars of its infernal prison.

To keep his mind off his Goddess, Christopher let his thoughts drift back to the disturbing dream from which his cellphone alarm had rescued him at six a.m. Actually, it had been a full-on nightmare which culminated with his being chained by the neck in a dark dungeon.

The scariest part had been awakening to an identical reality.

He really *was* shackled by the neck—to an overhead bracket in her pitch-black closet. Yes, he could free himself, and had done so once during the night, to empty a bladder painfully full of his Goddess' golden nectar; then had returned to the unyielding floor and his noose, which tightened itself automatically as he lowered his head to the blanket.

Would such nightmares become a regular occurrence? Or would

he eventually get used to his dark, hard, sleeping place, like a dog to his kennel, and even find comfort in its wretched familiarity?

"Turn in here, slave—by that Thai noodle sign!"

Her sharp command vaporized his aimless thoughts. They were off the freeway now, in a foothill community Chris didn't recognize, traveling down a tacky commercial strip between a lot of used car lots and Asian signage. He turned carefully, as directed, into a strip mall that featured the noodle shop, a mattress store and a plain brown stucco storefront identified by only a small neon marquee over the entry door. He deciphered the Oriental-styled script, "XANADU," and beneath, "Adult Fun 'n' Games."

Chris recognized the lettering from the pink plastic drawstring bag he'd carried upstairs from the Audi trunk. The bag containing the brand-new toys that the two Goddesses had later used to tie him down over the loveseat and beat him till he was screaming and sobbing into his panty gag.

Chris experienced both fear and excitement as he parked and sprang out to open the rear passenger door. Long, white-jeaned legs swung out first, led by the platform sandals that showed off lovely lavender-polished toenails, which she'd had him touch up just before they left. Rising gracefully now on tall cork heels, his Goddess overtopped him an inch or two, further enhancing her superior status. But, instead of walking away and expecting him to follow his customary step behind, she was digging into her Dooney and Bourke shoulder bag.

To extract the chain leash.

"Bow your head, slave." The command was delivered in an offhand way, as though this was everyday routine for them. Yet never had Goddess Kelly even hinted at anything like this. Chris was in total shock, sensing the last remnant of his personal dignity about to be shredded.

But he bowed his head as directed, knowing there was no option but to obey. He closed his eyes as the rattling metal noose slipped around his neck and was cinched tight.

The next instant he was yanked nearly off his feet. Opening his eyes, Chris scurried after his owner, his flip-flops slapping the asphalt, and just managed to overtake her in time to open the shop door so she could enter without breaking stride.

In the doorway, she nearly collided with a long-haired guy in heavy Goth makeup on his way out. On seeing Kelly—regal head high, shoulders back, bosom outthrust—the guy hopped instantly aside, making an extravagant flourish of his arm like a bullfighter executing a cape pass.

Kelly swept by without apparent acknowledgment, as did Christopher a second later, jerked along in her wake. He got a close-up flash of the Goth Guy's black mascaraed eyes and caught a muttered, envious comment from behind him:

"Lucky bastard!"

*

The irony was not lost on Kelly as she paraded her slave through aisles of S&M and B&D paraphernalia, every now and then dropping an item into the plastic shopping basket she had him carry. Only yesterday she'd condemned another woman for doing exactly this—dragging a hapless, hopeless male around this store at the end of a doggy chain.

That had been a crossroads moment for Kelly—and perhaps even more for Chris. Seeing in the woman's sadistic treatment of her male companion an indictment of her own female supremacist tendencies, Kelly had returned home fully prepared to relax her new household rules and restore some of the personal privileges and freedoms she'd just taken away. She would let him wear clothes again and address her without an honorific title, sit on furniture and eat at table and, yes, even allow him back in her bed. Yes, of course, she would still expect him to be properly submissive and attentive to her needs, but she would do her best going forward not to treat him as an inferior.

It was not she who had sabotaged all those sincere resolves, but her darling Christopher. Falling to his knees before her with nonstop tears and pleadings, he had fought passionately and with abject eloquence to hold on to his newly conferred slave status.

How could Kelly ever forget those tear-choked words? *"Please, Goddess! I don't want to be free! I want to be your slave. Always!"*

So she'd relented and agreed to grant his pathetic prayers, all of them, but only after an ominous warning: *"You realize, slave, there will be no going back from this?"*

In a submissive ecstasy, Chris had reaffirmed his choice—very possibly his last free choice as a man. Setting all her reservations aside, Kelly had embraced that choice with the entire force of her dominant personality. From that moment forward, she no longer felt obliged to regard Christopher as her husband, or even as a man, simply as a servant who existed to obey her commands and attend to her needs and whims, a creature to be used and abused as it suited her.

With that irrevocable decision safely behind her, Kelly was relishing every moment of this morning's public display of Christopher as her collared chattel. The erotic surge she felt between her thighs, and spreading throughout her body, was absolutely intoxicating. She especially enjoyed how quickly and closely he was learning to follow her, even to anticipate her every movement, in order to avoid any precarious tension on the leash.

My smart puppy is learning to heel! Ideally he should be stark naked, like he was with me and Carmen last night.

The only hiccup in her happiness was the minor worry of being spotted by someone who knew her, and of salacious gossip getting back to her employer and damaging her professional reputation.

But the odds were heavily against that happening in this remote suburban setting. All the same, maybe next time she should wear a wig. In any case, these delicious little domme-and-slave outings should probably be a seldom thing.

Not that she would bother telling Christopher that.

Giving his choker chain a quick come-along, Kelly stepped into an aisle given over to a bewildering array of what Carmen had called "impact toys." In addition to the familiar crops and canes, paddles and leather straps, she browsed racks of strange-looking ticklers and slappers, quirts and tawses, and multi-strand floggers of every sort.

The final rack was devoted to whips, from single-tails on up to the classic cat o' nine. There was even a six-foot, coiled bullwhip, discounted to half-price from three-hundred dollars. "Not for beginners!" cautioned a sign.

Kelly was content, for now, with her little starter kit, but she couldn't resist a few airy practice swings with a pricey "Prussian leather" dogwhip. Then, as if seriously contemplating its purchase, she dangled it above the shopping cart, noting with pleasure the flicker of fear in Christopher's eyes.

"Oh, well, maybe next time," she said with a regretful sigh, returning the little whip to the rack before giving his neck chain another onward tug.

In none of the well-stocked fetish fashion aisles did she see anything she liked, for herself or her slave. Dressing Chris as her French maid, or zipping him into bizarro leather or PVC gear, didn't appeal at all. Of course, she could do it to him, but why? She much preferred the primal power trip of having a stark naked male at her beck and call—or just in chains and cock cage, if he had to wear something.

As for herself, well, judging by the gaudy sleazewear on prominent display, Xanadu wasn't likely to make her Top 100 list of favorite fashion boutiques anytime soon.

She did come to a full-stop at a circular rack of t-shirts with a special section marked "For Obedient Slaveboys." Kelly started clicking through the hangers before holding one up for Christopher to see.

"How about this one, sweetie?"

It was black with a boldface white banner that proclaimed "MATRIARCHY NOW."

"Wouldn't you be proud to wear this while running errands for me?"

"Yes, Goddess."

"Silly me! Why am I asking you, as if you had any say in the matter? You're a medium, right?"

"Large actually fits me better, Goddess."

"Well, I want it nice and snug, so medium it is." She went through the whole section, pulling out several more imprinted tees of pink and white and purple. Chris saw the slogans as the shirts went sailing into his basket, one after the other:

FEMALE SUPREMACY FOREVER
#OWNED BY MY MISTRESS
CHASTITY SLAVE
WOMEN IN CHARGE – THE NATURAL ORDER OF LIFE
KEEP CALM & OBEY WOMEN
I BELONG TO HER
WOMEN RULE

"And look," she said, tearing off a perforated card, "if I fill this out, they'll make up a special that says PROPERTY OF whoever. But do I really want my name advertised around the neighborhood on a slaveboy shirt? Don't think so."

They'd reached a wide central aisle, visible from most parts of the store as well as in the elevated security mirrors and CCTV cameras she'd been noticing. She was aware, too, that she and her leash-led slave had drawn every eye from the instant they entered the store.

"Just one more purchase, sweetie, and we're done. But first, I want you to get down on your knees and kiss my feet."

Kelly had expected at least a slight hesitation at this public mortification, or perhaps some inane, time-wasting question, such as "Do you mean right here, Goddess?" Instead, to her immense satisfaction, Chris obeyed instantly, falling to his knees on the dark-stained red carpeting. He planted his face on her extended left sandal, then covered her exposed toes with eager kisses.

"Now the other one, slave."

"Yes, my Goddess."

An abrupt cutoff of the piped-in background music caused Christopher's response to be eerily audible throughout the store. Hearing the obsequious tone of his own voice triggered an out-of-body experience. It was as if Chris was looking down at himself, or rather the pathetic creature he'd become, groveling on the grubby carpet and slobbering on a woman's sandaled feet in plain view of a half-dozen customers, all men.

He sensed how he must look to them, and how they were probably reacting. With amused contempt, he supposed. Though one or two must surely be grinding their teeth in envy just like that Goth kid at the front door.

"Enough, slave. On your feet!"

The command was punctuated with an upward jerk on his chain. Again Chris found himself stumbling and scrambling after his Goddess. She was striding now toward a back corner of the store.

It was, he saw as they drew near, a torture chamber stage set. Despite the campy, hokey arrangement—corner dais with blood-red shag rug, matte-black walls festooned with fake spiderwebs, grotesque furniture props highlighted by pink baby spots—Chris experienced a quick flutter of fear. It was easy to envision himself strapped naked onto that man-sized wooden bondage wheel and turned every which way but loose, or having his head and arms locked down into those hinged wooden kneeling stocks.

"But it's way too big for my car," he heard his Goddess complain.

Chris assumed she was joking about the difficulty of taking home one of those monstrous contraptions. But he turned to find her talking to a skinny, bearded guy with spidery, tattooed arms poking out of a leather vest. They were staring, not at the bizarre stage set, but at what looked like an ordinary workout bench off to one side.

Chris noticed a series of straps and buckles along the sides of the bench, and on front and back vertical supports. The bench's function quickly became obvious, and Chris recalled that, besides the ball gag, this was the only piece of B&D equipment Carmen had specifically recommended to Kelly. There could be no mystery about who would be buckled into all those restraints—if the damned thing could actually fit in the Audi.

"No problem, Ma'am," the bearded floor salesman was saying. "Comes disassembled. Just slap it together when you get home. Got a couple right here in understock, matter of fact, Ma'am." Crouching, the salesguy slid a thin cardboard case from beneath a nearby display island.

Kelly looked skeptical. "Well, *I* could do it easily, of course, but I never lift a finger. As for my slave… well, does he look particularly handy to you?"

Chris stood, head down, hearing himself verbally reduced to a complete nonentity.

"With all due respect, Ma'am," the salesguy was saying, "yes, even he can do it. Assembly takes about twenty minutes max with just one little wrench that comes in the box. How about I give you a special price for both of these?"

"I only have the one slave, sweetie. Unless you're volunteering to help me start a stable."

The bearded guy swallowed hard. "Uh, you're like kidding, right? Because, I mean, if you're really serious, Ma'am, I, uh—"

"Too late, sweetie, you shouldn't have hesitated. Now, slave, do you think you can carry that big box to the checkstand all by yourself, or do you need the nice man to help you?"

*

The checkout island was perched high above the sales floor, affording an overlook of every aisle. Its sole occupant was a heavy, Hawaiian-featured woman in a rainbow-hued muumuu, name-tagged "Heather." She rotated on her captain's chair to scan the items Chris handed up from the basket. Besides the t-shirts, there were only three—another pair of Velcro flexicuffs, a red-rubber ball gag with adjustable head strap, and a pair of what looked like leather oven mitts with lockable wrist straps.

"There's a ninety-nine-cents special on all the DVDs in that rack beside you," the checker lady said, reaching down to hand-scan the long, flat cardboard box containing the disassembled bench. "I'm pretty sure there's some heavy femdom in there somewhere."

"Thanks, Heather, I'll just have a look. I took away his TV privileges, but maybe I can find something educational he can watch."

Even with eyes properly cast down, Chris caught several titles from the dozen or so Kelly now passed up to the woman: "Whip Mistress From Hell," "Under Her Desk" and "Return to Slave Island."

"After you scan the t-shirts, I'd like him to wear one home."

"Any special one?"

"You pick."

"What about this?"

"Perfect. Can you snip off the tag? Here, slave, take off that grungy t-shirt so I can put the new one on you."

Chris did as told. Only after she'd forced the new, tight pink tee down over his slim torso was he able to glance down and read the upside-down block letters marching across his chest:

SHE'S THE BOSS OF ME.

"Truer words were never silk-screened," Kelly said with a throaty chuckle. "Heather, would you be a dear and shitcan his old shirt?"

"No problemo. You know, there's another lady who comes in sometimes with her subbie on a dog chain."

"Does she wear Western shirts and boots?"

"That's her."

"I'd actually like to talk to her. Is there a particular time she comes in?"

"I saw her in here yesterday. But we got some of her cards over here." Muumuu Gal swiveled and plucked something off a cluttered corkboard behind her, then handed it down to Kelly. "Why don't you keep the card and give her a call? That's why people leave their contact info."

Kelly studied the engraved business card a moment before reading it aloud: *"Brenda McClintock. Metal Sculpture and Spot Welding. Custom Slave Collars and Shackles.'* What do you think, slave? Veddy interesting, *n'est-ce pas?* Thanks for the tip, Heather."

"That's what they pay me for. Hey, your boy looks real cute in his brand-new subbie shirt."

"Doesn't he, though? Come on, slaveboy. Let's get you home. I can't wait to try out your new punishment bench."

*

CHAPTER TEN ~ VIGNETTES

There it stood, padded black-leather top over shiny chrome frame, sturdy leather straps for ankles, neck, waist and wrists. While trying not to think about all the ways it could and would be used, Chris couldn't help admiring his own handiwork.

You put that together. By yourself. Without Goddess Kelly's help.

She had ordered him to get right on it the instant they got back from Xanadu—right after fixing her an omelet for lunch. It hadn't been easy, sorting out all those fasteners and straps and struts and matching them up to the exploded drawings, then trying to make sense of the poorly worded captions so he could fit everything together in the right order. It had taken the best part of an hour, nearly three times as long as the salesguy had claimed.

But he'd done it.

Before going to announce his success, he stretched facedown on the bench to make a last check of the placement of the six restraining straps—the top pair for his wrists, the bottom two for ankles, plus the two bench-spanning straps in between for neck and midsection.

"Anxious to try it out, are we, sweetie?"

Chris whipped his head around. Goddess Kelly stood in the doorway, wearing her favorite mocking smile and the same all-white outfit, deliciously loose tanktop and tight jeans.

"Uh, sorry, Goddess," he'd said, not exactly sure what he was apologizing for. The naked slave scrambled off the bench and fell to his knees before her, forehead to the floor, the default position for greeting his Goddess. Her bare foot slid under his face. Chris commenced kissing and became instantly aroused—*painfully* so, as she hadn't gotten around to removing his chastity cage.

"Good job, sweetie!" she said, eyeing the assembled bench as she switched feet to let him continue his oral devotions. "I hope you don't have too many parts left over. We don't want it collapsing in the middle of our fun, do we?"

"No, Goddess. I was careful."

"Very good. But you must be famished. I don't think I gave you dinner or breakfast, did I? So I've brought you lunch. Lift your face and look." Chris obeyed and saw her setting down the plate he'd served her earlier. She'd left a few forkfuls of omelet and scraps of toast. As a slave, he was not permitted utensils.

"You're welcome to all the rest, sweetie."

"Thank you, Goddess." Chris crawled forward, hands behind his back as he'd been taught, then lowered his face to the plate and began pursuing the morsels of cold food with his mouth and tongue, trying not to push them off the plate. He did his best to minimize the unavoidable sucking and slurping sounds.

He heard her giggle at the uncouth spectacle he must be making, then seat herself on the bench. He hoped she wouldn't step on his head, as she'd done last night when she'd made him drink water from the big bowl. If doing so amused her, of course, he had no grounds to object.

"That's enough, slave. Stop slobbering up my leftovers and crawl to me. Oh, dear, that's so gross! You've got little bits of egg and cheese and chives and crumbs all over your chin and your mouth, even on your nose." Kelly slapped repeatedly at the lower half of her slave's face, then wiped it roughly with her hand, back and forth. "Now lick your lips for me and let me see. That's a little better. Too bad that water bowl isn't handy to dunk your face in.

"Now place your chin right here into my hand and look up into the eyes of your Goddess. You have a very full chore list for the rest of the day, as you know, but I want to take a moment and say a few words to you about our little adventure this morning.

"First of all, I want you to know that I'm extremely pleased with you, slave. Not for putting together this little kindergarten do-it-yourself kit, but for how you behaved at Xanadu. That was a big step for you, making your public debut as a collared and leashed slave. And perhaps it was scary, too? Hmm? Just nod your head. Yes, I thought so.

"You've been 'outed' now, to the world—but most of all to yourself. Outed as a lady's slave, an inferior creature to be leashed and led around in public. Like my little dog. I mean, you're simply not a man anymore, sweetie, and you'll never be one again. You do see that, don't you?"

Chris nodded again. His throat was too congested for speech. And, for some idiotic reason, his pulse was pounding.

"But really, it's a great honor for you, being owned by a superior creature like me. You can take pride in that. So, all in all, I think you should be feeling pretty good about yourself. Now, please, don't go all weepy on me again, because I have a bit more to say.

"The second thing is, you're not going to be punished for the rest of today, I mean if I can possibly help it. What do you say to that?"

"Thank you, Goddess. I—I don't deserve it."

"Of course you don't. And, in fact, it's not really a reward for good behavior. More like a brief holiday. *Extremely* brief, because the fact is, for the rest of your slave life, sweetie, as long as I own you, you're not likely to experience another day without being punished. I'm quite serious. Starting tomorrow we're going to be instituting what are called daily maintenance spankings or whippings, or whatever implement I decide on. It's standard practice among female supremacists, I'm finding out, and it makes perfect sense. A slave needs to know, every morning of his life, that he'll be receiving a certain number of lashes or strokes from his female owner, just for starters. It has nothing to do with corporal punishment. That's an entirely separate category. Maintenance whippings are given simply as a daily reminder to the slave of his inferior status." She paused to punctuate her words with a medium face slap, something she often did to ensure his full attention, then added, "Surely you can see how very effective that will be, sweetie, in preventing any silly thoughts above your proper station?"

"Yes, my Goddess." Chris felt the truth of her words sink deep into his submissive soul. With a daily beating at her hands, how could he forget, even for a second, what he'd become?

"But all that starts tomorrow, so make sure you enjoy your little slave holiday. Now, before I send you back to your chores, I'm going to give you a special reward for being such a good little puppydog on your first outing. Help me out of these super-snug jeans so you can properly worship your Goddess in all her glory."

*

The t-shirt was white with big black lettering:
STAY CALM & OBEY WOMEN!
It must have been readable from forty feet away, judging by all the curious stares and sidelong glances Chris got Monday morning on his three-block walk from their condo complex to the local Goodwill store, trundling his shopping cart behind him.

Chris felt his owner's presence every step of the way, almost as if he was still leashed to her. Not just because of his new "subbie shirt," as Kelly now called them, borrowing the phrase from the Xanadu checkout lady. No, he felt Kelly's total ownership, as well, in the metallic clench of his cock cage, and the acrid aftertaste of her warm, morning cocktail, and most painfully in the enduring butt-throb from his very first maintenance spanking, which she'd administered before leaving for work. It had turned out to be two-dozen no-nonsense swats from her new laminated wooden paddle.

Get used to it, 'cause you're gonna get it like that every day for the rest of your life.

Never again would Chris be able to cruise carelessly along these familiar streets pretending to be a regular guy. By requiring him to wear the demeaning subbie shirts whenever he left the condo, his Goddess was ensuring that his daily errands would be outings in every sense of the word.

And yet, the sleepy-eyed girl behind the Goodwill dropoff counter took scant notice of Chris, let alone his shirt. She was too busy texting to give more than a glance at his two garbage bags of used clothes before scribbling out a donation receipt.

Maybe it won't be so embarrassing after all, Chris told himself, as he towed the now-empty cart out the door. Nobody cares anymore about tattoos or facial piercings, so why would they notice t-shirt slogans?

This frail hope was dashed moments later. He was detouring his wheeled basket around the metallic prow of a Dodge Ram pickup that was protruding into his crosswalk when he heard a shouted insult:

"Hey, faggot, nice t-shirt! And that old-lady shopping cart, nice touch!"

Chris glanced up at the high cab and saw a scraggly-bearded kid in a backwards camo cap leaning out.

"What'd she send you for today, wimp? Heavy-duty Tampons?"

"Matter of fact she did," Chris replied.

His heart was pounding, but he was extremely proud of his quick comeback. In fact, he couldn't wait to tell Goddess Kelly when she got home. She'd instructed him to respond to all comments, pro or con, by affirming and, if necessary, defending his belief in female leadership. And that's just what he'd done.

His self-congratulation was short-lived. The redneck kid gunned the massive pickup, and the high-decibel explosion propelled Chris and his little cart on a panicky dash to the opposite sidewalk.

The really weird thing, Chris thought as the Ram truck roared off and he was able to gather his senses, was that feminine supplies really were on his morning shopping list. Along with a squeeze bottle of Nair for Men. The local supermarket, with its well-stocked pharmacy aisle, was his next and final stop. As for the nasty crack about his "old lady" basket, well, the collapsible, easily stored cart was really quite handy for marketing. A necessity, really, since Chris had no access to a car when Kelly was at work.

Anxious now to get back to his household chores, Chris moved quickly through the supermarket aisles, retrieving the dozen or so items on his list—milk and eggs, a pound of her favorite coffee beans, fresh fruit and greens, and a forty-count box of Kotex pantyliners.

Not Tampons, you stupid redneck asshole!

Chris wheeled his cart toward his favorite checker. Lois was plump and placid, with Shirley Temple curls, beaverish incisors and pale blue eyes shrunken behind thick-lensed glasses. Never once had Lois kidded him, or raised so much as an eyebrow, about anything he'd placed on her conveyer. She would simply scan even the most embarrassing items, whether vaginal itch relief cream, or iridescent nail polish or the latest issue of *Vogue*, *Shape* or *Women's Health*, with a shy smile and a sweet absence of editorial comment.

And so it was today.

Until Lois turned to hand him the register receipt. Then those blurred blue eyes of hers came into sudden sharp focus and did a startled double take on his white subbie shirt with its black-lettered motto:

STAY CALM & OBEY WOMEN

"OMG," gasped Lois, clapping a palm to her rosebud mouth. Hot pink infused her plump cheeks.

"I'm sorry," Chris blurted, genuinely concerned, "if my t-shirt offends you. The thing is—"

"Don't apologize! It's really, really cool! Where'd you get it?"

"My wife bought it for me. It reminds me always to obey her, because, you know, women know best."

"OMG, that's so *true!* And so, you know, like really hot!" She bit a plump underlip. "I've got to get one for my boyfriend!"

It was Chris' turn to be shocked. Who'd have thought that shy, hefty Lois had, or would ever have, a boyfriend? Let alone that she'd turn out to be, well, at least, a domme-in-the-making? Kelly had been quite frank about her hope that the subbie shirts would function as conversation-starters, especially with girls and women who crossed his path, and might thus help spread the gospel of female supremacy. It sure looked like that was happening.

"Hey, could you like tell me where I can buy one?"

"On the Internet, I'm pretty sure."

"Great, thanks!" Lois blushed pink again before turning to greet her next customer, a bent-over guy with a gnarled fistful of coupons and a big bottle of Tennessee sipping whiskey. As Chris rolled his cart toward the exit, he took a quick look back and saw her plump cheeks still aflame.

*

CHAPTER ELEVEN ~
SELECTING A BULL, PART 1

Kelly swiveled her leather recliner to face the window wall of her high-rise corner office. She'd just spent an exasperating hour on the phone with her company's newly acquired resort property in Bermuda, unsnarling an inexplicable series of botched convention reservations for one of her major clients. Now, for respite and reward, she decided to treat herself to a ten-minute online shopping spree.

She touched up the browser on her personal iPhone and brought up a favorite designer boutique. But, instead of focusing on the five-inch screen, she found her attention drawn to the windowed panorama beside her desk.

Down below in the adjoining marina, a two-masted sailboat was motoring out toward the main channel, catching the afternoon sun in its sails. Always a lovely sight. But something about it had snagged her attention.

Of course! From the position of the smaller mast—forward of the helm—it was a ketch, the same basic rig as Henry Malcolm's boat. The one he kept in the Mediterranean and had been texting her enticing photos of. Henry the Incorrigible. The roguishly handsome, fifty-something South African was still stalking her from halfway around the world—in between running his various companies and playing with millionaire toys.

"You know, Kelly Ann," ran his most recent, oh-so tempting text message, *"nobody has to know about us. What if, next time you fly over to check out your Monte Carlo operation, I dock the Astarte across the Italian border in San Remo & sneak you aboard for a little cruise along the Ligurian*

coast? No crew, no itinerary, no ports of call, no bathing suits. Just a jug of wine, a baguette & me & thee, skinny-dipping in paradise!"

Squinting down through the afternoon dazzle, Kelly saw a blonde in a thong sunbathing on the sailboat's foredeck.

Okay, that could be her in a few weeks, if she merely juggled some items in her travel schedule. With Henry at the wheel. And the Italian coast sliding scenically alongside. And a teak-paneled stateroom waiting for them below.

She could see it all. Well, except the thong part. Tying a string bikini around *her* superabundance would be beyond absurd. Like pasting a decal on a 747. Anyway, according to Henry, except for a spray coat of sunblock, they'd both be stark naked.

Was Henry Malcolm man enough to carry that off? Most definitely, she thought, slipping her fingers under the waistbands of her skirt and silken panties. What would that whipcorded, sun-baked body of his look like stripped to the buff?

Specifically, how well was he hung?

Now she really was wet down there. She really *did* want to fuck Henry. "God, yes!" had been the full-throated shout in her mind, and almost the whisper on her lips, after their first deep-dive kiss overlooking the golf course in British Columbia—incredibly only nine or ten days ago!

But, before the steamy proceedings had gotten completely out of control, Kelly had called an inexplicable halt. To Henry's bewilderment—and, frankly, to her own rueful regret ever since. With their lips locked and their hands all over each other, wasn't it a bit late to be invoking her self-imposed rule against mixing sex with business? And, really, what was so wrong with a little resort hanky-panky with a prospective client? Wasn't she in the hospitality biz, for heaven's sake! And, after wildly exceeding her sales goals three years running, wasn't her job safe from any whispering campaign?

Damn right it was!

The only open question was upward mobility—all the way upward. Because the title Kelly Ann Sheffield coveted was not even a divisional vice presidency, but that of corporate CEO. And she didn't want to come up even one rung short of the top because of some tiny notation in her personnel file. No affair was worth *that* career price.

Abiding ambition, in other words, trumped unbridled lust.

Heaving a considerable sigh, Kelly swiveled away from the marina overlook and refocused on her iPhone browser. She really should text Henry back her regrets—reluctant but final—and take the poor man off the hook.

But, dammit, it was such delicious fun to keep on playing him— the macho big-game fisherman—at the end of her own line. It was, curiously, like owning and tormenting her helpless slave, another way of demonstrating supreme female power.

It was even more fun playing one off the other—inflaming Christopher's submissive jealousy as she had several nights ago, by comparing his pathetic, housebound existence to the virile, globetrotting South African:

"Henry Malcolm is everything you're not, Slaveboy," she'd explained with *withering scorn. "He swaggers, while you grovel. I couldn't tame Henry if I tried, and, believe me, I have no intention of trying."*

And describing for Chris that first passionate kiss with Henry: *"I absolutely melted in his arms! Like Scarlett O'Hara being French-kissed by Rhett Butler!"*

And making it explicit that, though she hadn't yet fucked the older man, it was her sovereign right to do so: *"Whatever happens or doesn't happen, it's none of your business—unless I choose to tell you. As I explicitly told you when we got married, ours was not and never would be a marriage of equals. I have absolute freedom. While you—well, you live under my absolute control."*

Who would have guessed that so much sadistic, sexual pleasure could be derived from merely threatening to cuckold one's adoring slave, then further humiliating him with detailed descriptions of his masterful rival?

Just think how much more exciting, and cruel, actually going through with it would be.

Kelly intended to find out. Which meant keeping Henry on the string as a viable, imminent cuckold option—a "bull," wasn't that the term?—until she could stage manage the whole performance, to maximize her slave's agony and her own dominant jollies.

With her mind swarming with erotic images, she no longer felt like browsing fashion sites or even online shoe shopping. Instead she called to mind some mildly fiendish ideas she'd had for stripping away Christopher's few remaining freedoms.

Could the Internet help her accomplish any of them? *Let's just ask Google, shall we?*

A few verbal hints to the search engine genie were enough to fetch her back a cornucopia of possibilities. Kelly clicked on the top site and got an illustrated page for something called the "TimePad," a metallic red padlock with a digital counter.

With growing, malicious delight she began reading the product description:

"The TimePad looks just like a regular padlock, but with an embedded countdown timer from one minute to 23 hours… Once the timer is set, you can't open the lock until the designated time… Only when the TimePad reaches zero will the lock magically open."

Isn't that *exactly* what she was looking for? *Why should she deny herself the thrill of really and truly chaining up her slave?*

With this simple device, she could do away with the nightly honor system she'd been forced to use with Christopher. No longer would he be able to free himself from his sleeping noose at will. Once she locked his neck chain into the TimePad and set the timer for six a.m., her slaveboy would be helplessly imprisoned in her closet until it was time for him to get up and start his early morning chores.

Maybe I'd better restrict his fluids before bedtime, she thought with a sly smile. Or give him an empty jar. Or spread an absorbent puppy pad beneath him.

Kelly clicked the purchase button and, quickly supplying her credit card info, opted for expedited shipping.

There another idea she wanted to check out, along similar lines. She'd already password-locked Chris out of her old laptop, deleted the browser and newsfeeds from his cell phone, along with his music and radio apps. But what about her big screen TV? Should a Supreme Goddess have to rely on her slave to self-enforce her rules and prohibitions? Of course not. Her TV should remain locked till she settled herself in front of it. Nor did Kelly want to rely on parental-blocking software. She demanded a total physical lockout.

Surely the Internet could help her with that.

Indeed it could, she discovered about thirty seconds later. For twenty-five dollars, Amazon offered a small "black box" known as the Power Plug Lockout. On one side of the box was a short power cord you plugged into the nearest wall socket. On the other side was a built-in socket where you plugged in the TV. On top of the small box was a single keyhole. Turn the attached key and you cut off power to the television—or anything else you plugged into the lockout box.

But couldn't Chris just pull the TV plug out of the box?

No, he couldn't, she learned in the next sentence. Once the key was turned and removed, the TV plug was locked in place. As the first five-star customer review put it:

"Once you take that little key out, there's no way short of power tools to remove the plug. It's locked in the box!"

It seemed Kelly was going to be keeping two magic keys in her possession, one for Chris' cock cage and one for her big screen TV.

She selected Amazon's "1-click" purchase and one-day shipping. By tomorrow night, the TimePad and Power Plug Lockout should both be installed, joining the spiral chastity device as permanent fixtures in her slave's ever-constricting life.

Her control over Christopher had now exceeded all her fantasies. Well, almost all.

Why did it turn her on so to do these things to her sweet boy?

This was one of the main things about Chris that had excited her from their very first ballroom dance. How easily she'd been able to take control of him and steer him backward, a sweet-faced, movable mannequin with a helpless hard-on!

Besides, she reminded herself, he'd begged her to make him her total slave. Which is exactly what she was doing. And there was no earthly reason she couldn't take his enslavement further yet. Although, for the moment, she'd run out of fiendish ideas.

Kelly closed the phone browser. But, before switching back to her work computer, she decided to check her personal email. She still had ten minutes before the three o'clock videoconference with the corporate brain trust in Chicago. As usual, she had all her bullet-points prioritized.

Kelly finger-scrolled her inbox and, spotting nothing of immediate interest, was about to exit when a familiar cyber-name popped into view—"pennywise."

Three years ago, when Kelly had been hired right out of college, the West Coast PR director, Penelope Wise, had taken Kelly under her wing. Until, a year ago, that is, when the free-spirited, fortyish executive had cashed in her stock options and flown off to the South of France to marry a famous travel writer. Penny's emails were always chock full of salty comments and toxic gossip, not only about mutual acquaintances in the biz, but the many glamorous and outlandish folk she seemed to bump into in the course of her ceaseless travels, from Montevideo to Macau.

Five minutes remained before the meeting. Time enough, Kelly decided, to take a peek at Penny's latest. The instant she did so, another familiar name leaped out at her—*Henry Malcolm.*

Speak of the sexy devil!

Could Penny know about her and Henry? Impossible! Especially since there wasn't anything to know. Not yet. And maybe not ever.

Kelly zoomed in on the paragraph:

"If I hear aright, Darling Kell, you folks have hired Henry Malcolm's outfit to bulldoze and rebuild that dreary old railroad resort up in the Bugaboo Mountains. My main recollection of Henry, until quite recently (see below!!), was of his casting a predatory eye on you during that epic two-day yacht party in Nassau Harbor—and you a just-married lady! Had I been his quarry, I'd have rolled over on the spot and let him munch and crunch me for lunch. (A girl can dream, can't she, even at an advanced age?) Lately, though, it seems, the ageless Sir Henry the Lion-Schlonged has been making a less than chivalrous name for himself up and down the Côte d'Azur, luring luscious Eurobabes onto his 60-ft. loveboat..."

Kelly felt shock, then gathering fury. How dare Henry stock his stateroom with sweet young things, apparently with the same cruising pickup line he was using on her!

Well! It would be an ice-cold day in Hades before she ever went sailing, or fucking, with Henry Malcolm.

Thank you, Penelope!

Now, as it just so happened, Kelly had a replacement candidate in mind to cuckold Chris with. A gorgeous candidate decades younger than Henry. And, in her present mood, Kelly didn't see why she should let this particular young stud get any older before trying him on for size.

It was three o'clock sharp. Department heads would be filing into the conference room, picking up coffee and croissants from the credenza while the Chinese techie girl fiddled with the video conference controls. Well, they could all just wait for her one more sweet minute.

Her text to Carmen was short and to the point:

"Re: Our little chat about ur snackilicious pilates teacher -- I may be ready 2 rumble."

Carmen's reply, which came through as Kelly exited the elevator on the top floor, was equally to the point—and punctuated with three rocket ship emojis:

"U won't be disappointed. He's even bigger than Hector if u know what I mean! 🚀🚀🚀"

*

CHAPTER TWELVE ~
SELECTING A BULL, PART TWO

Christopher was on hands and knees, sponge-scrubbing the lower tier of kitchen cupboards, taking special care to clean around all the hardware. Earlier, before dinner, Goddess Kelly had come into the kitchen to hurry him along on his preparations and found a sticky residue under a brass drawer pull. This was an infraction so serious that she'd promptly bent her naked slave over the butcher-block island and beaten his butt with a wooden spoon.

Worse for him, in the midst of his punishment, he had pleaded with her to stop because his glutes were still on fire from the morning's maintenance paddling. Chris had earned an additional dozen for this backtalk and disrespect of female authority.

You've got to do better, he reminded himself now, kneewalking to the next cupboard. And so, while he scrubbed, he began murmuring his slave mantra, concentrating on a particular section that had just been revised: *"She owns me... It's her right to own everything... I obey Her totally..."*

But that wasn't quite right, not any more. Tonight at dinner, while scraping her leftovers into the new metal dog bowl at her feet, she'd dictated a new phrase to be inserted right after *"to own everything"*:

"It's her right to take lovers."

Chris quietly recited the alarming addition over and over as he worked, including the familiar phrases before and after:

"It's her right to own everything... It's her right to take lovers... I obey Her totally..."

Why was she making a big deal about this just now, her right to take lovers? Kelly had declared her unconditional sexual freedom from the very start of their relationship. Over the years, of course, he had done his best to convince himself she was not truly serious about this. And so far as Chris knew, she had never exercised that particular freedom.

Was all that about to change? Was she finally going to fuck that old South African construction tycoon? Or maybe that muscular slave of Goddess Carmen they kept talking about, the one with the really big dick?

One thing he knew for sure, there were no empty phrases in his slave mantra. Every single one rang true.

"It's her right to own everything," for instance.

Chris had never had much money. Back in college, he'd run up serious credit card debt, and Kelly had helped him clear it. In the aftermath, she'd assumed complete financial control. Chris had been stripped of everything, a condition that persisted to this day. He had no money, and no access to any. He had no bank account, no ATM card, not even the small weekly allowance some submissive husbands apparently got from their strict wives. He was originally permitted to carry only a ten-dollar bill for emergencies, which had recently increased to a twenty, plus a debit card for household shopping, and Goddess Kelly monitored that account online every single day. Any unauthorized purchase, as Chris had learned, would be punished severely.

So *"It's her right to take lovers"* was no idle threat. She was going to exercise that right sooner or later—and it was sure looking like sooner.

The door chimes sent a surge of electricity through his naked body. Chris sprang to his feet and scurried into the adjoining service porch, where he pulled on the top subbie shirt from the stack atop the dryer. Sweatpants followed in a hopping, slapstick panic. Then he stopped, staring at the sliding wooden door that led into the front room.

Did Goddess Kelly expect him to resume his door-opening duties wearing his new slave uniform? She hadn't told him so. And it was always risky to do anything without clear instructions.

Lucky for him, as he dithered, he heard her footsteps approaching the door. Then they halted and, for several moments, Chris heard nothing.

Was she peeking through the wide-angle door viewer, maybe to see if it was Goddess Carmen?

At this prospect, Chris felt his cock come alive. The Cuban bodybuilder-domme was almost as sexy, and intimidating, as his own Goddess. And the two together turned him into instant male jello.

But his surging cock was overruled by his sore butt. He couldn't take another beating.

Please, Goddess, not tonight!

Then he heard the door open. "You must be Kelly." A masculine voice, rich and rumbly. "I'm Jason."

Chris wanted to die. His nightmare had just arrived. Not some old South African fart, but a young stud, judging by the sexy voice.

Was it going to happen tonight?

"Thank you for coming, Jason," Goddess Kelly said in a throaty, sexy purr. Chris heard the door click shut. "I saw you once before, you know, while I was parked outside Carmen's condo. You walked right by me. Did she tell you?"

"She did. I hope it's okay, by the way, I didn't bring any of my equipment. She said this was just a, you know—"

"A get-acquainted interview, yeah. Carmen swears I can absolutely trust you to be discreet. Is that true, Jason?"

"Don't worry. She gave me this whole lecture when she hired me about keeping her private life private, I mean with her being on that TV show and all. She even makes me hand over my cell phone until I leave. The thing is, Kelly, I never talk about my clients, and I work with some really well known people. They all know I can keep my mouth shut."

"Good. It's really important we're straight on that, Jason. But you can keep your cell phone. I'll trust you not to take any pictures or videos and post 'em on social media." She laughed. "Would you like some coffee?"

"That'd be great, thanks."

"Good. I'll get my husband to make us a fresh pot."

Their voices began to fade as they moved toward the dining room. Chris stuck his ear to the door jamb, desperate to hear more. But Jason had dropped into a gravelly whisper, like he might be telling a dirty joke. And maybe he was, because something had just triggered Kelly into a burst of bawdy laughter.

Chris whirled, grievously wounded, then hurried back into the kitchen. When Goddess Kelly came in to tell him to make coffee, she needed to find him busily scrubbing cupboards, not sneaking around.

And he *did* feel like a sneak. Like he had as a child, when he'd tiptoed downstairs to eavesdrop on Mom and Dad or grownup talk at a party.

They were in the dining room now. Back on his knees, scrubbing, Chris could hear their subdued voices behind the swing door—not the words, but the vocal interplay of growly baritone and husky contralto.

Then he heard the little shop-door jingle. Chris' reaction was pure panic. "Whenever you hear this sound," Goddess Kelly had warned yesterday, giving a quick shake to a little silver service bell she'd just bought at a gift shop, "I'll expect you before me in slave position within five seconds. Is that clear?"

Springing to his feet, Chris pushed open the swinging door.

They were at the dining room table, Kelly in the low-cut, black satin camisole she'd slipped into after coming home. Leaning far forward, as she was doing now, she seemed in imminent danger of slipping spectacularly *out* of the loose garment.

As for her guest, Chris hated him on sight. The only flaws he could find in his manly good looks were a toothy grin and some pitting on his cheeks above a neatly trimmed beard. But could you really fault someone for growing facial hair to cover up old acne scars? The sun-faded tanktop was a bit much, though, showing off not only his gym muscles but the fact that he'd once completed some obscure marathon.

Chris moved forward, merely nodding his deference. This was a major lapse in slave etiquette, but there was no way he was going to fall to his knees before Goddess Kelly with this grinning bastard looking on. He was even willing to risk the further ignominy of a face slap.

Astonishingly she let it pass—at least for now—and spoke to her guest instead:

"Jason, I want you to meet my husband, Christopher. Christopher, this is Jason West. He's a personal trainer and also teaches Pilates. And he comes *very* highly recommended."

Jason got to his feet, extending his hand. He was an inch or so taller than Chris. "Pleasure to meet you."

Chris feared a bone-crushing, but the man's grip was merely firm and friendly.

"Jason and I have been talking," Goddess Kelly continued, "about maybe having him come by once or twice a week to work me out. He's going to really help me strengthen my core, aren't you, Jason?"

"That's the plan." Jason smiled as he sat back down.

"Sounds great," Chris said, his mind in total freefall. "Is there something I—"

"Make us a pot of coffee," Kelly said. "Unless you'd prefer decaf, Jason?"

"Decaf, if you've already got some. Don't make it just for me."

"Of course he'll make it just for you. That's what he's for. I'll take decaf as well, Christopher. Ask our guest if he takes cream or sugar."

"Black's fine, thanks," Jason cut in. "And, by the way, dude, I like your t-shirt."

Chris suffused with embarrassment. He'd forgotten about his subbie shirt. A furtive down-glance showed him which one he had on:

I BELONG TO HER

"Uh, thanks. I, uh… I guess I never ran a marathon."

"No, you certainly didn't." With a small gesture, Goddess Kelly shooed him away. "And, Christopher, please keep the kitchen door closed. Jason and I have more to discuss, and we'd like to do so in privacy. Knock before you return with the decaf."

"Yes, Ma'am," Chris said, his head bobbing.

He turned and exited, his face now on fire, just like his spoon-bruised butt cheeks.

*

Kelly was relishing every moment of the three-way scene. The actuality of subjecting Christopher to such delicious humiliation, while knowing how much farther she intended to take it, was making her seriously wet. And unleashing a whole chain of seismic tremors epicentered between her thighs.

Jason was a huge part of that, of course. Close up, he was even more of a stud than he'd seemed walking by her parked car that evening outside Carmen's condo. Sitting there in her parlor was this well-groomed wild animal, the complete antithesis of her emasculated slave. Oh, maybe Jason was a bit too conventionally handsome, with his Prince Valiant hair and chiseled profile, and beards had never really been her thing. But his was trimmed sort of cute and piratical, like Kevin Kline's in *Pirates of Penzance*, one of Kelly's favorite movie musicals. And the facial scarring did give him a bit of a rough edge.

Mainly, though, Jason West screamed "SEX" without even trying. The vibe was effortless and irresistible, implicit in that easy grin and resonant voice and those tiny squint lines at the corners of his blue eyes.

Hasta la vista, Henry Malcolm, and you can take your floating girl-trap with you!

"Jason's no gigolo," Carmen had explained over the phone. "He really is a first-class personal trainer and Pilates teacher."

"I get that," Kelly had said. "But you just said he works exclusively with female clients, and that if he's attracted, well—"

"Oh, he likes the ladies, no shit, and they *love* him. And he's incredibly hung, like I been telling you. But he's very picky when it comes to any extracurricular stuff. But if things click with a client, which is like a total no-brainer in your case, and obviously with me, then, yeah, he's been known to schedule extra playtime at his basic hourly rate. Believe me, if Jason wanted to lower his standards and jack up his prices, he could make a fucking fortune, or a fortune fucking, however you want to say it."

But how would Jason feel about playing the role of "bull," Kelly wanted to know, especially if the hubby or boyfriend remained on the premises during the cuckolding?

"Well, there *was* a small problem," Carmen had admitted, "when Jason met Hector, and saw those Popeye arms of his and all those gang tats. So I had to promise that, whenever Jason comes over, I'll put Hec into heavy bondage and lock him in the spare room. But with Christopher, you won't have to worry. I mean, you've totally deballed the poor guy. Who's going to worry about what *he* thinks?"

And so it had proved, Kelly thought, judging from their initial encounter. Jason's attitude toward Chris had seemed to be one of amused contempt. Almost the way she herself had come to regard her slave husband. What really mattered, of course, was Jason's attitude toward *her*. Which was why she'd dressed to slay. Or at least mortally wound.

"I take it you bought him that shirt?" Jason said, turning to her.

"Yes, he has a whole collection of them. I make him wear them whenever he goes out shopping."

"And he doesn't object?"

"He wouldn't dare. Christopher does exactly what he's told, or else. I assumed Carmen had briefed you about our arrangement."

"She said it's basically the same sort of deal she has with her own, uh…."

"'Slave.' That's the label Carmen and I prefer. It doesn't leave this room, but just like Hector, Christopher is my complete and utter slave and domestic servant." Kelly leaned forward again, providing her guest another peekaboo vista. "Is that a deal-breaker for you, Jason?"

"It's intriguing, Kelly, I'll put it that way. Though I'm not sure I really get how it works. Femdom, I mean. That's what your lifestyle is called, right?"

"You can use that term, if you like."

"But isn't it a consensual deal? You each play your roles, right, domme or sub, whichever floats your boat? And then you got these limits and safewords and like that, which you both agree on?"

"No, it's not like that. Maybe with some couples, but not with me and Chris. Or Carmen and Hector. I guess she didn't go into detail."

"Well, I didn't ask many questions."

"But now you're curious?"

"Kind of, yeah."

Kelly had been checking Jason's vital signs. So far, his big easy grin seemed unaffected. She decided to push things a bit, see how he'd react.

"Okay, since I can rely on your discretion, I'm going to give you a quick peek behind the curtain. We're not just 'female led,' or 'femdom,' Carmen and I. We're what are called female supremacists. That means it's our way or the highway. No safewords, no limits. Sure, Chris is free to leave. Theoretically, anyway. But if he stays, then he gives up every other right and freedom and lives under my absolute control." Kelly paused. "I guess that makes me a cruel, heartless bitch, doesn't it? Or maybe, just maybe, you find it a wee bit *intriguing*. Isn't that the word you used a minute ago? Hmm?"

So here was a moment of truth. Was she making him squirm, ever so slightly? If so, that might indicate Mr. Jason West had a secret submissive streak, like most hetero guys in her experience, once she focused all her weaponry on them.

"Well, I can see how it could be a real turn-on, you know, being bossed around by Marilyn Monroe or the Queen of the Ninja Warriors." He grinned again. "For some guys, anyway."

"But not for *you?* You like to call the shots, don't you, Jason?"

"That's the way it usually works. And most of my clients seem to like it."

"Maybe I will, too, when I'm one of your clients. It can get tiresome—always being in charge. The thing is, sometimes a girl *has* to show a bit of initiative, just to get things rolling. Take this nice, polite little chat we're having, for instance. I think we both know what the next step is, so what's to prevent us from taking it?"

"What next step?"

"Let me put it this way. Would you mind if I kissed you, Jason? Or am I supposed to wait for you to make the first move?"

There was a definite twinkle in his eyes. "No, go ahead, knock yourself out, babe." Jason leaned toward her, as if to facilitate a kiss. Kelly, already on her feet, ignored this.

His chair was just far enough from the table that, with two steps, she was able to slide in and plant her bottom on his blue-jeaned thighs, twisting her busty torso toward him as she twined her arms around his strong neck. As she did so, she felt a small python begin to uncoil beneath her right thigh.

My God, he really was *huge!*

She leaned in harder, compressing her breasts against his chest. When he deliberately didn't react, she touched noses with him, staring owlishly into his eyes.

"Hi, there, Jase."

"Hi, yourself."

"I forgot what I came over here to do."

"I think you were going to kiss me."

"Oh, was I? Like this?"

She pressed her lips softly against his, enjoying the furry tickle of his mustache, then slid her hands up into his thick hair, pressing his face even closer against hers to ratchet up the kiss. His eyes were shut tight now, she saw, opening hers for a second, but his nostrils flared, drawing in the air that, sweet seconds later, warmed her lips with his exhalation.

So far, she thought, Jason was behaving like a perfectly docile boy, almost like her Christopher. Was he just playing along with her aggressive game, or had she really pushed secret submissive buttons?

Let's find out, shall we?

His hands came up to caress her cheeks, but she had something else in mind. Seizing his right wrist and, with her other hand, lifting the scalloped bottom of her satin cami, she guided his big palm exactly where she wanted it.

"Holy Mother of God," he breathed, hefting the full quivering weight of her.

"Religious awe, I like it! Why don't I arrange things a bit so you can really worship them?"

"Now? With your husband due back any second?"

"He's also my slave, remember? And what does it matter if he sees you on first base or second?"

Leaning back, Kelly used both hands to tug the satin garment up over the great, bouncy bulge of her bare breasts. Then, cupping her palms beneath the great twin globes, she lifted their heaviness up to his eager face.

No baby could have zeroed in and suckled more greedily, Kelly thought. Jason's face and grasping fingers moved right, then left, then laughing at his absurdly futile attempts to take one of her prodigious breasts entirely into his gaping mouth. Finally, as he settled to work nursing on her erect right nipple, from deep in his throat came a long, drawn-out growl of primal pleasure.

This, Kelly knew, was an experience from which he would not soon recover.

She really wanted Christopher to witness it, but she decided it was already time to wean Jason—to leave him desperately wanting more. Besides, she craved more deep kissing. So she withdrew the goodies and lowered her cami, snaking her arms back around the big man as her lips found his again.

Next she bit his underlip. More of a nibble, really. Not enough to draw blood, as she had the other day with Christopher. But enough for Jason to target her with a point-blank stare.

"You're really asking for it, aren't you?" he said hoarsely.

"So what if I am? What are you going to do about it, big boy?"

Jason's response was to wrap her up in his powerful arms and crush her gently against his chest. Giving him her sexiest smile, Kelly closed her eyes and parted her lips, taking in his warm breath and then, inevitably, his questing tongue.

There came a timid knock at the kitchen door.

Kelly unglued herself from the dizzy-making kiss, just enough to gasp an impatient command: "Come in, slave."

"Yes, Goddess," Christopher answered automatically, shouldering open the door while holding the black lacquer serving tray in both hands. As he turned to behold the monstrous scene, he felt his whole world lurch sideways and dissolve. The cups began to chatter.

"Oh, for God's sakes, Christopher! Just put the tray down and go back to your chores! We're not finished yet."

Chris managed, somehow, not to drop the tray, but, in his anguish, set it down with a cup-rattling thump. Had his Goddess not been otherwise occupied, this unforgivable clumsiness would have gotten him a well-deserved face slap.

But, back in passionate face-lock with her new macho man, Goddess Kelly hadn't even noticed.

Chris whirled and fled for his life.

Back in the kitchen, his legs turned to jelly. Putting a palm to the wall, he slid slowly down, ending up curled on his knees and sagging into a corner, his staggering heart in utter despair.

It was the end of his world. He meant nothing to his Goddess now. Less than nothing.

*

"Now what do you think?" Kelly asked. "Can you imagine being a woman's slave?"

She was still not quite sure how she'd managed to extricate herself from this gorgeous man and return to her chair close beside him.

Jason's gaze remained fixed on the rise and fall of her bosomy breathing. "Probably better if you don't ask me any complicated questions right about now." He flashed his trademark grin. "I think my brain got unplugged."

"Possibly it's because all your blood went someplace else." Kelly made no attempt to conceal her avid glance down at the elongated bulge in his jeans. "Anyway, I thought I was asking a fairly simple question. After seeing that teensy weensy demo, what do you think about our lifestyle, Carmen's and mine? Where the woman is always on top? And I mean in every way there is."

"Well, obviously it works—for you and your—your guy. I forget his name."

"That's because it doesn't really matter. Just call him 'slave.' I do."

"I'd rather not."

"Call him Chris then. Obviously my rules don't apply to you. At least not yet."

"Well, *that's* a relief, I suppose." He grinned. "Look, Kelly, please don't get me wrong. You obviously got the reaction you wanted from me, right? And, believe me, I'm ready to clear as much time on my schedule as you can use. But when it comes to sex, I guess I'm just hopelessly conventional. I gotta be the *guy*, right? Like in dancing, you know? *Slow* dancing, I mean."

"Don't tell me. You like to lead, with the girl's cheek on your manly chest?"

"Yeah, I do. I hope that doesn't disqualify me."

"No, Mr. West, it doesn't. It sure as shit doesn't."

So, the verdict was in, and it suited her just fine. So far it looked like "Jason" and "bull" would go together like "De Sade" and "Sacher Masoch." Slaveboy material he most definitely wasn't. And thank God for that. Because didn't civilization still need a few of these red-blooded Neanderthal types around? Like for a terrorist takedown or a hostage rescue?

Or maybe just a good hard fuck?

When you wanted brute force, what good were battalions of subbies and sensitive metrosexuals?

She took hold of Jason's thick wrist and turned it to glance at the face of his steel-banded watch. "Alas, it looks like my interview time is almost up. But we're all set for—when is it again, Jason?"

"Wednesday night, you said, at nine." He paused. "I don't have anything scheduled after you, by the way."

"Well, I like the sound of *that!* Maybe I'll have Christopher fix us a late dinner."

"I don't eat when I'm working. And, remember, I really *am* going to work you out. And I'm just talking Pilates now."

"Of course you are, big boy!"

Kelly saw him to the door, where she leaned in for a last, long kiss. In the course of which she did something she'd wanted to do while on his lap, but somehow had gotten distracted from. She put her hand on his pants to feel the sheer size of him.

"Oh là là!" she exclaimed in playful French, breaking off the kiss. Joking aside, as he continued to swell and harden under her touch, Kelly felt her knees go wobbly. He was, as Carmen had said, *really, really big.*

Jason, meanwhile, could only grin and slowly shake his head. As if to say, Aw, shucks!

With a rueful smile, she shut the door on her beautiful new stud, then leaned back against it. She remained there for several minutes, letting her breathing subside, before going to check on her slave.

*

She found him huddled in a corner on the floor, whimpering.

Seeing him like that, knowing the suffering she'd inflicted, only added to the incredible erotic high she was on. She bent down and placed her hand on his shuddering shoulder.

"Are you okay, little slave?"

At this bit of feigned tenderness, Christopher's whimpering gave way to despairing sobs.

"Tell me how you feel. Turn and look at your Goddess."

He twisted toward her, but could not meet her gaze. As his tears began rolling, he turned his ruined face back to the corner. Kelly leaned closer, heard his stammering attempt to answer, "I—I—," amid all the sobbing and snuffling and hopeless convulsions. She was on the verge of slapping him to bring him out of it when he managed finally to choke out three words:

"I—I feel—defeated, Goddess."

Then, to her surprise, Kelly did feel some genuine sympathy for her suffering slave. She stooped down beside him and ruffled his hair.

That's good, sweetie."

"It is?" came the pitiful response.

"Yes. It's *very* good."

He turned back to her, a look of faint, puzzled hope breaking through his wretchedness. "Why? Why is it good?"

"I'm going to tell you why. But first, you must take off your clothes—as you should have done the instant you heard the door close on my handsome guest."

And next time Jason comes over, she thought, I'll make you serve us in your birthday suit so he can see how much smaller you are.

"And when you've taken off your clothes," she went on, "and folded them neatly, then come to my chair and sit on the floor and listen carefully." She made a double clap of dismissal.

Kelly settled in the recliner, but kept it in upright position. She wanted to look down from full regal height as her slave approached.

She was pleased, a moment later, to see her naked boy coming to her on all fours, head lowered, without her having expressly demanded that. Truly, he was learning his place.

"You may curl up at my feet, slave, and hug my calves. Would you like that?"

"Yes, Goddess," he said, still not daring to look up. "Thank you, Goddess!"

"Now I will explain why it's good that you feel defeated. For too long now, as I've told you, you've been thinking that you are a man. Despite all the evidence to the contrary, don't ask me why. Because tonight you saw what a real man looks like. And you know you can never be that—not to me, certainly, and probably not to any woman."

Chris was whimpering again, sounding like a pitiful puppy, and clutching her leg for dear life. Yet, to his credit, he had nodded in agreement at each particular of her indictment.

"Some of this is my fault," she went on, "as I've said before. I've been so totally absorbed in my career, I just didn't have time to deal with you properly. As a result, you've gotten all kinds of ridiculous notions about what you are.

"But those days are gone. Ever since you failed to pick me up on time at the airport—what was it, just a week ago, or less?—I've begun to do what I should have done long ago. And that is to reduce you to the status you truly deserve, sweetie. Which, of course, is my complete inferior, to do with as I please. It's not only what you deserve, but what you need. And now, I think, what you've actually come to crave. Isn't that so?"

"Yes, Goddess," Chris said, laying his cheek against her thigh as he continued to clutch her strong calves. It was true. Even in his utter desolation, he could still feel the familiar submissive bliss in being at her feet, clinging to her strength while her Goddess words washed over him.

"So, you must always remember this—what you are and what you are not. You don't belong in my bed. That's only for a real man, like Jason West. And now that you've met him, it's no wonder you feel defeated. It's good that you feel that way, because you need to stop dreaming about things far above your station, things that can never be." She tipped his head up. "You see that, don't you, slave?"

He nodded again, gulping. "But—but—"

"But *what?*"

"What if you get rid of me?"

"Is that what you're afraid of? Oh, I see. Well, let me think."

She ruffled his hair absently again as she thought about her answer, and savored to the full the awesome and delicious power that was hers as a slave owner. "Well, I can't promise that I'll never get rid of you—now don't look so devastated—but I will say this. As long as you obey me in everything, follow all my household rules, and accept all your beatings, and always remember your place, and perform all your duties, to the best of your ability, from morning till night until you are exhausted, and then go obediently to my closet to be locked up until it's time to start all over again next day, then I don't see why I should want to get rid of you. Do you?"

"No, Goddess. I don't."

"But I should counsel you, if you know what's good for you, you won't give me even the tiniest reason to be displeased with you from now on. Does that make sense?"

"Yes, Goddess, it does."

"Very good. Now, slave, I want you to kneel up right beside me. I know that was hard for you tonight, meeting Jason. You can see how strong and handsome and manly he is and how happy I was to be with him. Because of this, you might have trouble going to sleep if I sent you right to my closet. So I'm going to give you something to help you calm down."

Kelly crossed her arms, taking hold of the satin cami at either side. With an abrupt gesture she stripped it off over her head and flung it away, exposing her magnificent breasts to the kneeling slave.

"Come here to me, sweet boy, where you belong."

She cradled his head, drawing his face into the fullness of her left breast. Christopher began greedily, but soon settled into a slow, steady suckling that seemed to soothe his fears and calm his submissive soul. Soon enough, his upper body was corkscrewed over the chair arm, his face buried in her flesh. He was whimpering again. But this time, she knew, from sheer happiness.

*

CHAPTER THIRTEEN ~
MORE DESCENDING STEPS

Christopher took a morning timeout from dusting and vacuuming the Mistress Bedroom to inspect himself in front of her standing floor mirror. Last night, before locking him—first into his cock cage, then into her closet—Goddess Kelly had slathered him all over with Nare for Men.

A dozen minutes later she'd wiped off the thick goo, then had him stand before her as hairless as a prepubescent boy, including chest, underarms and crotch. A prepubescent boy with a full salute.

"Tell me," she'd asked, brows arched and arms folded, "do you still feel like a man?"

"No, Goddess," Chris had answered honestly.

"Why not?"

"Because I'm *not* a man, Goddess."

"No, you're certainly not, are you?" She'd reached out to caress his rigid cock, then to cup his hairless testicles, and finally, shockingly, to apply a vicious squeeze that made him grunt and fold to the floor where he lay doubled up and groaning.

"Stop that noise and get back on your feet, slave," she'd commanded. "I was simply shrinking you so I can lock you into your cage and put you to bed."

Chris had clamped his jaw to silence and done as told. But, when she reached again for his groin, his hands flew up reflexively.

"Hands behind your back, slave!" she barked.

"I'm so sorry, Goddess!" Chris pleaded, knowing he'd done an unforgivable thing. "I didn't mean to, it was just—"

But retribution was already en route—an upswing of her sandaled toe directly to his exposed testicles. Pain exploded in crippling waves. The grunts and groans from the earlier ball squeeze were as nothing compared to his howls and gasps as he doubled up again and rolled on the floor at her feet.

"How many times have I told you, you are *never* to lift a hand against me? Not even to protect yourself from anything I choose to do to you. You are my property, to do with as I please. When will that finally get through to you, slave? Answer me!"

"I'm sorry, Goddess," Chris groaned between sobs. "It'll never happen again."

"Prove it! Back on your feet with your hands behind your back."

It was so hard to obey, but there was no choice. He felt like a prizefighter climbing off the canvas as he staggered to his feet and stood fearfully and unsteadily before her, sucking air.

"Your legs are shaking, slave, as well they should. Perhaps you know what's coming next?"

"Y-yes, Goddess."

"What is it? What do you think I am going to do to you?"

"You—you're going to—to—kick me again."

"Indeed I am. And *where* do you suppose I'm going to kick you?"

"In—in the balls."

"Right again. And this time you're not going to raise a hand, or turn away, or move a muscle, are you?"

"No, Goddess, I'm not." Chris looked down, inwardly cringing while remaining perfectly still as ordered. Despite his panic, he found himself idiotically admiring her sexy, pearl-tipped toes peeking out of beaded thong sandals, and actually priding himself on how carefully he'd applied the polish.

"And *why,*" he heard her say, "are you not going to protect yourself?"

"Be—because, like you said, I'm your property, Goddess… to do with as you—"

"Blah-blah-blah! Do you think this is some kind of a slave quiz where the correct answer gets you off the hook? Eventually you're going to learn what those words really mean—and learn it so well you'll never forget it. Look at me!"

Chris forced his glance upward. Her gray eyes danced with cruel mischief as her right knee lifted with the slow, deliberate grace of a ballerina. She held the pose, balancing on one leg with the other raised and flexed to strike, a long, gleeful moment before unleashing her kick. Chris cried out a split-second before the sickening impact that dropped him a third time, face-down at her feet.

A little impatiently, Goddess Kelly waited for all the writhing and gasping and moaning to subside a bit, then knelt down beside his shoulder and spoke gently:

"I won't make you stand up again just now, slaveboy. But turn over so I can lock you up for the night."

Chris obeyed, face clenched and eyes shut. He felt her fingers working deftly below, slipping the cold steel base ring over his now-shrunken penis, then over his aching balls, one after the other. Next the spiral cage was twisted on and snapped into the base ring, followed by the closing click of the tiny padlock.

"Now that you've had a moment to recover, up on your feet. I want to have a final look at you before you go in the closet."

She made a complete circuit. He stood, quivering slightly as her lacquered fingernails traced an equatorial line around his hairless crotch and thoroughly battered buns.

"Well," she said, coming full circle, "Goddess Carmen was right again. This is exactly how males should be kept, without clothes or body hair.

"The problem is, I can only use this depilatory cream on you every three days. So, if even one hair pops up in the next two days, no matter how tiny, you'd better shave it off before I see it. Or I'll have to take you in for laser treatments and solve the problem permanently."

The painful memory of those kicks was still with him as he stood, regarding his naked form in his owner's mirror very much as she had last night. And, Goddess knows, his testicles still hurt. But he had more immediate concerns. Carefully, he lifted his caged penis out of the way in order to inspect the wrinkly folds of his ball sac, searching for the slightest traces of stubble. He didn't want to give Goddess Kelly any pretext for laser-zapping his follicles, although, oddly, he wasn't sure why the idea troubled him so.

Satisfied, he turned his back to the mirror, and, with the aid of his owner's heart-shaped hand mirror, bent and twisted to inspect his backside.

Chris was shocked by what he saw.

No new hairs, thank Goddess! But his butt cheeks and the backs of both thighs were disfigured with bruises and welts. He saw not only the expected crimson and pink blotches from this morning's harsh maintenance paddling, but lurid purples and indigos from the crop and strap applied under Goddess Carmen's supervision two nights before. And, older still, were the fading traces of plum and saffron left by that brutal weightlifter's belt.

Then an odd thing happened. Shock and revulsion began to fade, just like the livid bruises, to be replaced by a peculiar sort of pride. He realized, once again, that he was actually proud to bear these marks of his Goddess' power and cruelty. He was seeing them not as ugly scars, but as badges of honor, showing his complete submission to her supreme authority.

And as indelible signs of her ownership. Even, perhaps, of her love.

Are you crazy? Are you out of your freaking mind? The more she beats you, the more she loves you? Is that what you really think?

I don't know. Maybe yes. What other hold did he have on her? At least this was one thing he could cling to when all seemed lost.

Because, of course, Christopher now had a rival, a cocky, good-looking bastard who was about to displace him in Kelly's favor and in her bed.

In this one thing, however, no rival could displace him. Not if he was willing to suffer the worst cruelties his Goddess could inflict and each time crawl back for more. She would have to keep him close, if only to assuage her cruel lust. In this way, and perhaps this way alone, Chris reassured himself, he could secure his place forever at her glorious feet.

*

There was one implement Kelly had yet to use on Christopher—the whippy little bamboo cane. By reputation, the harshest of them all, and Kelly couldn't wait to see its effects. And she needed to do *something* when she got home to get her mind off Jason West, who was scheduled to come by the following night to rock her world—not to mention her slave's!

But an E. coli outbreak at her company's Singapore hotel kept her on the phone with clients well into the evening, rescheduling or relocating short-term bookings. She had a prosciutto panini sent up from the street-level café, then phoned Chris to go ahead and eat without her, so long as he did so out of his dog bowl on the kitchen floor. It was nearly eleven when she finally dragged herself home.

Even then, she might have found time for a quick cropping were it not for the two UPS cartons sitting atop the console table near the entryway. After kissing her shoes, Chris stood to hand her the utility knife—as a slave, he was forbidden to open any mail or packages, even those rarities actually addressed to him. She started on the slightly larger box, slicing it open and plucking from a nest of Styrofoam noodles a black plastic cube with an attached power cord.

"What is it, Goddess?" Chris was overcome by a queasy curiosity.

"It's called a Power Plug Lockout box, sweetie." She handed it to him. "You need to crawl behind the entertainment center and unplug the TV and plug it into this box instead. See, right here on the side? Then you unwrap this cord and plug the little box directly into the wall outlet."

Chris did as told, then handed Goddess Kelly the black box, which was now plugged into the wall with the TV plugged into it.

Kelly turned a small brass key in its slot atop the black box, then instructed Chris to press the power button on the TV remote. He did so, but the screen remained dark.

"I get it," Chris said. "It's a cutout switch."

"Exactly. So when I turn the key back to the 'Power On' position, the TV works. Go ahead, push the button."

Chris touched the remote, and the big HDTV screen came alive. A busty redheaded weathergirl in a wispy blue minidress pranced across a moving temperature map. The instant Kelly turned the key 'Off,' the screen went black.

"Watch closely now. I'm going to remove the key and drop it into my purse," which she did, "where I will keep it until such time as I want to watch TV. Which means, sweetie, your TV watching days are over."

"But I never turn it on anymore, Goddess Kelly. You forbade it."

"Of course you don't. But you *could*, theoretically. Only now you *can't*. Because I've removed even the temptation for being naughty and disobeying me. Shouldn't you be thanking me for that?"

Chris nodded bleakly. "Thank you, Goddess."

"But perhaps you're secretly wondering if, the minute I leave for work each morning, you couldn't just remove the TV plug from the black box and stick it back into the wall. Hmm?"

"No, Goddess." But she was right, of course. He *had* thought of that.

"Okay, I want you to try that right now. Pull on the TV plug as hard as you can."

Chris did. The plug wouldn't budge. It was trapped in the box somehow. The gizmo was foolproof.

"Now, think back. I believe I've removed some other potential distractions from you in the past few days. Can you remember what they were?"

"My computer access, Goddess. And all my iPhone apps."

"Very good. And why do you suppose I did that?"

"So I won't be distracted from… from my housework and… and from thinking about being the best possible slave to you."

"Right again. Shouldn't I get another 'Thank you, Goddess'?"

"Yes, Goddess. Thank you."

"Now let's take a look in the other box, shall we?"

Kelly used the knife again, then lifted out a large, red metallic padlock with a digital counter. "This is also for you, sweetie. Since it's already way past your bedtime, we can try it out right now."

Chris was instructed to go to the bathroom and relieve himself, then return to Goddess Kelly's walk-in closet to be locked up for the night.

"And with this padlock timer, I can *really* lock you up. Isn't that fun?"

Chris nodded, a lump in his throat. Awash in equal parts alarm and excitement, he hurried off to do her bidding. When he returned, she was adjusting the chain leash that was secured through the clothes pole bracket. She pointed to the floor, where she'd spread his sleeping blanket and pillow.

"On your knees," she said crisply, "but kneel up, so I don't have to bend down to put this on you."

He obeyed, heart pounding as she looped the chain noose around his neck, exactly as she'd done last night.

"Don't be frightened, little slave." She snugged the noose tight, but left enough slack in the rest of the chain so he'd be able to lie flat on the blanket. "Your Goddess is just keeping you safe in her closet where you belong till morning."

Now she produced the red padlock with its digital timer, opened the shackle and slipped it through a link close to the noose ring. Chris couldn't see the padlock now, but could feel its solid weight beneath his jaw, tugging his neck chain downward and keeping it tight.

Then, with an ominous *snick-click*, he heard the padlock snap shut.

"You can't see this part, sweetie, but I'm setting the digital countdown timer. Right now, by my watch, it's eleven twenty-four. So six a.m., when you need to start your chores, will be in approximately six hours and thirty-six minutes. So I'm pressing the 'Hours' button until it reads 'six,' okay, and now the 'Minutes' button till the counter reads 'thirty-six.' Almost there. Okay, now I press the 'Start' button, and *voilà!* The LED letters light up, and the countdown begins. When it reaches zero-zero-zero, the lock will open and you'll be free—but not a second before. Now lie down, slave, just like a good little doggie chained up in his mistress' closet."

But when Chris lay on his side, the padlock pressed into his neck. He pushed it this way and that on the pillow, to no avail. He turned on his back instead, resting the heavy timer in the notch between his collarbones. He'd have to get used to it, as it was obviously going to be a fixture of his nocturnal life from now on, just like sleeping on the closet floor.

"Comfy, sweetie?" came the teasing voice above him. Her sandaled toe prodded his caged cock.

"Yes, Goddess Kelly," he lied, not daring to utter a word of complaint.

"Isn't it exciting, knowing we're not playing silly pretend games anymore? That you're really chained up in my closet for the night— or for as long as I want you chained up?"

"Yes, Goddess," he said meekly, realizing that what she said was actually true. In fact, she'd be able to see how excited he was to be chained up in here, except for the steel cage that kept his cock from standing straight up.

Her face hove into view, her goddess gaze drilling right through him to the very bottom of his craven soul.

"Good night, sweet slave," she said, pivoting and walking away. "Dream of me."

Then the light went out and the closet door shut, leaving him locked in total darkness except for the faint cigarette glow of the LEDs beneath his chin.

*

Ten minutes later, naked save for her plum satin kimono—the very one she'd threatened to make Chris wear when she'd sent him on an errand down to her car—Goddess Kelly lounged back in her leather recliner. With one hand she tipped a crystal flute of Prosecco to her lips, while her other hand, lower down, guided her Hitachi Magic Wand precisely where it could do the most good. While she sipped and self-eroticized, she watched a favorite episode of *Downton Abbey* on the big screen. Funny how these lavish, period dramas never failed to stimulate her. She particularly enjoyed the contrast between the languid hauteur of the well-bred young ladies of the house and the measured bowings and scrapings of the family footmen.

How easily she would have fit into such an aristocratic existence!

Maybe I really am Cruella!

And why shouldn't she be? Hadn't she acquired the role direct from her own mother, a North Woods lumber heiress who still rode roughshod over her hopelessly doting father when and as needed? Kelly Ann had simply taken it all to a new level with poor Christopher. Who, thus far at least, seemed to crave living in an absolute gynarchy every bit as much as she did.

Codependency, wasn't that the term?

And tomorrow night she would take the most irrevocable step of all, bringing Jason West into her home. And into her bed. And deep into her insatiable pussy. With Christopher in passive attendance. Thinking about it set a kaleidoscope of erotic images spinning in her mind.

So much for watching *Downton Abbey!* Her focus now entirely inward, Kelly tilted farther back and parted the satin flaps of the shorty kimono to let the purring wand perform its deep, interior magic.

It wasn't long before her back began to arch and her bare heels to dig into the footrest. While her lovesick captive—within easy hearing distance—was driven to the brink of madness by the drifting sounds of prolonged ecstasy.

*

CHAPTER FOURTEEN ~
FIRST CUCKOLDING, PART ONE

This was Christopher's morning for a thorough vacuuming and Swiffering in living room and dining room. It meant moving every piece of furniture so he could dust the underside and clean the exposed floor, whether carpeting or hardwood. It usually took around thirty minutes, if he kept at it steadily, which he needed to do, as his chore list was always very long. But, as he was repositioning the final piece of furniture—a heavy Biedermeier-style dining table—he was hit by a crushing wall of fatigue. In a half-faint, he felt his knees give way as he folded to the floor and his tailbone hit the carpet.

He cried out. The impact had reignited butt cheeks already superheated from his morning paddling. He rolled sideways, wishing fervently he could crawl onto the loveseat or stretch full-length onto the Goddess bed. A slave, of course, was forbidden even to think of such things. But Christopher did so anyway, daring to imagine he was not only in her bed, but snuggling beside her, clinging like a puppydog to her luscious, curled leg.

The way he used to do. The way she used to let him.

Last night in her closet he'd slept very little. No matter how he'd turned or squirmed, there was no escaping the infernal weight and bulk of the heavy padlock timer fastened tightly around his neck. Self-pity had flared into bitter resentment at his cruel treatment, then deepened into hopelessness with the realization that this nightly curse would be his for the rest of his life.

How was he supposed to endure it, on top of everything else? Endless hours of solitary constriction and confinement, with only a blanket between his hipbones and the hardwood floor?

If only she'd left him a pair of her worn panties to intoxicate his senses and calm his nerves. But she'd forgotten it. Or deliberately denied him this small precious comfort.

And now, as he lay curled fetally, half under the dining table, Chris began to whimper, and then to weep. They were tears of self-pity, as they'd been last night. How little she seemed to appreciate how hard he worked for her, or how desperately he adored her.

But, of course, there was something far more threatening than neglect in the immediate offing. Something that would happen in only a few more hours, not long after his glorious Goddess came home and he served her the sausage and white bean cassoulet he was slow-cooking for her.

The threat had a name. Jason West.

The so-called Pilates teacher who looked just like one of those bare-chested bastards on paperback romance novels. A big grinning pirate on a tilting deck, with one hand on the ship's helm and the other around the waist of a half-naked wench.

Jason West was making a housecall. The first of many, no doubt.

"He's going to really put me through my paces," Kelly had said this morning by the front door as Christopher groveled before her, kissing the pointed toes of her black patent leather pumps.

Her meaning couldn't have been more plain. Jason West wasn't coming over to train her, but to fuck her. And Kelly had made no effort to conceal her kittenish excitement at the prospect. She flaunted it, clearly gleeful at the torturous effect on her lovesick slave.

"Carmen says he's really gorgeous—not just his face, he's obviously good-looking— but all over, every manly inch of him! Now why are you making such a pathetic face? Don't you want me to find a man who can give me what I need? Who can make me happy? I mean really, really happy?"

When he'd hesitated, she prodded his steel-caged penis with her toe. "Well, don't you? And be warned, slaveboy, you'd better come up with the right answer."

"Yes, Goddess," Christopher managed to squeak out, "I want you to find a man who can—" But she'd already turned away, stepping across the threshold and pulling the door firmly shut behind her, leaving him to his chores and hopeless thoughts.

So, this terrible day, which had always been coming, had finally arrived. Chris' only option was to accept it. No, not merely accept it, but embrace it.

She is everything, I am nothing.

How many times had he repeated the simple formula while saying his slave mantra? Now was the time to live out the truth of those words. To bask in his Goddess' glory. To rejoice in the unlimited gratification of her carnal appetites —her right to fuck whenever and whoever she wished. While he remained locked in perpetual chastity.

Before she'd taken away his Internet privileges, Chris had read about femdom marriages in which serially cuckolded husbands not only acquiesced to their wives' complete sexual freedom, but were tasked with bathing and dressing them in sexy outfits before their dates. And some husbands who were required to do even more demeaning things, both during and after those dates.

Chris remembered wondering how a man could allow himself to be so totally degraded. He would soon find out.

*

The chimes had sounded while Christopher was Swiffer-mopping the kitchen floor, the final step in his after-dinner cleanup. He froze, hoping and praying Goddess Kelly would answer. It was shameful enough to be sent scurrying to greet the man who was coming to make love to his wife. It would be even worse to do so in the ridiculous outfit he was being made to wear for the occasion. His black "subbie shirt" proclaimed in bold white letters that he was #OWNED BY MY MISTRESS, while white-lace boxer briefs clearly revealed the chastity cage beneath.

"A special present for a special occasion," she'd said with a snicker upon arriving home, handing him a pink Xanadu bag containing the pansy-ass shorts. "I want you to put these on tonight for our special guest."

Again the chimes sounded, with no sounds of movement from the living room—where, Chris knew, Kelly was reclining and checking her email. In a panic, he pushed out of the kitchen, aiming himself at the door.

"You're keeping him waiting, slave," came her low, menacing voice as he skirted the Laz-E-Boy. "And you're going to be punished for it later."

Chris quickened his steps and pulled the door open. There stood the conquering hero, right out of Central Casting. In stark contrast to Chris in his sissy outfit, Jason West reeked of manliness. A sun-bleached tanktop and side-slit gym shorts showcased domed shoulders, a deep chest, and arms and legs knotted with muscle.

Chris thought he saw an amused glint in the bigger man's light-blue eyes, but there was no accompanying sneer. Just a lazy grin that crinkled his eyelids and bunched the pitted cheeks above the neatly styled beard.

"Chris, right? How ya' doin'?" Jason extended his big paw. As Chris took it, there was a creak from the recliner behind him, and Jason's gaze refocused deeper into the room.

"Invite him in, for God's sakes!" came Goddess' Kelly's sharp rebuke. "Where are your manners?"

Chris bowed, then stepped aside with a beckoning gesture. "Sorry, Mr. West! Please come in."

The big Pilates teacher brushed past him, toting his gym bag. Chris noticed the breadth of the muscled back and the way the shaggy, rock-star hair showed off his thick, superhero neck.

He's everything I'll never be! And Chris knew his cause was lost.

Over his rival's broad shoulder, Chris could see Goddess Kelly on her feet now, facing them. He was intimately acquainted with all her workout gear—he handwashed them, after all! But she stood before them now in an outrageous, never-before-seen ensemble, into which she must have changed while he was doing the dishes. Candy-striped spandex leggings hung low on her flaring hips, then plunged into a deep frontal V, baring her navel and several inches below. A jumbo sports bra in shockingly see-through nylon mesh was obviously stressed to the max, yet woefully unequal to her spectacular dimensions.

Chris went weak in the knees, barely noticing the erectile pang from his caged and swollen cock.

"Kelly, you, uh—" Jason spoke in a hesitant growl, absent his usual nonchalance. "I can see you're, uh, going to make this, uh, very difficult for me."

"Difficult? Why?"

"To, uh, concentrate on, uh, Pilates."

"Pilates? Is that why you've come?"

"Uh, well—"

"Come here, you beautiful man! I've been thinking about you all day."

From directly behind, Chris watched Jason drop his bag and kick it sideways with his foot, then step forward like a muscular automaton to take her outstretched hands. How could any man not obey such an irresistible summons?

The two perfect people stood at arms' length a long moment. Chris couldn't see Jason's expression, but the look of smoldering lust on Goddess Kelly's face was almost scary in its laser-like intensity. If she'd ever looked at Chris like that, he'd have melted on the spot!

Now she did look his way, but with unmistakable exasperation. "Stop staring at us, slave, it's impertinent! Go away and make yourself useful. Maybe our guest would like something to drink. Would you, Jason? He'll fix whatever you like. Or I'll send him out to the store to buy it."

"Uh, no, thanks, I'm fine. If, uh, you're ready, maybe we should, uh—"

"Ready? My God, am I ever ready!"

She pulled the big man all the way to her roughly, kissing him full on the lips as her arms snaked around his strong neck. It was a long kiss, with faces locked and mouths working hungrily, a kiss that twisted Christopher's guts. Yet he couldn't look away. When at last their lips parted, it was only an inch or so, just enough for Kelly to bark out a sharp command:

"Go away, slave, and clean something, why don't you? I'll ring the bell if we need anything."

Summarily dismissed, Chris fled the room in panic. But not fast enough to shut out the greedy vocalizations of their resumed passion. Reaching the kitchen, he let the spring-hinged door slap shut on the exploding nightmare, then fell forward to his knees on the tile floor.

*

Kelly had not meant it to go like this. She had planned to take her sweet time with the preliminaries. She'd pictured herself sitting on Jason's lap again and shoving her tits into his manly pecs and teasing him a bit, maybe whispering in his ear as she twined her fingers in his hair.

While poor Christopher looked on, of course. When he wasn't scurrying to and fro, serving them coffee and dessert, and being scolded for taking too long or being too clumsy. It would all be such delicious fun!

And just a warmup for the main event.

But the instant she'd seen all that man-candy standing in her doorway, with his cowboy squint and lazy grin, all her plans had gone right out the window. She wanted Mr. West and she wanted him now. She wanted to sink her claws into his tawny torso and fill his sensuous mouth with her tongue.

Just for starters, of course. And she wanted to do these things right in front of her cringe-worthy husband, then watch him slink away on command.

The idea that either man would resist her program in any way never occurred to her. And she was being proved right. So far, Jason West was being every bit as obedient as Christopher. How easily she had brushed aside Jason's earlier resolve that any playtime between them come only *after* a serious session of Pilates! Which is why, surrendering herself to this gorgeous stranger, she'd never felt more in erotic control, more sovereign in her authority over the weaker sex.

Why, she wondered suddenly, had she waited so long to do this in her marriage? When, by simply exercising her natural female supremacy, she could have it all, whatever she wanted, whenever she wished?

After this first flagrant display of her powers as cuckoldrix, both men would have learned their assigned roles and would perform as directed on subsequent visits. Jason would be her lover, on call for as often and long as needed, while Christopher, especially by the end of this incredible night, would be reduced to absolute slave status, more eunuch than man.

They would do as she said, both of them. The muscular hunk, his fingers fumbling frantically at the front zipper of her sports bra, and the sissified slave surely cowering now in his see-through shorts on the other side of the kitchen door, attuned to every lascivious sound.

*

CHAPTER FIFTEEN ~
FIRST CUCKOLDING, PART TWO

Goddess Kelly was right, of course. Christopher had his ear glued to the doorframe, just as he'd done the first time Jason had dropped by

Only this time his Goddess and her new guy weren't doing much talking. Their mouths and tongues were otherwise occupied. But Chris did manage to catch one coherent exchange when they apparently came up for air. "How am I doing so far?" Kelly spoke in a teasing tone. "Am I your worse student ever?"

"Well, you're a handful, I'll say that."

"Only a *handful?* You underestimate me, sir!"

Christopher ground his teeth, hating himself for listening, yet unable to move, even though his ear cartilage was starting to ache from being pressed against the door molding.

After more soft moanings and throaty purrings there came an urgent whisper from his Goddess: "Wait right here till I arrange things with my slave, and I'll come back for you."

"Don't worry, babe," Jason growled, "I'm not going anywhere."

Babe? Chris had never heard his Supreme Goddess referred to in such an insulting, sacrilegious way. He half-expected the instant report of a face slap. But she only giggled. Obviously slave rules didn't apply to macho lovers.

What Chris did hear next were naked footsteps—hers—padding quickly across the dining room. He sprang up and fled the kitchen, dodging down the short hallway and into the guest bathroom, where he dropped to his knees between the toilet bowl and the wall. Hiding from the wrath of his Goddess.

She found him only seconds later. He could sense her standing over him, knew exactly how she would look, the menacing set to her jaw, the fire in her eyes.

"You were spying on us, you little rat! Don't lie!"

Without waiting for an answer, she kicked him hard in the ass. Even delivered barefoot, the impact drove him forward, the top of his bowed head banging into the facing wall. He howled in pain, then began sobbing, his shoulders shaking and the tears pouring down.

"Now listen up! Since you can't seem to stop spying on your betters, I'm going to gratify your sneaky little soul. And we'll just see how you like it." She grabbed his elbow. "On your feet!"

Chris was yanked up and roughly after her, down the corridor. His Goddess still wore the candy-striped tights, but she was topless now, her spectacular breasts gyrating side to side as she hustled him into the shadowy Mistress Bedroom, past the canopy bed and then into the long walk-in closet. Chris expected to be led straight to the secured chain leash and noose-locked into it. But she halted just inside the closet door.

"I'm going to leave you right here, slave, with the door slightly open, just like this, so you can kneel down and peek through the crack." With a hand to the top of his head, she shoved him to his knees. "Now, tell me what you see."

"I see your bed, Goddess."

"My Goddess bed, yes, exactly. The one you're never be allowed to sleep in again. Isn't that so?"

"Yes, Goddess."

"And do you have a very good view of it?"

"Yes, Goddess. But the room is kind of dark."

"Don't worry. I'm going to switch on one of the bedside lamps so you won't miss a thing. In just a few minutes, you'll see me bringing in Jason. And we'll be absolutely out of our minds with lust. Actually, we already are. I bet you could tell that from your sneaky little eavesdropping, couldn't you?"

"Yes, Goddess."

"I should hope so! I don't think my pussy's ever been so gloriously wet. Certainly not with you. And you, lucky boy, you'll get to see absolutely everything that happens on that bed, crouched here in the dark like a little spy in your little hiding place, in your little subbie shirt, watching your superiors fuck their brains out. You'll get to see how a *real* man makes love to a woman like me. Of course, you'll probably want to play with yourself while you're watching us, won't you, the way sissy slaveboys love to do. But with your little peepee all locked up, I'm afraid there's nothing you'll be able to do about that, is there, sweetie?"

"No, Goddess, there isn't."

"Now, remember, you're not to look away until I give you permission, or I come for you. Even if it takes all night—and, God, I hope it does!—you are to remain right here where I put you, on your knees, watching us. Now, are you all done crying, because we can't have any of that. You'll just have to suffer in complete silence. I don't want to hear the slightest peep out of you, is that clear?"

"Yes, Goddess."

"You're sure?"

"I'm sure. I won't cry."

"Okay. I'm going back to my gorgeous lover now. I can't wait to get his clothes off." Her bare feet squeaked on the hardwood as she turned and slipped out of the closet, leaving the door ajar. On the other side of the bed she paused to turn on a table lamp. Then, in apparent afterthought, she pulled a scarf out of a drawer and, shaking it out, draped it over the lampshade, casting the bedroom in a sensuous, apricot glow.

It was an exotic, even romantic touch, something never done for him. He'd never been special enough.

On his knees, through the six-inch opening, Christopher's view was not only of the big four-poster, but through it to the open bedroom door beyond and straight down the corridor, which was illuminated by only a single wall sconce. Chris peered down this dim passage, waiting for something he desperately did not want to see.

He heard them before he saw them. Earthy giggles from his Goddess and a man's heavy footslaps. They appeared at the end of the hallway. Kelly was cradled in his arms like a bride, a sight that pierced Chris through the heart. He had tried to carry his bride like that on their honeymoon, but had stumbled slightly—Kelly was a big girl, after all—and gotten promptly slapped for it.

"When a gentleman lifts his lady fair," she'd scolded him, "he doesn't grunt or stagger."

The big Pilates guy made it seem effortless, chuckling as he shuffled forward with his beautiful burden—she was quite naked now, laughing and kicking the air in mock protest, both arms locked around his strong neck. The only mishap came as she twisted around in his arms to kiss him and thus blocked his vision, causing him to blunder sideways into the wall. Jason made a joke of this, stumbling on in what was now a playfully exaggerated zigzag, even pretending to drop her once, which set them both to laughing, Kelly hysterically.

Chris had forgotten how much he loved Kelly's impish, little girl side, given to frightful shrieks and peals of childish delight. But he hated seeing it on flagrant display for another man.

They were halfway down the hall now, silhouetted by the wall sconce behind them. Chris squinted, focusing below her cradled thighs at a vague thrusting shape.

Then Christopher realized what it was—his rival's jutting penis.

Kelly had boasted that Jason was really big down there, but Chris couldn't really tell, not in the half light with the thing pointing straight at him. Only as they emerged into the room's apricot glow and Jason pivoted to lower his prize to the four-poster's gold satin sheets, did Chris get his first good look at the man's vaunted equipment.

Shit! It was even bigger than he'd feared, standing straight up now against Jason's six-pack abs. Chris found himself wondering how, even when flaccid, the thing fit into Jason's pants.

Or, cartoonishly large as it was now, into Goddess Kelly.

All of her recent putdowns about his own "little boy peepee" had been no more than simple statements of fact, the slave realized now. Stood naked beside Jason West, Chris would look little-boyish indeed. Especially with all his pubic hair removed and his own little dagger no doubt shriveled up from shame and embarrassment. The Pilates teacher, on the other hand, seemed like a born exhibitionist, a man who liked having all his assets on display...

His pirate grin and hairy chest and tapered torso. And, of course, that world-class schlong.

Goddess Kelly, reclining on her bed now with one leg drawn up, reached both arms up to her new man in theatrical appeal, as though playing directly to her hidden audience of one.

Obliging, Jason kneewalked onto the mattress toward her. She grabbed his cock like a wagon handle and yanked him forward till he

137

tumbled on top of her, causing another burst of mingled laughter.

"Time out, babe!" Jason protested. "What did you do with him?"

"With who?"

"Your husband, remember?"

"Oh, you mean my *slave*. Let's see, what *did* I do with him?" Kelly giggled mischievously. "Oh, now I remember! I locked him in the guest bathroom. I put him in there whenever I don't have a use for him. It's very convenient. And don't worry about him. If you need anything, I'll get it for you. Tonight I'll be your slavegirl, sweetie."

Jason levered Kelly up off the mattress. Chris watched them kneeling torso-to-torso in the apricot light, deep kissing now, their hands swimming all over each other. He wanted to throw up, but his penis was desperately trying to get hard—and would have if the steel cage hadn't choked it off.

Would Chris be playing with himself now, as Kelly had snickered, except for his chastity cage? Was he *that* pathetic?

Yes, I am!

On the bed, the naked lovers tumbled sideways, still locked in their embrace.

They're like movie stars, Chris thought. While he was one of the faceless nobodies, munching popcorn in the dark and living vicariously through the hugely glamorous people up on the screen.

And the show was just getting started. Kelly now rolled the muscular man over onto his back, wrapped both hands around his huge cock and began licking its swollen head.

Oh, no, Chris thought, *she's not going to—*

But an instant later she did. Opening her jaws wide, she tried to swallow him whole. Chris expected a gag reflex as the huge appendage slid into her gaping mouth and up her throat, but her lovely head just kept sliding up and down the swollen shaft on which her fingers were interlaced.

Never had she done that to, or for, Chris. Not even close! From the first night she'd taken him back to her college apartment, Kelly had made it clear he must never expect that.

While she, of course, demanded and got endless oral service.

Yet Jason wasn't content with his passive role. He began bucking and thrusting his hips, upwardly fucking her mouth.

Did she really like that? As if in answer, Kelly mouthed the huge cock even more greedily. *She couldn't get enough!* Finally, when Chris thought he could stand no more, Jason stopped thrusting and nudged her head away. Had the bastard just shot his load up her throat? No. His big dick slid out, as rigid as ever, slapping his belly again as he knelt up to face her.

Kelly grinned back at him in sluttish challenge, leaning far back on her haunches now, her oversized, sloping breasts sweat-sheened as her legs splayed wide.

"I want you inside me," she commanded. "Right now."

Instead, Jason dipped his bearded chin into the exposed cleft of her sex. From his low angle, Chris could no longer see what his rival was doing, but of course he knew. He could hear the wet, disgusting sounds the man's mouth and tongue were making as they invaded Goddess Kelly.

And the nonstop, passionate responses he was evoking.

Over the next twenty or thirty minutes, by Christopher's reckoning, his Goddess came at least three times, the final one a breathless, gasping climax beyond anything he'd ever been able to produce in her. So much for Christopher's oral skills, which Goddess Kelly had so often praised. He'd just been outperformed by some musclebound stud. A guy she barely knew. On his first try.

*

But Kelly wasn't comparing the cunt-licking skills of her new lover with those of her slave husband. As much as she'd relished setting up this whole scene to give Christopher a ringside seat at his own cuckolding, she wasn't thinking of him at all. For her, right now, Jason West was the only man in the world.

Except he wasn't doing what he was told. She was trying to push his head away, but there seemed no strength in her arms and no escape from his insatiable tongue. Finally, as the nonstop clitoral excitement again became unendurable, she kicked and thrashed and yanked his long hair until he finally lifted his grinning, satanic face.

"No more, you bastard!" she gasped. "I want you in me this minute. Do you understand?"

"Guess I got carried away, babe."

"Guess you did. But first, before you do anything else, come up here and kiss me."

He glided up till his lips nestled into hers, tasting pungently of her womanhood.

"Ready for me now, babe?"

"I was ready ages ago. Get in there where you belong!"

"If you insist."

She felt him then, just the tip of him. Then more. Then *much* more. And realized that, *Houston, we might have a little problem. Make that a big problem.*

No, she thought, this can't be happening.

She'd intended to yelp and squeal about how huge Jason was when he first tried to stick it in, entirely for Christopher's benefit, of course, knowing how that would torture him.

But she didn't have to pretend. Jason really was huge. So large, in fact, she was suddenly truly afraid he wasn't going to fit.

Which, aside from being cruelly ironic, would break her heart. She wanted him so badly, and she wanted him now.

"How're we doing?" Jason asked, still probing cautiously.

"Wait," she gasped. "It's really hurting."

He withdrew instantly. "Sorry, babe. It's my fault. Honest to God, sometimes I wish I was smaller."

"No!" Kelly dug her fingers into his shoulders, binding him to her. "I'm going to have you inside, every glorious inch of you. Just be patient with me, lover."

Okay, girl, think! Compared to you, Carmen's a little Smurf girl, and she can take him inside. And so, according to her, can several of Jason's other female Pilates students.

Kelly recalled a specific exchange they'd had on Jason's size:

"Honestly, I didn't think there'd be an issue, because, you know, Hector's hung pretty good. I mean, you've seen him, right? But even Hec didn't prepare me for what Jason's got between his legs."

"What did you do?" Kelly had asked.

"This is going to sound way too simple, but it's like the old Nike slogan, you know?'"

"You're telling me *that's* the secret? You just *did* it?"

"Not exactly. More like I just let go—and let *him* do it to me."

"But what does that mean?"

"I like to run things, just like you do, Kelly girl. But with Jason, that doesn't work, not with sex anyway. I had to surrender completely. Turn myself into, you know, his little slavegirl. At least for the night."

"And that worked?"

"Oh, my God, did it ever!"

Could it really be that simple, just a mind game? Kelly decided it was worth a try. She dug her fingernails into Jason West's meaty shoulders again and breathed into his ear:

"I'm ready for you now, darling. Please go slow, but don't stop— even if I tell you to—till you're all the way in."

"You're sure?"

"Absolutely, my darling," Kelly lied.

"Okay, but don't worry, babe. I'll take it real slow."

There were a couple of bad moments right at the start. But the big lug, bless him, concentrated on the task at hand, brow furrowed, biting his lip. While she concentrated on her part, the letting-go. Each time the flaring pain of penetration seemed too much, Kelly stopped fighting him and just surrendered more territory.

Finally, to her astonishment, she realized his enormous member was in all the way, filling her to bursting. The success of that moment was shared in a look of mutual delight. It felt to Kelly ike they were two kids who'd just broken into a candy store.

"You know, babe," Jason flashed a sly smile from an inch away, "that's only phase one."

"Oh, really? There's more?"

"Uh-huh. Are we ready to give phase two a try?"

"Oh, yes, my darling! We are so ready!"

It began as a slow, rhythmic to and fro, helping her get used to his sheer size and only hinting at the power held in check. Kelly's vaginal spasms receded. Then, magically, even those bearable pains turned into unbearable pleasure—toe-curling, cunt-creaming pleasure.

"Faster, my darling!" she sang into his ear. "Don't hold back!"

He did as told, moving more quickly now, thrusting deeper.

Holy fuck, it was like she'd been a virgin till now! There'd been a couple dozen guys since that hunky blond lifeguard at the country club when she was seventeen. But never before, Kelly realized, had she been thoroughly and properly fucked.

She dug her nails into his muscled flesh and forgot completely about her slave. There was only Jason, filling her cunt and her heart and wiping out her mind. Before she knew what hit her, she was coming, like being swept off your feet by a wave you never saw. Then wave after wave had their way with her, carrying her off to the far horizon.

*

Hearing Kelly's first primal screams, Chris had nearly rushed from hiding to her rescue. Then those early agonies had swiftly subsided, giving way to unmistakable ecstasies. And Chris knew all was lost. As he was soon to discover, their sexual Olympics had just begun.

Jason was stretched full-length atop his Goddess now, humping and flexing his big butt muscles. Chris had been allowed penile penetration maybe three times in all his years with Goddess Kelly, never on top. Always she'd mounted him in the female superior position, in total control of the proceedings. No matter how wildly she gyrated above him, he had to remain perfectly motionless and was forbidden, of course, to ejaculate.

Now it was his Supreme Goddess who was pinned down, her hips rising to meet the endless belly-slapping thrusts from above. "Oh, Jason!" she was gasping now, "Don't ever stop!"

Jason didn't. He seemed as relentless as an industrial drilling rig, in fluid, synchronous motion, from his calves, flexing upward, to his mouth, sealing hers in an endless respiratory kiss.

And, of course, there was the part Chris couldn't see. The part that was claiming Kelly for its own with every plunging stroke. A claim being validated, again and again, by her helpless cries of completion.

After each earth-shattering orgasm, Jason would cease his labors and lie perfectly still deep inside her, patiently waiting for Kelly's gasps and shrieks to subside and her breathing to slow and steady. Then, barely perceptible at first, the undulant flex and thrust of the muscled buttocks would resume, and the whole cycle would begin again. Over the next several hours Chris lost track of how many times Jason was able to repeat this incredible feat.

At last the marathon man could hold off no longer. Jason's muscled neck stretched forth, his head tipped far back and his throat let out a roar of brute triumph as he erupted in a head-to-toe shudder before collapsing atop his totally exhausted partner.

The meaning was clear to Christopher. Jason West had just taken his wife. From now on, she belonged to him.

He's everything to her now. And I'm nothing.

On the bed, though the fucking had stopped, thank God, the lovemaking continued—in more tender ways. The lovers clutched and kissed and whispered secret things. Then they were quiet together, though still love-locked. Or so it seemed. But after all that bellowing and shuddering, how could Jason still be hard inside her? How could that even be possible?

Finally, from their silence and stillness, Christopher judged them to be asleep. After a few more minutes, he nearly nodded off himself. Then he was roused by a flicker of movement on the bed. Jason again? Yes! The big glutes and hips and the muscled slabs of his lower back had resumed their slow, insidious motion.

Incredibly, the horse-hung bastard was at her again!

Couldn't he leave her alone for five minutes? She was a Supreme Goddess, not a personal fuck toy. But Kelly was responding, writhing slowly beneath him once more. Then whispering urgently in his ear. Chris watched Jason nod slowly and begin to move faster. Until she cried aloud:

"Oh, my God, Jason, you're ruining me for any other man, you know that, don't you, you lovely bastard? I swear, I can feel every inch of you inside me!"

*

At some point Kelly's spirit had seemed to take leave of her body. She'd looked down at her own physical self being endlessly pummeled and pounded by this beautiful Neanderthal she'd taken to her bed. It was actually frightening. And she would definitely need to rest and recover. Call in sick. Be hand fed and catered to by her slave.

Despite this, she knew, soon—very soon—she would want Jason West back in her bed. He was going to be an essential part of her world from now on.

*

Chris woke with no memory of having fallen asleep. Still in the dark closet, but curled now on his side. He rolled up, back to his kneeling position next to the slightly open door. Then stared out.

The Mistress Bedroom was still bathed in apricot-tinted lamplight. But the bed was empty, the gold sheets wildly askew.

Panic flooded in. Where had they gone? Had they left the condo together? How long had he slept? And what would she do to him when she got back, to punish him for falling asleep? Would she beat him bloody? Or—worse, infinitely worse—would she just open the door and boot him out of the condo? In shorts, sandals and subbie shirt?

He heard their laughter then. They were coming back to the room.

Kelly appeared first, giggling and jiggling in all her glory, her naked

Hercules right behind her. And Chris saw, for the first time, the big man's cock in its natural state, flaccid and dangling. It was still intimidating, easily twice as big as Chris' got when fully erect.

"I hate you!" Goddess Kelly was saying peevishly, with a pouty toss of her pixie-coiffed head.

"Really?" Jason growled. "That's how we're saying our good-byes?"

"You expect me to forgive you—for running off and leaving me? In my hour of need?"

"I'm pretty sure we took care of all your needs, babe. That was the plan, anyway."

"In that case, I take it all back. You're a God among men. There, I've said it." She turned now and leaned against him, her palms stroking his thick pectorals. "But do you really have to rush off, lover? Just wait a bit, and I'll get my slave to make you breakfast."

"Let the poor guy sleep. I'll pick up something at Starbucks. Then I'll go home and collapse into a nice long coma."

"A happy coma, I hope."

"Extremely, babe. Now kiss me good-bye." Jason looped a heavily muscled arm around her swan neck and tugged her closer.

Kelly leaned into the kiss, her heavy breasts compressing against his chest. When they finally separated, Chris saw, to his astonishment, Jason's huge cock once again at full salute.

He wasn't the only one to notice. Jason and Kelly were both eyeing it now.

"Well, well! Seems like someone isn't so anxious to run out on me."

"Kinda looks like it, doesn't it?"

"Maybe he needs a little something to remember me by?"

Taking the erect cock firmly in hand, Kelly lowered it to horizontal. Standing on tiptoe, then, she carefully impaled herself, inching forward and gritting her teeth till they were mated, groin to groin.

Christopher nearly gasped out loud. But Kelly wasn't done. Lacing her arms around Jason's neck to keep their bodies interlocked, she lifted her legs and wrapped them tightly around his thighs.

The big man stood, looking slightly foolish, before taking a lurching step with his delightful burden toward the canopy bed.

"No," she snapped, "don't put me down! I want to be fucked

right here."

Obediently, Jason began rocking back and forth in place, palming her ass cheeks as she slid in and out, laughing and gasping and urging him on. They came together, his Goddess wailing like a lost child as Jason bucked and thrust into a final trembling spasm, then stood, breathing mightily, still holding her in his big arms.

Their final farewell took place at the front door, blessedly out of Chris' sight and earshot. He heard the condo door open and close, then her naked footsteps returning to the bedroom.

Still on his knees, Christopher lowered his gaze, waiting for a word or touch from his Goddess to decide his fate.

But the footsteps stopped some ways off. Then Chris heard the slight creak of the Spanish oak bedframe, the sibilant sigh of the vast mattress, a longer, heavier sigh from his Goddess.

Chris dared to open his eyes.

Goddess Kelly lay back in a tangled nest of pillows and satin sheets. Her brazen pose and careless nudity reminded him of the "Naked Maja," a Spanish master painting he'd studied in college. As if sensing his adoring gaze, her face inclined toward his hiding place. She spoke huskily:

"Come here, slave."

Chris stood, or tried to. But, after so many hours on his knees, he faltered and fell. In a panic, he tried to gather himself.

"Don't bother, just crawl to me. I prefer you on your knees."

He crawled to her bedside, heart racing. As he neared, she half-turned toward him. Never had he felt more in awe of his Goddess— and more unworthy.

"I know you fell asleep for some of it, slave. I should punish you for that, but I'm too weak to lift a hairbrush, frankly. You saw most of it, though, didn't you?"

"Yes, Goddess, I did." His response was faint and pitiful-sounding.

"So now you know what a real man is, don't you?"

"Yes, Goddess, I do."

"I wanted you to see that. So you'll never again forget your subordinate place in my life. I also wanted you to see how much sexual pleasure I'm capable of. With a real man in my bed and a real cock in my cunt. You agree I deserve that, don't you?"

"Yes, Goddess. I do."

"And you're happy for me, aren't you? Happy that you've been completely replaced by a man who can give me what I need and what I deserve? A *real* man? Not some pathetic wimp who lets himself be slapped around and sleeps on the floor like a dog?"

"Yes, Goddess, I'm—I'm happy for you."

"Well, that's the right answer, of course, even though you didn't deliver it with sufficient conviction. We'll work on that. You'll learn. I'll see that you have many opportunities to learn. Now, let's see. I need you to do several things for me."

"Yes, Goddess."

"Going to work is out of the question, obviously. I'm not sure I can even stand up. I need you to call Todd, around eight-thirty. Tell him I won't be in today, and maybe not tomorrow. Tell him I have a stomach flu and can't even come to the phone. And really, I am having these cramping pains in my belly from Jason's incredible big dick. My God, Christopher, I've never been fucked like that before! But I'll tell you one thing. I'll be fucked like that *again*. As often as I can get it and as much as I can stand.

"But what else was I going to tell you? Oh, yes. So you'll call the office a bit later. And in a few minutes, after you drink all my golden nectar as usual, I'll have you run me a hot bath and kneel on the bathmat and wash me all over, then dry me and lotion me and then put me to bed and give me a long massage till I fall asleep. Would you like to do all that for me?"

"Yes, my Goddess, oh yes! I—I—"

"Now don't start crying again, for heaven's sake. Keep yourself together, because right now there's something else I need from you."

Kelly reached down languidly and peeled back an edge of satin sheet that was partly veiling her golden triangle. As a sly smile wrinkled her lips, she used her fingertips to comb the pussy hair back from her labial flaps. They were redder and puffier than Chris had ever seen them.

"Do you see what that big wonderful man did to me, slave?"

"Yes, Goddess."

"And you see how wet and sticky he left me? My bush and all down my thighs. Even my bellybutton is a gooey mess. You see that, surely?"

"Yes, Goddess, I do."

"Well, like they say, I've been rode hard and put away wet. I need some TLC, wouldn't you say?"

"Yes, Goddess," Chris said reverently, dizzy now with submissive yearning despite the grossness of what she'd just exposed.

"Can you do that for me, slave?"

"Yes, my Goddess. I can."

"In fact, you'll love doing that, won't you? As a sacred duty to your Goddess?"

"Yes, my Goddess, I will."

"Would you like it to be one of your regular duties from now on? Whenever Jason comes over to see me?"

"Yes, Goddess."

"Then you're going to get your wish. You'll have other duties connected to his visits, or any other dates I may want to have. But we'll start with this one. Do you know what it's called, what I'm asking you to do?"

Chris *did* know. He'd read about it on the Internet, before she'd taken away his access. "It's called cleanup duty, Goddess."

"That's right. I need my little slaveboy to climb up here on his knees and perform cleanup duty on his Goddess while she lies back and dreams of her exciting next time with her new lover. Will you do that for me now?"

"Yes, Goddess, I will."

"You understand, it's not just my Goddess juices you're going to be slobbering up?"

"Yes, I understand that, Goddess."

"Jason really filled me up, so you're going to find gobs and gobs of his sperm, and I expect you to swallow every bit of it. Is that clear?"

"Yes, Goddess."

"And I expect you to enjoy it."

"I will," Chris lied.

The thought of tasting Jason's man-goo made him want to throw up. Yet, after feeling he'd lost her forever, Chris was thrilled to do anything for his Goddess, no matter how disgusting and degrading.

Moving onto the bed, he kneewalked carefully forward between her widespread thighs. Viewed close up, her blonde bush was indeed matted with congealed ooze, her swollen labia glistening with sticky droplets. Yet it was still the most entrancing sight in all the world.

Evidently he was taking too long surveying the scene. Kelly

reached and grabbed him by the ears, yanking his face into her crotch.

"Just get on with it, slave!"

So he set to work on his sacred new duty, starting with soft kisses and long slow tonguing of her luscious inner thighs.

As he did all this, he was engulfed by a wave of profound happiness. There was indeed something sacred, he thought, in the unspeakable intimacy between abject slave and omnipotent Goddess. Something Jason West would never experience, no matter how many times he brutally fucked this woman or went down on her. Worshipping Goddess Kelly in this privileged way, Christopher felt himself being drawn inexorably toward the heavenly center of the feminine universe.

*

CHAPTER SIXTEEN ~ COLLARING AND MORE

It took Kelly three weeks after that first cuckolding to make all the arrangements for what she wanted done to Christopher. Although these plans of hers were to affect him in extreme and intimate ways, it did not occur to her to share them with him.

Why should it? When Kelly thought of Chris at all, which was less and less these days, certainly it wasn't as a husband whose opinions mattered, or even as a man to be respected, but as her rightful property to do with, or neglect, as she saw fit.

Had he not begged her, tearfully and on his knees, to impose exactly this kind of diminished existence on him—to be disregarded as a person and treated only as a slave?

He had. She was merely keeping her side of that unequal bargain.

And, so, when they started out together early that Saturday morning in the Audi—Christopher driving, Kelly in back reading her weekend edition of the *Wall Street Journal*—he had no inkling of what was about to happen to him. But he certainly seemed happy, she'd noted, catching his worshipful backward glances in the rear-view mirror. Happy and surprised, no doubt, to have his Supreme Goddess all to himself for a change.

Jason West, after all, had become such a large part of her life these last weeks. He was spending almost every night with her now. (Sorry, girls, but I stole him fair and square!) As a consequence, Christopher had been banished, with blanket and pillow, down the hall to sleep in the tiny guest bathroom where, most nights, he was locked in to keep him further out of their way. Jason didn't like her slave underfoot,

149

and what Jason liked, or didn't like—well, that did matter to Kelly.

As for poor, neglected Chris, Kelly rarely spoke a word to him, except to issue an order or verify that one had been carried out as specified. She had even been lax with his punishments of late, except for the routine face slaps she used to summon his full attention.

But wasn't that how relations *should* be between owner and slave? It was only natural that Christopher was having a tough time adjusting to his greatly reduced status, or, more accurately, to his utter insignificance. But today's appointment should help him with that, she thought, by rendering that inferior status official and irrevocable.

A quick eye-flick up from the *Journal* showed her an approaching freeway overpass. "Get over in the right lane and turn up the eastbound ramp," she instructed.

"Excuse me, Goddess, but isn't that the freeway we took to Xanadu?"

Kelly rattled her newspaper in annoyance. "Did you just say something?"

"I was just thinking out loud, Goddess. If you want me to take you back to Xanadu, I remember exactly how to get there. That'll save you having to—"

"Did I ask for your input, slave?"

"No, Goddess."

"Be quiet then! You'll be told what you need to know." For that impertinence, he deserved an immediate head slap. But not, alas, while he was driving.

Twenty-five minutes later Christopher was told to exit the freeway at Latigo Canyon Road. As this was several offramps beyond the one for the sex emporium, they were obviously heading elsewhere. Just where, as he'd lately been reminded, was of no concern to him.

And yet, way down in his gut, Chris had a feeling that it *did* concern him, or *would*—in a big way.

After three or four quick turns, with Goddess Kelly calling out the directions, they found themselves in horse country. The two-lane blacktop was now twisting up into a narrow, tree-shaded canyon with hillside ranches on both sides. Rustic signs, mounted over incline driveways or on mailbox posts, bore cutesy names. Like Zephyr Hills. Studly Acres. Relatively Stable.

"It's just coming up on the right, slave. Turn in at that big iron gate."

Chris eased the Audi over, coming to a stop before a wide, wrought-iron gate, atop which curlicue letters spelled out "McClintock Ranch."

"Pull up to that little box and identify yourself."

Chris did as told, rolling down the window beside an access control box and pushing a call button. A tiny squawkbox buzzed and a scratchy male voice asked him to state his business.

Chris relayed word for word what Kelly said in his ear: "Kelly Sheffield to see Ms. McClintock. We have an appointment."

"Drive on up and I'll come out and show you where to park."

There was an electric buzz, a metallic clunk, then a steady motor whine accompanied by a squeak of wheels as the gate retracted slowly sideways. Chris drove in through a tangled tunnel of wild oaks and up and around a long switchback.

On top, they emerged into a sunny clearing. On their left, several horses stood in a white-fenced field of grass. Straight on was a long, weathered barn with a half-dozen, horse-sized Dutch doors. The one-story ranch house, over on their right and shaded by eucalyptus, was less picturesque, with plain beige stucco walls, a tile roof and a long wooden porch.

A skinny young man in loose bib overalls and no shirt underneath stepped off this porch and started toward them. The closer he came, the younger he looked—early twenties, Chris decided. His hair stuck out in all directions, close-cropped and straw-colored. A faint blond mustache was paired with an underlip "soul" patch.

"You can park it over there," he said, approaching Chris' open window, "under that big pepper tree."

Chris did so, switched off the Audi and sprang out to open the door for his Goddess. He smelled horses and hay, heard a buzzing of flies and the boy's boots crunching through the gravel. Then Goddess Kelly emerged from the back seat and Chris stood back a moment, transfixed as ever. Even out here in the boondocks and dressed in tight jeans and a loose, off-the-shoulder top with plunging, elastic neckline, Kelly radiated star power.

But his admiration was ill timed. The young man rushed past him and fell to his knees, then, to Chris' dismay, began audibly kissing her sandaled toes as she extended them, left and right. As this groveling devotion continued, she swung an accusatory look at Chris, as if to say, *Why can't you be more like him?*

Eventually, though, the superior woman tired of the ritual and prodded the young man's face away with her sandal, ordering him to his feet. As he complied, Chris dropped to his own knees—but too late. His Goddess had already pivoted away and was now striding off toward the ranch house with her new devotee eagerly in tow.

"My Mistress is just finishing up with Satan," Chris heard the young man say as he caught up to them. "She'll join you on the porch in a few minutes."

Kelly and Chris both turned toward the horse barn where the young man's spindly arm was pointing. A woman on horseback was coming down the lane at an easy trot. Reaching the front corner of the barn, she leaned back in the saddle and reined in her big black mount.

The young man was already launched at full gallop toward the barn, overalls flopping, boots churning gravel. "Sorry," he called back over his shoulder, "I have to go!"

He's a complete zealot, Chris thought. *The way I should be.*

The young man got there just as the woman swung down from the saddle. Chris watched him take the reins and lead the big black toward the barn, saw the morning sun ripple like molten gold across its sweat-sheened flanks.

As the woman began walking toward them, Kelly hissed into his ear: "This time, slave, don't forget your manners!"

Chris wasn't taking any chances. When the woman was still several strides off, he was already down on his knees, forehead on gravel, hearing her boots crunch closer with a jangle of spurs. He quickly inventoried what he'd glimpsed before flinging himself face-down. In her fifties, he'd guess, big and broad-shouldered and mannish-looking in faded ranch shirt and fully packed corduroy jeans that thigh-whistled with each stride.

Then he smelled leather and horse manure and had his head prodded, none too gently. He opened his eyes to see a pointed, steel-capped toe at the tip of his nose. He began kissing it.

"Pleased to meet you, Ms. Sheffield." The voice above him was gravelly and ragged-edged, like a football coach's. "I'm Brenda McClintock. Brenda or Big Brenda, I answer to all of 'em."

"I'm just plain Kelly. Thanks for fitting us in, Brenda."

"My pleasure. Never too busy to put a boy in his place. That him down there in that cute little Female Supremacy shirt?"

"That's him."

Chris heard an evil chuckle far above him, and the booted toe slid back, replaced by its mate. Chris resumed kissing, until the foot flexed, exposing the soiled bottom to his face.

"How about a little sole kiss down there, slave?" The woman's explosive guffaw degenerated into a coughing fit. "Then lick it, and lick it good."

Chris commenced to kiss and lick her filthy boot sole. The disgusting task gave him a weird, defiant rush. *See, Goddess Kelly. I know my place, too!*

"Bring him on up to the porch and you and me'll sit and go over a few things. How about some coffee?"

"Love some."

"I'll have Quintin fetch it soon as he finishes up with Satan. Hey, that's enough down there. Get up and follow your mistress."

On the porch, the two women seated themselves in side-by-side log chairs. Chris knelt by his owner's sandaled feet with his gaze correctly lowered, but did manage a few quick peeks at their formidable hostess.

Despite her mannish looks and a strong tobacco aura, the big woman inspired in Chris feelings of excitement, as well as naked fear. Was it from being outed again as an owned slave and treated so dismissively by these superior women?

That was part of it, for sure. But there was more. Something about Brenda McClintock pushed all his submissive buttons.

Not her looks or shape, obviously. Like Kelly, she was big-busted, but the resemblance emphatically stopped there. The older woman was wide-bodied and thick-legged. No makeup softened her harsh features, and her short, salt-and-pepper hair could have been hacked off with pruning shears.

Perhaps it was the occasional twinkle in those cold blue eyes, and a mirthful twitch every now and then at the corners of that coin-slot mouth. The woman had a playful streak, he thought, though no doubt a sadistic one.

Brenda McClintock, he decided, would tolerate nothing less than total surrender from any hapless male who blundered into her orbit, and she would relish the ruthless exercise of her power over him. No wonder Quintin had sprinted to grab the reins from her hands.

And very soon, Chris sensed, it would be his turn to experience that power firsthand. But Kelly wouldn't have brought him all the way out here for just another punishment session, not with Goddess Carmen so close by. It had to be something else. Several possibilities came quickly to mind, inflaming his imagination and vainly swelling his caged manhood.

"So," Brenda said now, as if reading Christopher's agitated thoughts, "does your slaveboy know why he's here?"

"No, I didn't bother to tell him. But we've discussed it before, and he's been begging me for it, actually."

A collar! Chris thought, with a charge of excitement. *His Goddess was finally going to give him her collar!* And it must be a very special one, since Mistress Brenda was involved. Would it be of hand-tooled leather, like a fancy horse bridle?

"No problem. He doesn't have to know ahead of time. But for the other thing, if you decide to go ahead—"

"There's no 'if' involved, Brenda. We're definitely having that done, too."

"Well, there is a slight hitch with that. He has to sign a standard consent form. In advance. Sorry if that spoils your little surprise."

"Why on earth do you need his consent? He's just a slave."

"I know, it's silly, and I'd prefer to do without it, but my lawyer insists. A very high-powered lady, by the way, and a slaveowner herself."

"Then we'll do whatever the high-powered lady says."

"Don't worry. You'll still get a big reaction out of him when he sees my equipment. Ah, here's Quintin. Do you take sugar or cream?"

"Just plain, thanks."

"Two black coffees, Quint, and some of those scones from Trader Joe's."

"Yes, Ma'am." Quintin curtseyed and about-faced, then hurried into the house. The crisply executed protocol was not lost on Goddess Kelly. Why did seeing a male cringe and defer to female authority always give her such a rush?

"This is going to be fun," Brenda said, extending her corduroy-jeaned legs and crossing her spurred leather boots. "Mind if I ask your boy a few questions?"

"Go ahead. He's all yours."

"Hear that, slaveboy?"

"Yes, uh, Mistress—"

"'Mistress Brenda' will do just fine. Do you know what you're here for today, slaveboy?"

"No, Mistress Brenda, I don't."

"Your owner is going to collar you today. With a little help from yours truly. You had no idea?"

"No, Mistress Brenda. But I've been hoping."

"Have you now?"

"Yes, for a very long time. It's something that—"

"Whoa! That's way too much talking from a slave! I'd better have you right over here in front of me where I can slap you next time you run off at the mouth."

His heart racing, Chris hurried over to Mistress Brenda, who spread her big legs, directing him to kneel between them. When he saw her right arm lift, he braced for a blow. But she was merely reaching toward the coffee tray Quintin was now holding toward her.

After the skinny slave served her and then Goddess Kelly, Mistress Brenda beckoned him back to her side. "You should have served our special guest first, slave."

Her swinging slap sent both the boy and his now-empty tray flying. "I'm so sorry, Mistress Brenda, and to you, Goddess Kelly." He about-faced on his knees this time, picked up the tray and crawled to the nearest corner where he cowered, head down.

The big woman ignored all this, turning her attention back to Christopher. "Now, slaveboy, refresh my memory. What was I just saying to you?"

"Something about your wanting to slap me but not being able to reach—"

"Right, that was it!" Big Brenda carefully set down her coffee, then delivered an open-handed blow to Christopher's cheek with sufficient force to knock him sideways against her big left thigh. By the time he was able to gather his wits, he realized she'd gone right on speaking, and he had no idea what he'd missed.

"—of course, your mistress could have just taken you to PetSmart, but she wanted yours to be very special. It's stainless steel, an inch high and fairly thick, and it's gonna be welded permanently around your scrawny little neck. How does that make you feel, slaveboy? All tingly and gushy deep down inside your inferior little slave soul?"

What Christopher actually felt right then was a jolt of pure terror. "Did you say 'welded,' Mistress Brenda?"

"Haven't you been listening to me?" She slapped him twice more, forehand and back, then grabbed his neck to steady him. "Yes, your collar will be welded on. Forever. Tell me now, doesn't that make you feel all giddy and gooey, slave? Because it damn well ought to."

"Yes, Mistress Brenda. It d-d-does."

"And maybe just a teensy-weensy bit scared, too? Hmm? Like maybe scared shitless?"

Chris swallowed hard. "That, too, Mistress Brenda. The part about welding, that does scare me, I confess. But now that I'm thinking about it, I'm also getting, well, really excited because—"

This time her big hand just clamped down over the bottom half of his face. She kept it there for long frightening moments before letting him gulp air. "My word, he does go on and on, doesn't he?"

"I'm afraid he does," Kelly chuckled. "I had to shut him up on the drive over here. He's extremely keyed up this morning. I didn't mention it on the phone, but I've only recently gotten around to cuckolding him, so he's terribly insecure about his place in my household just now. The idea of a permanent collar, even one that's welded on... well, it's probably very reassuring to him."

"Of course, it is. A collar, or a cage, means everything to a slave. It gives them comfort and security. They're just like dogs in so many ways. Let's see now. I went ahead and had the engraving done exactly the way you said. No last-minute changes, I hope?"

"No, just the one word. That's all he needs."

The two slavemistresses continued to chat, sip their coffees and sample scones while their males knelt in appropriate silence, eyes cast down. Christopher, despite being allowed to wear clothing and the warmth of the morning, found himself shivering.

After what seemed an eternity of chitchat, the two women set down their cups and went into the house, with Quintin darting ahead to open doors for his Mistress and Christopher bringing up the rear. The little procession made its way through a big room with Navajo rugs, leather sofas and flat-screen TV, then through a large sunny kitchen with granite countertops and stainless-steel appliances, then out a back door and across a smaller yard toward a large shed of corrugated metal. Ahead, through a gap in a wide sliding door, Chris spied the distinctive green and yellow gleam of a John Deere tractor.

Inside, Brenda hit some wall switches, and a bank of overhead fluorescents clunked on, lighting up a large interior space. The big tractor, with its bewildering array of attachments and spare parts, occupied only half the shed, Chris saw. The rest of the concrete slab was given over to a workshop with long workbenches and free-standing islands of power tools. Chris recognized some of these—table saw, band saw, drill press, lathe. Other machines were less familiar—for metal-working, he supposed. A big wheeled dolly holding tall metal cylinders with attached valves and hoses—that had to be for welding.

"Okay," Kelly said, "now I'm really impressed!"

"Actually, this is my late husband's shop. Alex did all our kitchen cabinets and made those two Adirondack chairs on the porch."

"Excuse my asking, but was he—"

"My slave? Of course. He even made his own cage. He became an excellent welder and metal-worker, and he taught me, as well. Which comes in mighty handy, as you're about to see."

She led them to a high workbench and motioned Kelly into one of two revolving barstools with back- and armrests. To Christopher's considerable surprise, he was ordered into the other chair, while Brenda remained standing with her slave in his usual place at her feet.

"Here's the engraving you asked for." Brenda handed Kelly a stainless steel rectangle about the size and shape of a standard Band-Aid. Craning his neck a little, Chris was able to read the big block letters inscribed in the matte-finished metal. They formed a single word in all-caps:

SLAVE

Along with the expected submissive rush, Chris felt a small pang of disappointment. It was the right word, of course. Yet it seemed so *impersonal.*

But Mistress Brenda wasn't quite done. She now brought her other hand from behind her back and held it open to reveal a second steel plate. This one read:

PROPERTY OF GODDESS KELLY

Yes! Chris thought with a euphoric rush. I want *that* one!

"I had my friend—the one who does all my laser engraving—make this extra one up in case you had a last-minute change of heart. Remember, once it's welded on him, it's not coming off. So I want you to be absolutely satisfied with your choice."

But Goddess Kelly was shaking her perfect head "no."

"That's so thoughtful of you, Brenda, and I know my slave would love that one. Look, you can see it on his face. His little peepee is probably trying to squirt inside its cage right now. But in my profession, especially at my executive level, I can't risk having even my first name 'out there,' so to speak."

"You don't have to explain. My friend threw this one in basically as a freebie." Brenda tossed the alternate engraving across the table to clink into a wire-mesh basket full of discarded pieces. "Plain old 'SLAVE' it is then."

She turned to Christopher, a tailor's tape suddenly in her big, calloused hands. She looped it around the base of his neck, then cinched it tight.

"Do his measurements agree with the ones I emailed you?" Goddess Kelly wanted to know.

"Close enough, fifteen inches, give or take. He's not a pencil-neck geek like my Quintin, but he's not exactly man-sized either. Hell, I could probably strangle him one-handed, the way I do my chickens."

"How tight is it supposed to be, the collar?"

"You want it nice and snug, so it doesn't slide around. But not so tight he can't breathe or swallow. And we have to leave a little room for the wet towel."

"What's that for?"

"So I can put in the steel rivets while he's got the dang thing around his neck. You don't want your property singed, do you?"

"No, I guess I don't." Kelly giggled. "At least not yet."

This lighthearted banter—the two superior females discussing him as though he wasn't propped up between them like a child in a highchair—whipped Chris' emotions into a submissive froth of excitement and dread. But what did his Goddess mean by that last puzzling comment, "At least not yet"?

Brenda, meanwhile, had been rummaging through a big sorting bin and now lifted out a hoop of matte-finished stainless steel about the same width as the engraved band. It was shaped like a pair of large calipers, with the opening just wide enough to accommodate his neck.

Brenda stuck some reading glasses on her nose and squinted down at a tiny peel-off label. "Fifteen and a quarter. That should do him fine."

"How thick is it?" Kelly wanted to know.

"Three-sixteenths. We could go with heavier stock, if you'd like. But an inch-high collar any thicker than that would really weigh him down. And three-sixteenths matches the thickness of the engraved plate."

"No, I trust your judgment completely."

Opposite the gap in the caliper jaws, as Brenda now demonstrated, a hidden hinge allowed the metal hoop to open and close. The big horsewoman sidled behind Chris, shoving her heavy tits against his shoulder blades as she leaned in to fit the cold steel band around his neck.

It was heavier than the chain-link dog collar he wore at night. A lot heavier. But its main effect was on his heartbeat, which was spiking again, and on his emotions, which were all over the place. Chris was about ready to swoon into the capable hands of this large, intimidating female.

Abruptly his stool was swiveled toward Goddess Kelly. Brenda was holding the engraved strip across the front gap to show how the finished collar would look.

"What do you think, hon?"

"I love it!" Kelly clapped her hands in girlish glee. "That one word says it all! But can you really weld it on *with him in it?*"

"Just watch." Brenda touched a stubby forefinger to each end of the laser-etched plate. "I'm gonna put in two little weld rivets here and here, then two more on the other end, and, presto, change-o, he's got that hunk of metal around his neck for life." She leaned forward, her big-jawed face suddenly so close beside Christopher that he could smell her tobacco breath.

"How does that make you feel, slaveboy? Knowing that in just a few moments, and for the rest of your life, you're going to be wearing a sign around your neck that identifies you as a woman's possession?"

Chris couldn't answer. His throat was constricted, his emotions on overload.

"Just have him shake his head 'yes' or 'no,'" Kelly suggested. "Better yet, why don't you ask him if his little peepee is trying to get hard inside its cage?"

"Well, slaveboy, is it? Is your little worm trying to flex its puny muscles down there?" Her curled forefinger snapped the tip of his caged penis through the cotton crotch of his sweatpants. Chris winced at the sudden, stinging pain, then swallowed hard and nodded vigorously. Both women were laughing.

Now Chris felt Brenda's thick fingers poking under the corner of his jaw. "Holy shit, his pulse is off the charts. Maybe I should give him a Xanax before he passes out."

"He'll be okay. He was just like that on our very first dance. I thought he was going to faint on me, but I got him through it somehow."

"Okay then, we'll get started. Quintin, a little help here. We're ready for that wet towel."

"Yes, Ma'am." Quintin threw a quick curtsey before dashing off to do his mistress' bidding. Moments later, after being soaked in the shop sink, a strip of folded wet toweling was stretched tight around the base of Chris' neck, with all the excess water trickling down under his subbie t-shirt. Chris looked down. His knuckles were bone white on the armrests. Behind him, he heard Big Brenda getting her equipment ready. He expected her to reappear in one of those hinged metal masks, wielding a blowtorch in hands made huge by heavy gantlets.

Instead she wore only a pair of clear safety glasses and garden gloves as she reached across the bench to snag the handle of what looked like a portable generator. There were lots of knobs and input jacks on one end, he saw, as she tugged it closer, plus a short hose that ended in a pointed metal fixture.

It had to be some kind of welding machine, he decided, and that little nozzle thingy must be the welding gun. Brenda pressed a switch, a red light winked on and the contraption emitted a faint, vibrating hum.

"It's awfully quiet," Kelly said.

"Hope you're not disappointed." Big Brenda chuckled. "You probably expected me to fire up that big oxyacetylene rig over there and attack your slave with one of my husband's cutting torches showering sparks all over the place. This is a portable arc welder, sometimes called a MIG machine. It's real handy for jewelry-making. In fact, it's almost like using a hot glue gun. But it does the job, and you'd be surprised how many referrals I get from the local B&D community."

Brenda fit the steel collar around his neck again, this time on top of the wet toweling, then rotated the collar opening to the back.

"You're gonna have to come around here, hon, where you can see the back of your boy's neck, 'cause that's where we're working. Now, Quintin, take those locking pliers and hold his nametag exactly where I place it. Okay. Right there, perfect. Don't move!"

Repositioned now, Kelly watched closely as the big horsewoman touched the superheated tip of the welding gun to one end of the engraved plate. The sound was exactly like one of those patio bug zappers. There was a second quick sizzle as the welding nozzle touched down again. Kelly caught a faint whiff of molten metal and saw a curl of blue smoke rising into the cone of overhead fluorescence. Two more buzzing zaps followed in quick succession as Brenda welded the other end of the steel plate to the steel collar, forging the circumference into a single silver hoop.

Mistress Brenda switched off the machine, then, as Kelly returned to her original place, swiveled the barstool and spread her hands in a theatrical gesture.

"I sure hope you like it, 'cause this is how he's gonna look for as long as he's on this earth."

Kelly studied her slave critically. "Can you take away the towel so I can see it on his bare neck? Or is it too soon?"

"The metal's still pretty hot to the touch, but, oh, well, like you said, he's just a slave." Brenda got a finger-hold on the wet toweling and yanked it out all at once. Chris' reflexive yelp was stifled by a fast face slap. "How's that?"

"Delicious! Utterly delicious! And it'll be even better when he's naked. But I guess I'll have to wait a few more minutes for that."

"Your turn to see, slaveboy." Big Brenda stuck a hand mirror in front of his face, then whisked it away with a hearty laugh. "Kind of a shock, isn't it, slaveboy? But don't worry, you'll learn to love it."

Kelly was feigning a casualness she did not feel. The shivers of erotic excitement were absolutely seismic now.

"I'll throw in a couple of O-rings and D-rings that fasten to the collar for attaching his leash or a choker chain or whatever. I could weld those on, too, if you want, but I think it looks a whole lot classier this way, more like—"

Brenda broke off abruptly. Neither Kelly nor Christopher was paying the slightest attention. They were staring raptly at one another.

What Brenda could not see, from where she was standing, were the tears welling in Christopher's eyes.

But Kelly could. They were tears of happiness, she knew. And gratitude, for her acceptance of his total gift of self. And imploring tears, too, begging her not to discard him. All the puppydog emotions that were so characteristic of her sweet Christopher.

She had an impulse to go and hug him and bury his slave face in her big tits. But she yielded to another impulse instead, taking out her iPhone and snapping the first photo of her darling boy with his new engraved collar. She sent it winging off to Goddess Carmen with a texted caption: "Mine all mine forever!" Followed by a string of emoji hearts.

When Mistress Brenda had spun him around and stuck that big hand mirror in his face, just like at Supercuts, Chris had been caught up in his own whirlwind of emotions. Pride was uppermost, of course, because being Goddess Kelly's slave meant absolutely everything. And yet, there had also been a twinge of shock, and even shame, when he flashed on his pathetic self. The collar, with the word SLAVE backward in the mirror, had been a whole lot larger than he'd expected. It was one thing to beg in secret to be a woman's slave. Another to have your servile status proclaimed to the whole world wherever you went. For the rest of your life.

Not that either woman had asked, or even cared, how he felt. Why should they? A slave's feelings were irrelevant. Besides, Goddess Kelly would know exactly how he was feeling. She always did.

As if to demonstrate this uncanny power of hers, she put her phone away now and pointed to the floor. "Here, slave, crawl to your owner."

This is exactly what Christopher wanted to do and where he most wanted to be in all the world.

"Is it really on me forever, Goddess?" he asked, happily curled at the base of her barstool.

"Yes, slave." She reached down and tousled his hair. "Didn't you hear Mistress Brenda? Your lovely new collar can never be taken off."

This wasn't strictly true, Kelly knew. During their preliminary discussions over the phone, Brenda had told her about a pneumatic crimping tool that could cut through the stainless-steel band without harming the skin beneath. But both dommes had agreed it was better if the slave believed his collar could never be removed inflicting severe damage to his neck and head.

Now with his cheek against his Goddess' bluejeaned calf, Chris heard a repetitive squeak. He looked around to see Quintin pushing a four-wheeled utility cart across the concrete floor toward them. As he came closer, Chris identified the three items in the cart's top tray—a small torch, a metal skewer and, incongruously, a large manila envelope.

"Okay, folks," Mistress Brenda announced. "Time for the main event." She snatched the manila envelope, opened the flap and drew out some papers.

"Is that the document you need him to sign?" Kelly asked.

"Yeah, like I said, it's a pretty standard consent form, the kind used by a lot of tattoo parlors and piercing studios. According to my lawyer, it basically protects them from any clients who might get buyer's remorse." Brenda placed the printed pages face up on the work bench. "Just have him sign here and here and date it."

"Did you hear that, slave?" Kelly said, prying Christopher off her leg. "Don't keep Mistress Brenda waiting."

Chris stood to obey, but couldn't help casting another fearful glance at the two items remaining on the utility cart. What he'd thought was a simple skewer, like for roasting marshmallows, was really more like a short ski pole, he saw now, but without the pointed tip. The steel shaft ended at a coaster-size metal disc.

"Am I—am I going to be tattooed with that, Mistress Brenda? And pierced?"

"Quiet, slave!" Goddess Kelly scolded behind him. "You'll find out what's going to happen to you soon enough."

"Actually, he's got to know in advance," Mistress Brenda said. "That's the whole point of the consent form." She sat Christopher back on the barstool, then slapped him with her big calloused palm. "Okay, slave, listen up, and I'll tell you exactly what's going to happen to you. Your mistress brought you to me today not just to have you permanently collared, but to have you branded."

"Branded?" Christopher repeated, not comprehending.

"Surely you know the word? Ever see any cowboy movies?"

"Yes, Mistress Brenda. It's just that—that I—"

Once again he was slapped to silence. "How about we show this boy of yours exactly what I'm talking about? Quent, get your ass over here."

"Yes, Mistress."

Quintin came and stood meekly beside his owner, facing away, head bowed. From his perch nearby, Chris watched Mistress Brenda quickly unbutton the side flaps and shoulder straps of her slave's loose bib overalls, then gave a yank that sent them sliding down his scrawny legs to puddle around his ankles.

The slave now stood naked from the waist down except for a small penis cage of solid metal. Just like Christopher, he'd been denuded of genital hair. That wasn't what Christopher was staring at, however. Nor did he take particular notice of all the bruises and welts, new and old, that blotched and striped the young man's lower back, meager buttocks and the backs of his stringy thighs.

What riveted Christopher's attention were the three initials seared deeply into Quintin's right ass cheek—a large "M" and "C" linked by a small "c." It was the logo Chris had seen in wrought iron over the ranch's entrance gate. The same design, he suddenly realized, displayed in gleaming silver on Mistress Brenda's big belt buckle.

"It's the brand for the McClintock Ranch," she explained. "My brand. All my livestock wear it. And wear it proudly, am I right, slave?" Brenda gave the burn scar on her boy's butt cheek a whipcrack slap, hard enough to make him leap forward and cry out.

"Yes, Mistress Brenda," he gasped. "Your slave is proud to wear the McClintock brand for the rest of his life."

"Damn right he is!"

Her implacable blue gaze now swung back to Chris. "I hope you realize what an honor your owner is about to give you this morning, slave."

"Y-y-yes, Mistress B-Brenda." He gulped. "I do. But—but is—is that the one I'm going to have on me, too?" Christopher's eyes rolled toward Quintin's exposed ass.

"Of course not! Your Goddess sent me the design for her own brand a week ago, and I made it up myself. Quintin, fetch it here. No, dummy, pull your slave overalls up first, so you don't trip and fall on your face."

Quintin bent over and tugged and buttoned up, then hurried over to the utility cart and brought the metal rod back to his owner. She turned it to show Chris the underside of the disk. Welded or soldered to it was a raised design, of steel or iron, in what looked like a backward ornamental script. It took Chris a moment to recognize the familiar "KS" in reverse. "KS" for Kelly Sheffield. The same fancy monogram Kelly had embroidered on all her bath towels and embossed on her personal stationery.

And was now going to have burned into his flesh!

Only the support of the barstool kept Chris from falling. As it was, Big Brenda had to slap him several times before he was able to refocus.

"I'm sorry, Mistress Brenda," he blurted out, "and Goddess Kelly. I—I—I didn't realize what was going to happen today."

"Of course you didn't. Your Goddess wanted to surprise you. But I had to go and spoil her fun. So, now that you know, why don't you tell your owner how proud you'll be to wear her brand, just like my Quintin?"

Chris turned to face his owner, trying to remember exactly what Quintin had said. "This slave will be proud to wear your brand, Goddess Kelly. For the rest of—of his life."

"That's so sweet of you, little slave. I knew you would be. That's why I had Mistress Brenda make it up extra large."

Christopher turned back to Mistress Brenda and stammered, "D-d-does it go in—in the same place?"

"Unless you'd like it on your forehead? 'Cause that could be arranged." Braying laughter drowned out Christopher's terrified "no." Then she slapped him between the shoulder blades, nearly knocking him out of the barstool. "That was a joke, slaveboy. Where the fuck do you think I'm gonna put it, except on your butt?"

"Will it—will it hurt, Mistress Brenda?"

Big Brenda's laugh detonated again. "Fuck, yeah, it'll hurt! Are you squeamish, slaveboy?"

"I-I-I think so, Mistress B-B-B—"

"'Think so,' my ass!" Goddess Kelly snorted in derision. "I hope you have a ball gag around here somewhere. I didn't bring mine."

"No need for one up here on the ranch. Your boy can scream as loud as he wants, no one will hear him. Hell, I'm getting all lathered up just thinking about it. But before I ask Quintin to fire up my branding iron—actually it's steel—let's get that consent form out of the way, shall we?"

Christopher tried hard to focus on the printed pages that were placed in front of him, but it was hopeless. Words and paragraphs swam before his eyes, while his heart was beating like a jungle drum.

He suddenly recalled something Goddess had said to him all those weeks ago when she'd started getting serious about all of this:

"You think slavery can't exist anymore, because, of course, it isn't legal. But you won't be living under the laws of this city, or this state, or even the good old U.S. of A. You'll be living under my laws and my absolute rule—a naked male slave, kept in chains, totally dependent on his owner..."

It was all coming true, every word she'd said. None of this was make-believe, just plain fact. In this modern day and age, there really were women who lived by their own supremacist rules. Who ensnared and subdued foolish males. Who collared and branded them and turned them into domestic drudges or mincing maids or anything else that amused them.

And his destiny was to be one of those males.

Suddenly his Goddess was at his side, supporting him as he started to slump in the high chair. "I've got you, little slave. Have you read it?"

"No, Goddess, I can't. I—I feel like I'm going to faint."

"That's okay. But first you have to do what you're told and sign the paper. And date it. In these two places, right, Brenda?"

"Right. And have him initial it, too, right beside those little checkmarks." Brenda gestured with a ballpoint pen, which she then handed to Kelly. Kelly transferred the pen to Christopher's now trembling hand.

"But I—I have no right to—to accept or refuse anything, you've said so yourself. I'm just a slave. I just do what you tell me."

"Then tell him to stop whining and sign the fucking paper," Brenda growled, "so we can get this show on the road."

"Don't worry." Kelly laughed. "I'll make it so simple even an inferior male brain can grasp it." With both palms, she turned Christopher's face to hers, staring deep into his submissive soul, and spoke breathily: "Do you want this, little slave? Do you want to belong to me forever and ever, and wear my brand till the day you die?"

Chris swallowed hard, but, of course, there was only one answer. "Yes, Goddess Kelly."

"Do you want it with all your heart and soul?"

"Yes, Goddess Kelly, I do." Though his responses came out sounding robotic, Chris meant them with his entire being.

She gave his forehead a queenly kiss. "That's all you need to say, slave."

Taking Christopher's still-shaking hand in hers, she lifted his forearm and carefully guided him in signing his name and adding his initials, then took the pen from him and dated the document.

"There," she said, handing everything back to Mistress Brenda. "All done."

*

Ten minutes later Christopher was standing, spread-eagled, in the adjoining tractor stall. He was securely cuffed at wrists and ankles and shackled above and below to twin steel uprights a yard apart, from which various tools and farm implements had been taken down.

He wore his spiral cock cage and his brand-new slave collar and nothing else. It was a warm morning with slanting sunlight bathing the big green tractor behind him. But Chris was shivering uncontrollably.

From terror and excitement.

Mostly terror.

A few feet away Mistress Brenda, back in her gloves and safety glasses, was applying the hissing blue flame of a propane torch to the raised metal motif on the end of the branding iron. Standing a little ways off, Quintin was recording everything with a handheld GoPro. Goddess Kelly, about ten feet in front of Christopher, was doing the same with her iPhone.

Christopher, between fast, shallow intakes of air, was mouthing the mindless phrases of his slave mantra over and over:

"Goddess Kelly is my Queen and Goddess… She is great and powerful… She owns me… I obey Her totally… I bow down and worship Her…"

The mantra was meant to calm and comfort, but somehow the magic wasn't working. Without his wrists being shackled to the steel posts above his head on either side, he would have collapsed on to the cement floor.

"How hot does that thing get?" he heard Kelly ask, as if in idle curiosity.

"On full blast," Mistress Brenda replied matter-of-factly, "it gets to around three-thousand Fahrenheit. But I only need to get your monogram half that hot. I think fifteen-hundred should do it. And judging from that dull red glow, we're just about there. Maybe you should leave the filming to Quintin and get over there next to your toyboy. He's looking pretty shaky."

"Good idea."

Kelly pocketed her iPhone and moved directly in front of her slave, inspecting him closely. Chris had a wild, panicky look, his eyes darting around. His shoulders and arms were shaking uncontrollably, and the muscles were quivering all down his legs. She reached around to check his butt cheeks. No quivering there. They were clenched tight. The poor thing was truly terrified.

"Are you saying your mantra, slave?"

"I—I was, Goddess! But then I forgot!"

"Keep saying it. It will help you get through this. Would you like to stare at my tits? Would that help calm you down?"

"Oh, yes, Goddess!" he gasped. "Oh, please!"

Kelly tugged southward on the elastic top of her off-the-shoulder blouse, spilling the great gelatinous globes out to his avid gaze. She'd gone deliberately braless this morning, so Christopher was able to zero in on those stupendous twin idols with all the fixity in his mind, trying desperately to banish all his panicky thoughts and fears.

But he couldn't help but hear the sudden cutoff of the hissing flame behind him, then the scuff and jingle of Brenda's big boots coming closer on the concrete slab.

"Do you need more time with him before I go ahead?"

"Give me half a minute. He's almost ready, aren't you, little slave? Ready to be brave and suffer for your Goddess?"

"Yes, Goddess Kelly!" This came out half howl, half sob. He wasn't ready or brave, even though he wanted to be. He'd seen how big Kelly's brand was, bigger than Brenda's. What he really wanted to do was break loose and run far, far away. It was too late for that, of course. Too late for anything now but total surrender to female ownership.

Kelly cupped her breasts and moved closer yet, thrusting her proud, rose-aureoled nipples only inches from his contorted face. "Do you truly worship your Supreme Goddess, slave?"

"Oh, yes, Goddess Kelly!"

"And are you ready to be permanently marked as mine?"

"Yes, Goddess! I am!"

Seeing her now in all her glory, Christopher realized how lucky he was to be branded as her living property.

"*Good.* Now recite your mantra again, and don't stop, no matter what!"

Kelly gave a quick head nod to Brenda as Chris began to mumble the sacred phrases, struggling to keep the panic from his voice:

"Her power is absolute over me... She owns me... I obey Her totally... She is in absolute control... She leads and I follow... Her decisions are final... I bow down and worship Her... I—

"Aiiieeeeeeeeeeeeeeeeeeeeee!"

A spear of white-hot pain had impaled his ass. The unbearable agony of that moment seemed to go on forever, though later on, during many compulsory viewings of the video, Chris would verify that the searing kiss of red-hot steel on his right butt cheek had lasted not quite two seconds. No matter. For him, those two seconds had constituted an unendurable eternity.

And they had forever altered his identity.

The effects were especially dramatic whenever his Goddess replayed those two seconds in silent slow-mo. Chris could see his body convulse, his head jerk back, his neck stretch and jaws distend in an unheard animal scream, before he went totally limp in his bonds.

Yet it was far better to watch the video in silent slow-mo than at normal speed with a full audio track. Because hearing the sound of the mortal shriek that had erupted from his bowels was like being branded all over again.

*

Goddess Kelly tugged her blouse back up and over her breasts. She felt genuine pity for her devoted slave's suffering. But those drops of pity had been swamped by a rising tide of more powerful and primitive emotions.

It was like Kelly had been transported out of herself and back through time to a long ago era of Amazon warrior women. Where she and her sister domme had dragged a captive male from the battlefield back to their campfire, then stripped and collared him before burning their tribal mark into his flank. Another male barbarian initiated into lifelong slavery to the Great Sisterhood...

It was the stuff of pure fantasy. Except for one thing. It had just happened. And the evidence was right there in front of her. A naked male slave, in stunned shock, hanging by his wrists and wearing her brand for the rest of his life.

Kelly slipped her hand from beneath her waistband to savor the sexual pungency of fingertips slick with her own juices. She couldn't remember sliding her hand down there, scarcely recalled the prolonged, exquisite moments of orgasm. What she did know for sure was that her whole world had been rocked by what she'd seen.

Her only real regret was that she hadn't seen it all. Standing here in front of her slave, she'd been unable to see the actual instant of contact. She'd heard the sizzle and scream, caught the barbecue whiff of just-seared meat. She'd seen her slave thrash and jerk in his chains. But she hadn't witnessed the red-hot die actually imprinting his flesh with her initials.

She'd watch it all later on video, of course. Over and over. But that was a poor substitute for the real thing.

Then a perfect solution occurred. Brenda had said it herself—that many dommes had their slaves rebranded annually. Why not do that with Christopher next year? Even better, why not perform the exciting ritual herself? With Brenda's help, of course.

There was another sharp hiss behind her. Kelly turned to see Big Brenda quenching the branding iron in a steaming water bucket. After a moment she pulled it out, still smoking, and waved it aloft in triumph with a broad grin.

"So what'd you think of our little show? Enjoy it, did you?"

"Yes," Kelly said softly. "Oh, God, yes!"

"I thought so. Not sure about your slave, though. He seems to have fainted dead away. Here," she handed Kelly a bowl of ice cubes, "rub these on his wound, very gently."

"Does that help with the pain?"

"No. But it keeps the burn from spreading and blurring the design. Then Quintin can help us unbuckle him and get him onto the daybed. Face down, of course."

*

This was like double role reversal, Kelly thought to herself an hour later. Here she was, driving her slave home. Not that he was exactly lounging back there, of course. He lay on his side, doubled up and facing backward, clad in only subbie shirt, new steel collar and loose-fitting sweatpants. Unseen, but carefully secured to his right butt cheek with a gauze wrapping, was a hydrogel burn pad.

Chris seemed to be drifting in and out of consciousness, in lingering shock, no doubt, and probably woozy from extra-strength Tylenols.

Kelly drove with extra care, amusing herself by thinking up dumb blonde-type lines she might use if pulled over for a traffic violation. Her favorite so far was: "Actually I just picked him up at a slave auction, Officer, but he doesn't have any papers. Can you help me think up a name for him?"

Kelly particularly liked this one because she'd been thinking seriously about stripping Chris of his name. Not only when addressing him, but even in her private thoughts. "Slave" was really all he was to her now, and the way she preferred to think of him.

His branding, according to Brenda, would take about a week to ten days to heal completely. During that time, the dressing should be changed daily and the wound checked for possible infection. Other than that, the ranchwoman had said, he was "good to go."

"Should I give him a break from housework?" Kelly had asked.

"I don't see why. I'm pretty sure I got a full load of chores out of Quint the very next day." Brenda had given a wink and a smile. "But I did cut back a wee bit on ass whipping."

Now, as she drove, Kelly remembered that first dance, when she'd swept this cute, incurably smitten young guy off his feet and steered him around the ballroom until he was out of his mind with submissive desire. Who would have guessed, way back then, that dance would lead to this? A man-shaped thing curled fetally behind her, collared and branded and utterly broken?

So where do we go from here? What was left to prove? Whatever she did to him now—and several interesting ideas did come to mind—she knew there would be zero resistance. Where was the challenge in that? Wasn't it pretty much game-over?

"Goddess Kelly?" The feeble voice from the back seat was barely audible.

"Yes, slave?"

"Are you—are you proud of me?"

"Yes, baby, I'm *very* proud." Where had that maternal tone come from? Kelly certainly hadn't meant to use it. Oh, well. "You were very brave for your Goddess."

He was weeping again. Whimpering actually, which was getting to be such a tedious habit. Another reason Kelly had come to view him with such utter disdain. But she continued her line of questioning, idly curious where it might lead:

"Was it very painful, slave?"

"Yes, my Goddess." He choked up again, then went on. "I can still feel it, Goddess. It really, really hurts."

"And it's going to go on hurting for a long while. In fact, Mistress Brenda says Quintin can still feel his sometimes, and that's from more than a year ago. But maybe that's a good thing, slave. Can you think why?"

"Because—because it'll help remind me what I am?"

"Yes, and also what you are *not.*"

Kelly paused, wondering if she should tell him the next part or wait for later. She decided to go ahead. He should have thought of it himself without being told, but he was obviously too far down into sub-space for his inferior male brain to function normally.

"Speaking of what you are not, slave, there is something else you should really be aware of, but I wonder if you are."

"What is that, Goddess?"

"Your branding will be completely hidden from view, even under swim trunks. But your collar won't. People will see it and know that you're a slave, whenever you go out in public, even on your little errands in the neighborhood."

"I've thought of that, Goddess." His voice was almost fading out now.

"And you think you can handle that, do you?"

"Yes, Goddess. I've been wearing subbie shirts for weeks and weeks now, so I'm thinking it'll be kind of like that only more so." There was a long pause before he added, "I'm just so proud to be your slave, Goddess. And I—I don't care who knows it."

"Well, that's the right attitude, of course. But you know, you won't be able to attend any more business functions as my husband. You do realize that?"

Now the pause was longer, much longer. Finally she prompted, "Did you hear what I just said to you?"

It took her a moment to identify the sound of muffled sobs. Only after a long while was he able to stammer: "I—I didn't think of that, Goddess Kelly."

"But it's so obvious. That slave collar is welded on permanently, as you know, and you can't really button a shirt over it, especially with a tie, because the metal is so thick that the collar will bulge out and look funny. Even if you could, your shirt collar wouldn't be high enough to cover your slave collar. I mean, you saw yourself in the mirror, sweetie. That thing is shockingly big. Would even a priest's collar conceal it? I don't think so, I really don't."

Chris was in hopeless freefall now. How had he not thought of that? His Goddess required him to play the role of husband—or corporate spouse, as she preferred to say it—only a few times a year. Mostly at holiday parties and special office occasions, like when she'd gotten her big promotion to West Coast sales director. Yet each of these occasions was highlighted in Christopher's memory, seeing himself in the elegant Armani suit and Hermès tie she'd bought for him, standing tall and proud beside the most glorious woman in the world.

But she was right, of course. He'd never be able to do that again. Not with this big hunk of slave steel around his neck. Why hadn't he thought of that? Why hadn't she?

Then he realized—she *had* thought of it, *of course* she had. She'd intended it from the start. The monstrous implications of that inevitability rushed at him, knocking his whole world off its axis.

"But—but what—what will you say, Goddess? When people ask where I am?"

"Well, let's give that some thought, shall we? It's not really you they'll be asking about, don't you see, but my husband. And obviously you won't be able to fulfill that function any more, not even in the official or legal sense. So that's something we'll have to take care of." She paused, waiting for the nonstop sobs to run down. At least she was helping him take his mind off his butt burn.

"It was never really going to work long-term, you know, being my slave *and* my husband. We tried it for, what, three years? Well, two, actually. And now it's simply over. I'll prepare the folks at work that I'll be getting a divorce. Now don't panic, little slave. I'm not going to let you starve or sleep under a freeway bridge. According to the terms of our prenup, you get six months of spousal maintenance payments. At least I think that's in there somewhere, though probably I should check."

Her slave was writhing around back there, she saw in the mirror, trying to lift and turn his head.

"Are you—are you going to get rid of me?" he gasped between sobs.

"Well, that's what we're discussing, isn't it?"

"But can't I stay on—not as your husband, but just as your slave?"

"Well, we'll see about that. But it's certainly good, isn't it, that I didn't get 'Property of Goddess Kelly' engraved on your collar? If I had, there's no way I could auction you off to another domme without having your collar cut off with a blowtorch. Which, if it didn't kill you, would certainly scar you enough to lower your resale value."

"But I don't want to be sold to another domme!" Her slave's voice was frantic now. "Please don't sell me, Goddess Kelly! Oh, please!"

"Quiet, slave! And don't you dare presume to restrict my options as a slaveowner. I know you want to stay on with me, under any and all conditions, and that's duly noted. But I'll just have to see if I can make that work—" Kelly paused before adding with special emphasis, "—for me and Jason."

*

CHAPTER SEVENTEEN ~
HAPPY-EVER-AFTERING

The naked young man in the steel slave collar ate his lunch from a dog bowl on the kitchen floor. When the bowl was empty, he got up and set it in the sink, wiped his face, then went back to his chores.

Funny way to celebrate a birthday.

He was twenty-six years old this day, and he had no one to celebrate it with. His mother had died long years ago, he was estranged from his father, and it had been the best part of a year since he'd heard from Wally, his old friend and college roommate.

Even on the unlikely chance that Wally had remembered the birthday and tried to reach him, the slave wouldn't have known. All email and Internet access was denied him, and phone service permitted with only one person. But that person, of course, was the only one the slave really wanted to hear from—and he wanted it so desperately. But she was faraway and hadn't phoned or texted.

Anyway, as he reminded himself on his way to the Mistress Bedroom, birthdays were meaningless now, a remnant of a former life. Like his name, which was no longer to be used or even thought of. He was only nameless male property now, his existence defined by the Superior Female who owned him. Without his service to her, he was nothing.

He accepted this. And yet, day by day, it still took getting used to.

Entering her long walk-in closet he switched on the overhead lights and let his admiring eye travel down the many yards of hanging garments, sectioned by season and type, and the designer handbags and purses in their glass-fronted cabinets.

His particular focus this day, as he moved to the closet's midpoint, was on his owner's shoe collection. There were currently seventy-eight pairs displayed on custom-built, slanted shelving, minus those taken on her trip, with ample space for future purchases. An adjacent tall-shelf unit displayed boots, twenty-three pairs in leather, suede and wet-look vinyl. Dozens of cross-trainers and running shoes nested in cubbyholes farther down.

Taking care of all these sacred items was one of the slave's many duties to his Goddess, one he'd been discharging proudly for years. But only recently had he been entrusted with reorganizing and systematizing the entire collection.

The initial phase of that challenging task had been completed just three weeks ago, filling him with slavish pride. He'd been prouder still when, after inspecting his work, his Goddess had let his arrangement stand with only minor adjustments.

What had once been a haphazard accumulation of pumps and sandals, espadrilles and platforms, slippers and flats, was now arrayed in logical rows by style, color and heel height. Three entire shelves were dedicated to her pumps, ranging from classic black (five pairs in varying heel heights) to peep-toes and slingbacks. Other shelves contained sassy spectators and outrageous contemporary platforms, strappy sandals and exotic espadrilles from boutiques all over the globe. Since each pair, after use, had to be cleaned, polished and, if need be, sent out for repair, two nearby drawers held an assortment of polishes, dyes and conditioners, along with silicon spray, soft cloths and brushes.

But there was still more to be done, his Goddess had explained just before leaving on her trip. Every pair had to be entered into inventory tracking software that could be sorted and searched by various shoe categories. For this project she'd given him back the use of her old MacBook (after disabling its Internet connectivity).

The slave approached the laptop now in its niche and summoned the spreadsheet he'd set up to her specifications. He was just a third of the way through the collection. He'd have to work faster at his data entry, maybe even steal more time from housework, if he was going to complete the assignment by her return.

But, instead of getting right back to work, the slave let his mind wander a bit. He couldn't help thinking about the place where he was standing. For two nights he had slept right here in the center of the long closet. On the floor, as a dog would sleep, chained to the overhead clothes pole. He had fully expected to spend every night there for the rest of his life. But that was not to be. For, on only the second night, Jason West had arrived like a conquering hero, and, ever since, the slave had been consigned to the tile floor of the guest bathroom.

In the half-year since that first cuckolding, what few privileges remained to him had been taken away, one by one, starting with his treasured status of househusband. He moved now on his endless circuit of chores like a zombie in the shadows. While another man—a "better man," as Goddess Kelly liked to remind him—shared her bed and lived the life of a swaggering satyr.

There was nothing the slave could do about any of this. He did as told, period. And so, banishing the dismal reverie, he reached for the next shoe to be entered into his spreadsheet. It took several retypings before he was satisfied with his description, "Stiletto sandals / nude colored / w/ankle fringe."

Then he paused.

Off to his right a fly was buzzing. Sandal in hand, he went to investigate. At the far end of the closet, he discovered the intermittent buzz was coming from an overhead fluorescent.

That meant a trip to Gruber's Hardware for a replacement tube. And that meant enduring another snide comment about his metal collar and subbie shirt from old man Gruber's mouth-breathing, teenaged son at the cash register.

"Hey, dude, does she like whip your butt, too?"

"Of course," he should answer. "And she makes me drink every drop of her piss, and I love it!"

He swung around to go back to his work on the laptop, then froze. At each end of the closet stood a full-length mirror, one right beside him now. In it, the slave had just glimpsed himself in startled close-up. Startled, because, even after a month of mandatory scalp shaving, it was still a shock to see himself completely bald. But that wasn't what had stopped him. The weird part was what he saw over his shoulder, reflected back and forth by the opposing mirrors.

An infinite, vanishing parade of bald, naked guys, all wearing steel neck collars and holding a lady's tasseled sandal. On the first few figures the backwards "KS" monogram was clearly legible.

Did the slave feel a twinge of shame at seeing this indelible mark of his chattel status? No. Rather, he was filled with perverse pride at being the property of a glorious Goddess. What happier fate could there be for an inferior male?

Impelled by these emotions, the slave raised his gaze to the tiny surveillance lens beside the ceiling smoke detector and cried aloud, "Goddess Kelly, I adore you and worship you!"

Was she watching at this moment? Not bloody likely, as the Brits would say. But she could be, that was what mattered to the slave. Seven tiny battery-operated cameras were strategically placed throughout the condo, all uplinking their feeds to the Internet via the WiFi-system. At any moment, from any point in the world, his Goddess had only to open an app on her iPhone or iPad to see and hear exactly what her slave was doing—or not doing.

Even now, four-thousand miles away in the South Pacific.

On her honeymoon.

*

Jason West—legally, now, Jason Sheffield—yawned hugely and stretched his shoulder joints. He was standing, buck naked, on the private terrace of their over-water, thatched bungalow overlooking Tahiti Lagoon. In their two weeks there, he'd deepened his tan, but the ridges of his sixpack had almost disappeared. What he really should do this morning, even before breakfast, was go for a hard run on the soft sand, then a hard swim straight out into all that turquoise perfection, followed by a lazy float back to the beach. Then maybe windsurf after lunch or paddleboard the lagoon. And don't forget kayaking and parasailing.

All that neat stuff was on their honeymoon list. So far they'd done none of it.

He yawned again, about-faced on the teakwood deck and headed back inside. A sigh of morning breeze parted the gauzy drapes, unveiling the bungalow's sizable centerpiece, a low-platform Tahiti bed. Sprawled enticingly across the king-sized acreage, and theatrically framed by tied-back canopy curtains, was a sight more breathtaking than the blue lagoon behind him.

Kelly Ann Sheffield. His bride, face down and bottom up.

A drop-dead gorgeous goddess if ever there was one.

And he was the lucky dude who'd won her and tamed her. At least in bed.

He recalled the wild, wanton look in her eyes last night on the ferry back from Moorea. She'd nibbled his earlobe, then, in a growly whisper and shockingly graphic language, told him exactly what she wanted done to her at the earliest opportunity.

He'd replied in a corny cowpoke drawl: *"Well, shucks, Ma'am, if that's what you really want, reckon I could maybe oblige you some."*

And oblige her he had, all night long. No wonder he was too wasted this morning for any additional exercise.

He moved on tiptoe, gliding up from the foot of the bed on braced arms, up and over those lascivious dancer's legs and pear-plump rump. Her head lay sideways on the pillow, her face concealed under a wayward spray of blonde hair.

His hand shot out, fingers bladed for a quick dive into the deep crease between her shoulder blade and right arm, then under to cup the compressed glory of one massive breast.

She didn't react. Didn't even turn to look at him. Puzzled, Jason gave a gentle tit squeeze, then withdrew his hand and used it to brush back those stray blonde hairs. Her visible eye was wide open, focused off to her right.

She was staring at her iPhone, propped against the bedside lamp.

"Look, sweetie. Isn't that precious?"

Jason crawled up behind her, resting his chin on her shoulder, cheek to cheek. The bright little screen was in her palm now, turned sideways to expand the image as she brought it closer. He recognized her home-security video app. Then, with customary disgust, her naked slave caught in the camera's crosshairs. In her walk-in closet, standing and staring at her wall of shoes. Probably praying to them.

Okay, so there was nothing wrong with a little kink, or even a lot. And Jason could dig the female power trip Kelly was on, and it was uber-sexy how far she'd taken it. But, really, wasn't it about time to send the poor bastard packing?

"I don't get it," Jason said. "What's he supposed to be doing now?"

"Watch. You'll see."

The naked man on the little screen reached and took one shoe from a crowded shelf. A stiletto pump with fancy fringe. Carried it to his face. Buried his nose in the opening. Kept it there a long time, obviously savoring the smell. Taking it in both hands, then, he began turning it and kissing it, toe and heel, vamp and sides, finishing up by licking the sole thoroughly before returning it to its place.

Jason couldn't contain his disgust. "Oh, for chrissake!"

"Well, I think it's sweet! It's one thing to tell a girl, 'I worship the ground you walk on.' Quite another to actually do it on a daily basis. And for the girl to see him doing it, secretly, with all his heart and soul."

He snorted. "I believe it's called a shoe fetish."

"And you're an insensitive brute! Why can't you be more like him?"

"Oh, yeah?" Jason grabbed his cock, which had returned to full battle readiness, and whipped it hard against the pink perfection of her right ass cheek.

"Ow! That hurts!"

"Is that what you really want from me, babe? To be more like *him?* Your little pindick slavegirl?"

"Well, perhaps I was a bit hasty. You do have your... um, finer qualities, I'll grant you that." Letting the phone slide from her fingers, Kelly heaved a vast, theatrical sigh. "What is it they say, women's work is never done?"

She steered the cleft of her beautiful buttocks toward his rampant erection. Then sent her fingers questing back between her slippery thighs to take him in hand and put him where he belonged.

"That's my big boy," she purred. "My big, big, sweet boy!"

It commenced immediately then, that interlocking mating dance practiced and perfected by them over so many hours for months on end, with Kelly continually striving for, but never quite gaining, the erotic initiative. This was a brand-new thing for her—sexual surrender to an alpha male, and one which had astonishingly expanded her orgasmic horizons. Up until Jason, Kelly Ann Sheffield had exercised willful control over every male in her life, man and boy, as far back as she could recall. Dozens of boyfriends before Christopher (as he'd been known) had been teased, tamed and discarded. Classmates and playmates of both genders had bent to her will, though only the boys had been eroticallytormented. Her very first conquest, of course, had been her quiet and courtly father, already emasculated by his wife before being thoroughly cowed by his precocious daughter.

Yet even in the midst of sexual surrender, Kelly's dominant nature would not be denied. Often, as she struggled on the precarious brink of bliss, it was the delicious thought of her slave, naked and knee-bent in her condo captivity, that took her over the final, shuddering edge.

What a head trip it was, while having her brains fucked out in paradise, to peek through a spyhole in cyberspace and watch her collared, housebound slave stick his ass in the air and his face in a dog bowl! Or lift and dust her crystal ballerinas, all twenty-six of them, each with meticulous care. Or engage in any of the silly makework projects she'd assigned him, like cataloguing all her fancy footwear.

Soon enough, though, her conjurings faded, atomized by Jason's relentless devotions. Her darling muscleman was on top now, grunting and gasping, the veins standing out on his neck and forehead. If he didn't drop his payload soon, she thought, he might burst a blood vessel. Besides, she was primed for the final fireworks, and the sooner he came, the sooner she could start pushing his glandular reset buttons.

What wicked fun it was to play with a helpless male, especially of the alpha variety! The way things were going, they'd be lucky even to make it outside today, let alone to the beach.

Ah, well, they'd just have to call room service again.

*

Goddess Kelly's flight wasn't due for another three hours, but her slave, in a fever of excitement, was already en route to the airport.

As well he should be. Never would he forget the terrible cascade of consequences after that night, just seven months ago, when he'd been late meeting her plane. Had he simply been on time that night—and not neglected his household chores while she was away—he might still be sharing her marital bed.

He'd lost all that—deservedly so—and was lucky that, after cuckolding and divorcing him, his Goddess had allowed him to stay on as her collared and branded slave. What truly terrified him now, as he steered the Audi through fast-congealing commuter traffic, was the possibility of losing even the little he had left.

The Goddess had confided, before leaving on her honeymoon, that she'd not yet made up her mind as to his final status. It was not reassuring, nor meant to be. She had no particular objection, she'd said, to keeping him on as a full-time slave, so long as he kept out of their way and remained excellent in all service categories. But, she had cautioned, if he became a nuisance with his incessant comings and goings with brooms and buckets and so on, and especially if he annoyed Jason, well—

"Then I'll just have to let you go, sweetie, won't I?"

No wonder he'd been in such an industrious frenzy every day of their honeymoon. The final pair of shoes had been entered into the database only yesterday. Every room was now adorned with fresh-cut flowers, every surface ready for a white-glove inspection. The Audi's slate-gray coat was washed and waxed to a showroom gloss, its interior vacuumed, polished and aerosoled with the smell of all outdoors.

And now, with her plane closer every minute, the slave was almost physically sick with longing for her. He'd behave himself, of course, when he saw her at the airport. There could be no falling at her feet or kissing her shoe tips. She'd be worn out from her eight-hour flight and anxious to get home. In fact, the slave would probably be lucky to get within five feet of her, what with her new husband standing guard.

But at whatever distance, just seeing her might cause him to squirt all over himself. It had been more than two months since she'd last let him out of his cage and squeezed him off.

Despite all this inner turmoil, the slave successfully negotiated the airport traffic and located the parking structure for Air Tahiti Nui. Minutes later he was seated in the baggage terminal directly in front of a giant arrivals screen.

Her flight, still somewhere over the Pacific, wasn't even listed yet.

So the slave sat back and began taking deep and desperate breaths. Which didn't help. He was an absolute nervous wreck. It was going to be a very long two hours.

*

His first glimpse of her was in a swarm of holiday refugees coming up the long ramp from U.S. Customs. She came striding up the incline in her platform sandals, tousled but radiant in a red-and-white floral sarong that clung precariously to her curves, held in place at the bodice, he saw on closer inspection, by a highly stressed coconut-shell buckle.

Only on second glance did the slave notice the man beside her, a tanned Tarzan in a tropical shirt. Arm in arm and stride for stride with his brand-new bride. Like maybe he was afraid of losing her.

The slave timed his move carefully. Just as the honeymoon couple reached the top of the ramp, he stepped out of the rope-line crowd and, with a nod of fealty, fell in on his Goddess' unaccompanied side, reaching for her rolling bag.

His reward was a flashing smile that, in a heartbeat, reasserted her supreme authority and acknowledged his appropriate submission to that authority. Yes, he wore the collar and brand of this incomparable she-creature, and wore them proudly. But it was that dazzling look of Dianic power that truly enslaved him, and had done so from their very first dance.

The slave went all tingly as he took her rolling bag.

Then she and Jason had swept past, and the slave hurried after to direct them to the carousel at the terminal's far end.

The long conveyer was already surrounded by passengers, their bags already thumping down the chute. The honeymoon couple found chairs and snuggled close while the slave went off to force a spot at the low rail. He stood there a long time, watching the circling bags. Amazingly, even over the mechanism's ceaseless clatter, his ears could identify his Goddess' quicksilver laughter.

That sound, usually so thrilling, today caused his heart to sink. Because it meant only one thing. The Goddess was truly happy with her new man.

When the now-despondent slave returned with all their bags stacked on a luggage cart, they took no notice. His owner' s eyes were unfocused, her mouth slack, while her Tarzan just sat there with a foolish grin and half his forearm under the flowery folds of her sarong.

The slave lowered his gaze and waited.

"Well," she said finally, and breathily, "why are you still here? Go fetch the car—and take our bags with you."

"Yes, Ma'am." It was the respectful form of address she'd instructed him to use in public.

"And be quick about it," Jason added with a smirk.

"You heard him," Kelly said with a dismissive wave. "Shoo!"

The slave scurried off, their derisive laughter still behind him. He didn't mind being insulted and dismissed by his owner. He was happy to be treated as her court fool whenever it pleased her; and, of course, she was free to slap him and kick him, mock him and curse him at any time, simply for her amusement.

But, clearly, the privilege of abusing the lowly slave had now been extended to her new husband. And, unless the slave wanted to find himself out on the street, he'd better get used to it—and fast.

Despite all this, as he steered the baggage cart across the airport street to the parking structure, down deep the slave was happy. Sublimely happy. All was right in his world. His beloved Goddess had come home.

*

Kelly Sheffield was being bad and loving it. Reclining now in the cushy leather embrace of the Audi's back seat, watching her lover fumble with the clasp of her Tahitian *pareo* until finally it fell open, spilling out one ginormous twin. Jason obviously couldn't help himself, after all those frustrating hours close beside her on the plane, having to keep his hands to himself, denied all those goodies to which he'd become so helplessly addicted. She closed her eyes now as he continued to fondle her breast while leaning in for a deep kiss. She purred in contentment as the fingers of his other hand slipped deeper inside the folds of the *pareo*, over her tummy and down into sweet ooze.

But why was it all so much sexier, knowing her slave was watching it all in the rear-view mirror and flagellating himself with jealousy? But it was, it absolutely was! Did that make Jason only a sexual prop in her primary relationship, the ongoing psychodrama between her and her slave? But that wasn't fair to Jason, surely. The man was a fantastic sexual athlete. His endurance was world-class; and, well, as for his sexual creativity, it was at least adequate.

But now she'd lost her train of thought, because Jason had just taken her left boob in both hands. Whatever was he going to do with it? Oh, dear, the sweet insatiable man was actually trying to stuff the whole quivering mass into his gaping mouth—

As if!

Kelly gasped in pleasure as he nibbled and sucked her erect nipple. Then she glanced up at the mirror, at beady eyes etched in pain, and spoke sharply: "Slave, can't you drive faster? And why aren't you in the diamond lane? I need to get home so I can be properly fucked by my husband."

"Sorry, Goddess. I'll hurry!"

"You'd better!"

The slave debated whether to veer immediately into the HOV lane and risk an expensive ticket, or wait for the first legal opening. He chose the latter, hoping she would not be infuriated at the delay. He needn't have worried. She'd sunk entirely out of sight now behind the front seat, giggling and gasping while the slurping and sucking sounds continued on her bared breasts. Those breasts that, for many months now, the slave had touched and tasted only in his dreams.

How could it be that, after two weeks in paradise, the honeymooners still couldn't keep their hands off each other? He'd been hoping his Goddess would have grown tired of her new fucktoy. Or, at the very least, that she'd exhausted him sexually.

But neither of those things had happened. The only person she was obviously tired of was him.

*

CARMEN: So tell me, Kelly girl, how was it?

KELLY: Have you ever seen Tahiti?

CARMNE: No, But it's definitely on my bucket list.

KELLY: Well, the truth is, I didn't see much of it either. Mostly the underside of a thatched roof. We didn't do all that much sightseeing.

CARMEN: I get the picture. Very vivid. Is he doing you right now?

KELLY: No, which is odd, I admit. I sent him out to the DMV to get his license renewed. Actually to get rid of him for a few hours, because I need some time by myself to decompress from... well, from all that Pilates work he keeps making me do. Strengthening my core, don't you know?

CARMEN: I bet. Look, I'll let you in on something. There's a hate group forming of some of Jason's former jilted clients. Which includes me, by the way. And what we're doing is, we're looking for an assassin—to take him out. Or, better yet, to take *you* out. 'Cause we want him back.

KELLY: Sorry, not gonna happen. I'm hanging my sign on him permanently. Oh, wait, I forgot. That's my slave who's wearing my sign around his neck, isn't it? And on his cute little butt.

CARMEN: I know, I know. You sent me the phone pic right when it happened, remember?

KELLY: Oh, yeah. Like I could forget.

CARMEN: You said you need time alone. But Christopher's still there, isn't he?

KELLY: Of course he's here, though I don't count him as a person, and he doesn't really have a name anymore. I took it away from him. On a whim, don't you know? But, yeah, he's here. He's always here. In fact, you wouldn't believe exactly where he is right now.

CARMEN: Okay, I'll bite. Where?

KELLY: Here are your clues. I'm in my breakfast nook, sitting down, and I'm multitasking. Having a third or fourth cup of coffee— freshly ground and freshly brewed by my slave—while I browse all my favorite gossip sites on my iPad.

CARMEN: You call that multitasking?

KELLY: Wait. While sipping and Web surfing, I'm also enjoying a leisurely, intermittent piss without the inconvenience of moving to another room. Isn't that efficient of me? And, from all that, you should be able to deduce my slave's present location.

CARMEN: Under the table. Between your legs.

KELLY: Exactly right. Licking my lips. And his. And hoping for more.

CARMEN: Goodie-goodie for you. But it's not going to work, you know.

KELLY: *What's* not going to work?

CARMEN: Keeping Jason and Chris under the same roof.

KELLY: Why ever not? Because I'm too greedy, and God will punish me?

CARMEN: You are, and He probably will. But that's not what I meant. What I meant was, Jason's gonna get tired of having another dick around, even if it's locked up.

KELLY: I don't recall giving the new Mr. Sheffield a vote on our domestic arrangements. Anyway, I think I detect a slight ulterior motive on your part. You want him, admit it. You've always wanted him. I'm not talking about Jason now, but my Christopher, as you persist in calling him.

CARMEN: I admit it.

KELLY: But if I gave him to you, then you'd have two slaves, and I'd have none. Not fair, boo-hoo.

CARMEN: You're wrong. I didn't have a chance to tell you, but last week I booted Hector out on his ass. Literally. I caught him in bed—*my* bed!—with these gorgeous black twins. When I was in

Vegas doing that big car show. Miss Senegal and her twin fucking sister.

KELLY: You're not kidding?

CARMEN: I can text you a picture of them all together if you don't believe me. So, yeah, I got no slave—zilch, zero, *nada*. You took my Pilates teacher *and* my favorite sex toy, and all I'm asking in return is a guy you're like basically done with. Who, by the way, I helped you break down and totally enslave.

KELLY: You forget. He's wearing my collar and my brand—for life.

CARMEN: I can live with that.

KELLY: I'll have to think about it, Carmen.

CARMEN: That's a big fat "no" if I ever heard one.

KELLY: Probably.

CARMEN: Blonde bitch.

KELLY: Yeah, I know. Look, meet me for lunch tomorrow and we can talk it all out over monster salads and sangria. One o'clock?

CARMEN: Make it two-thirty and it's a date. *Hasta mañana.*

Kelly hung up, eminently pleased with herself. She flexed her foot under the table and planted it on her slave's shoulder to detach him from her labia. Then moved it to his forehead and pushed harder this time, sending her slave over backward. He rolled up onto his knees, looking up at her like a puppydog, her piss tracks still visible on his face.

But seeing him like that, really, how could she prevent her heart from melting just a wee bit? He was much too cute and well trained to sell or trade or kick out or give away. Why couldn't she have it all? She could—and should.

"Slave, I'm going to tell you something I've never told you before. Do you want to hear it?"

"Yes, my Goddess."

"It goes all the way back to our first dance, remember?"

"Of course, Goddess. I think about that all the time."

"Of course you do. It was the greatest moment of your life. Anyway, I told you to meet me at Starbuck's after our dance class. But what I really thought about doing—it was really a wild, off-the-wall impulse—was to tell you to follow me to my car. It wasn't the Audi back then, but that little white Saab, remember? And, when nobody was looking, I was going to open up the trunk—which was awfully cramped and full of my smelly workout gear—and tell you to climb in. Would you have done that?"

"Yes, Goddess, I would."

He'd answered without hesitation, and she could see in his transparent face that he'd spoken the truth. "I was pretty sure you would. My idea was to close the trunk on you and drive off with you and make you my total slave from then on. We could always go back for your car later and then move you out of your apartment. And you'd really have done all that?"

"I would have, Goddess."

"Well, think of all the time we could have saved!" She wanted to tousle his hair, but, since he didn't have any, she patted his smooth dome instead. "Well, we got there anyway, didn't we, to your total enslavement, I mean? It just took a little longer. Now hurry and run me a hot bath and I'm going to let you wash me and dry me and powder me all over and... then make me lunch."

"What would you like me to fix you, Goddess?"

"You think of something. Can you do that, slave? Can you still think?"

"Yes, my Goddess, I think so." Kelly smiled at the unintended irony, but the slave had answered in all sincerity, eyes misted with adoration. She decided to reward him further.

"After lunch maybe I'll paddle your buns. No, I know! I'll use the cane on you. We've never really played with that lovely toy, have we? Not seriously, I mean."

"No, Goddess."

"But you want it, don't you, slave?"

"Yes, Goddess, I do."

"You want to feel my power and my cruelty, and the cane might be the perfect implement for that, don't you think?"

"Yes, my Goddess."

"And you know you deserve a good caning, don't you?"

"Yes, My Goddess."

"My God, you're starting to cry again! It really has been too long."

"Yes, my Goddess, it has." The slave was actually smiling now through his tears. Well, she thought, we'll just see how he feels after a nice long session with my bamboo cane! She was getting wet just thinking about it.

*

"I wouldn't push too hard to get rid of him, if I was you, slugger."

Kelly was speaking to her husband, lecturing him rather, as his responses were severely limited by the full weight of her cushioned hindquarters on his face. She luxuriated back against the headboard of her four-poster, having spent the last half-hour introducing Jason to the queenly pleasures and prerogatives of prolonged face-sitting. At this point she was abundantly satisfied, several orgasms to the good, though poor hubby was anything but. His magnificent body stretched supine and helpless before her, godlike phallus at full mast and handsome face swallowed in the deep, humid cleft of her buttocks.

"Yes, I know, darling, that he can be annoying, scurrying around on all his mindless chores, and he gets in your way sometimes. But you know my nature, darling, how impatient I can be when I don't get just what I want, when I want it. Kelly Ann needs a slave to boss around. Think about it. If we send him packing—and I'm not saying I won't, if you really insist on it—but are you quite sure I won't be turning *you* into my slave? Not just my pussy slave, because that's already happened, hasn't it? But *household* slave, too. Better think about that before you ask me to get rid of him."

Yeah, like that's ever going to happen!

That's what Jason *would* have answered, had he been able to make any sound other than a muffled grunt. There was absolutely no way in hell he was going to let Kelly, or any woman, turn him into the kind of pathetic worm she'd turned her ex into.

Oh, sure, he'd agreed to put his Pilates business on hold, leaving all his devoted clients in the lurch so he could be available full time. What the hell else was a guy supposed to do when he married a sex goddess? Say no? Even after six months, he couldn't get enough of her, and it was obvious she felt the same way about him. The important thing was, he was still his own man, still calling the shots.

Most of them anyway.

Besides, he could walk out the door anytime he wanted and pick up the pieces of his life in about fifteen minutes. Just make a few phone calls, round up some eager new female clients and he'd be right back in the old saddle.

There were other options, too, ideas and projects he'd toyed around with for years. Like that Pilates video concept, or the "Dream Lover" reality TV show idea he'd shopped around. The camera loved him, his killer chin and hero profile, that lazy, sexy grin. Several talent agents had told him that, not just gay ones either.

While he was thinking about all this stuff, Kelly climbed off his face, giving Jason something much more urgent to do—namely fill his lungs, deeply and gratefully, again and again. But even *in extremis*, he couldn't help watching his magnificent wife, in all her naked bounty, sashay away from him. Especially when she exaggerated the hip-sway, putting on an obvious show for him before yanking open the bedroom drapes to let in the remains of the day.

But the show wasn't over. Because Kelly's rear view was almost as sensational as her frontal, and not just because of that gorgeous ass. No, the crazy thing was, from directly behind her, you could still see those incredible boobs of hers—at least their outside curves, which bulged out well beyond the vertical lines of her back on each side. Jason was still fixated on this mouthwatering sight when Kelly plucked her empty margarita glass off the dressertop and shook it, rattling the ice cubes.

"Sweetie , I think Mama needs a refill."

Jason jerked forward to obey the implicit command, but, of course, could not. Not spread-eagled on her big bed with his wrists cuffed and lashed to the bedposts.

"Okay," he said, "but you're going to have to take these ropes off me first."

THE END

ALSO AVAILABLE FROM THOMAS LAVALLE:

DANCING BACKWARD:
AN ADVENTURE IN MALE SUBMISSION
An erotic novel of female domination and male submission

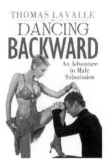

Little does Chris dream that when Kelly Sheffield makes him her dancing partner, it's only the first backward step in what will be a prolonged descent into complete and utter submission. One Amazon 5-star review calls *Dancing Backward* "the best piece of female domination erotica I've read!"

- *"A thrilling ride into submission!"*
- *"Awesome writing and a femdom plot that'll keep you aroused throughout!"*

DANCING BACKWARD 3:
A BELOVED SLAVE RECLAIMED

The 90,000-word finale of the three-part femdom epic, featuring

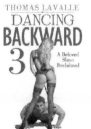

the concluding misadventures of Christopher and Goddess Kelly. These include a series of harrowing escapes and recaptures, provocative glimpses into strict female-led families and secret gynarchic societies—and the surprise ending of this most unusual love story.

- *"I couldn't put this incredible novel down!"*
- *"I just completed the third and final episode to this incredible journey into the world of FLR. You won't be disappointed in how this one turns out!"*

Made in the USA
Columbia, SC
25 September 2021